THE
LOCKET

KAREN R. RIVERS

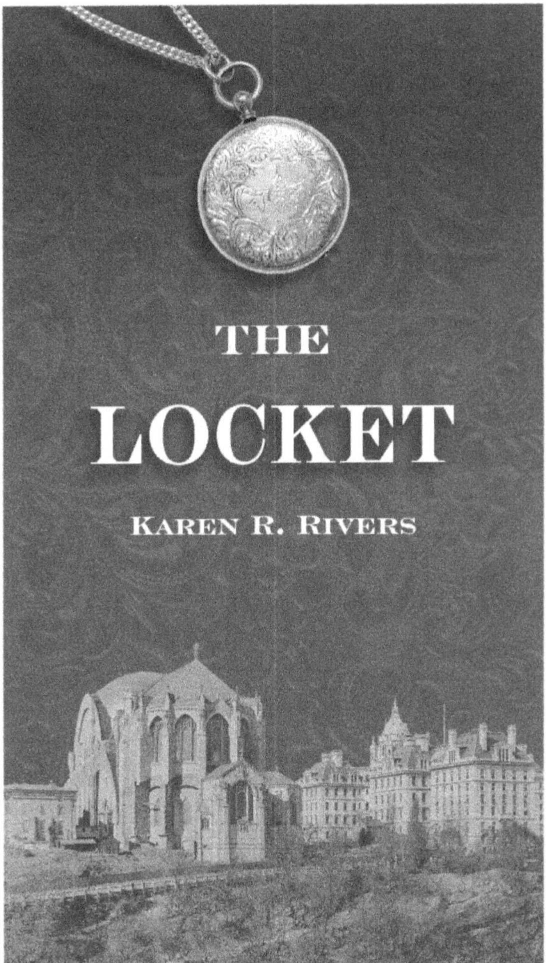

Cover design by Toelke Associates
www.toelkeassociates.com

Cover images courtesy of the Library of Congress

AUTHOR'S NOTE

The story that follows is a fictional account of life in New York City set in 1910, a time of great social and economic turmoil. Even as muckraking journalists exposed corruption in high places and workers joined together to fight for higher pay, the rich acted as though the Gilded Age would never come to an end.

But times were changing, not least thanks to a cohort of young college graduates who exchanged their comfortable enclaves for the city's slums. Working and often living in what were known as settlement houses, the graduates ran classes for immigrants and documented the conditions around them.

Much has been written about the rise of the union movement during this period and in particular the contributions of the Jewish intellectuals and radicals from the Lower East Side. The story I have set out to tell, however, is primarily about the Christian reformers—from the daughter of J.P. Morgan to the settlement house volunteers—who supported the workers' cause with money, legal challenges and appeals to morality. Their contributions were significant, but for the most part unsung.

PROLOGUE: DECEMBER, 2001

*T*he first thing Ken Breaknell was aware of when he woke up was the lingering smell of smoke. Despite the fact that he hadn't opened the windows in his Diocesan House apartment since late October, the smell had seeped into his room and even into the blankets he'd pulled tightly around himself after climbing into bed at 2 a.m.

In a flash he was back to yesterday: the knock on his door, the sight of the flames and smoke rising from the far side of the Episcopal Cathedral of St. John the Divine in the drizzly dawn, the sirens, the water, and finally, that moment after it was all over when he and the others had stood in the middle of the crossing, watching the shafts of sunlight pour in through the broken windows that were now open to the sky.

With a slight, involuntary shake of his head, Ken turned over and looked at the clock. He was surprised to see that it was only 6:30.

Mentally, he ran through the plans for the day that he and the others had agreed on in their late-night meeting in the Dean's house. His most important job was to prepare the afternoon evensong for the children at the Cathedral School. As the chaplain, he would be expected by the teachers to fill in what they could not: the details of the fire but more important, the details of what the fire would mean for them, and for the school.

Certainly today they would not have evensong in the

Cathedral; he would need to call the headmaster and ask to have the children assemble in the Commons Room instead. Beyond that? The staff had already been told that insurance would cover most if not all of the repairs, so he could assure the children that the Cathedral would be put to rights as soon as possible. Christmas services, the Cathedral staff had all agreed, should go on if at all possible, so the choristers would be able to tell their grandparents and uncles and aunts that yes, they should still plan on coming to hear them sing.

But he knew the children would be looking to him for something beyond all that—some assurance that the fire, coming just a few weeks after the September 11 attack on the World Trade Center, didn't mean their world was falling apart. Could he do that? Could he find some psalm, or some lines from the New Testament, to serve as the basis of a short homily that would have some meaning for them, and not just sound like empty grown-up words?

Ken sighed as he turned over and grabbed his pillow. *This was not what I signed up for*, he thought, even as he acknowledged to himself that the World Trade Center attack and the Cathedral fire were not the cause of, but only adding to, the doubts that had been growing in his mind for the past year.

Was he really cut out to be a priest, and specifically a parish priest? The idea had seemed so appealing to him when he was young, hearing his mother and father talk about the ways in which their Episcopal congregation in Minneapolis had been involved in the civil rights movement. Both from prominent African-American families, they had thrilled him as a child with their stories of travelling with college friends to participate in the March on Washington and later, while they were both graduate students in New York, listening to Dr. King's famous anti-war speech at Riverside Church. Even his name was a reminder of those exciting years: they had named him for an older priest at their church who had become something of a local celebrity for participating in the sit-ins in the South.

These days, however, it was hard to find anything glamorous

about day-to-day parish work. The issues were there—not just racial discrimination but also the growing gap between the rich and the poor that was visible everywhere around him in New York. But the city's leaders never seemed to feel any great urgency about addressing the problems and now, after the September 11 attacks, he doubted there would be discussions of anything but terrorism for a long time to come. Instead, Ken would continue to spend his time dealing with anxious school parents and bereaved relatives of people he'd never met.

Which left him…where? Turning over again, Ken deliberately pushed away the subject of his future and instead started thinking back to a conversation he'd had with Jack Cummings, a young fireman whom he'd met after yesterday's fire. Cummings and the others from the 113th Street firehouse had stopped to rest on the iron steps outside the south door of the Cathedral, all of them with sweat running down their soot-covered faces.

Cummings had told him that he'd been the house watch when the dispatcher's message had come through: smoke reported, from a fire alarm box on Central Park West. Within a minute and a half, he and the other five men on duty were driving down the hill, only to hear on their truck radio that the fire was at the Cathedral.

There was still no sign of the fire as they raced back up to Amsterdam Avenue and into the Cathedral grounds. But within a minute or two it was clear that it was coming from a make-shift structure used as a gift shop that had been built onto the side of the Cathedral where the north transept had been started but never finished.

"Me and two of the guys said we'd see what we could find up there," Cummings had told him. "We got a hose from one of the other companies and headed for the steps. We didn't have the water on, though. They always say, 'Never open a line into the smoke.' You want to know you have fire before you open up into it."

Suddenly, they'd heard on their radios that the fire had been located in a small room in the back of the gift shop. That was a signal to get out as fast as they could, since the flames were already shooting up through the building. Ten minutes later, the roof collapsed.

It had only been in talking with Cummings that Ken realized just how much of a near-disaster the fire had been. Even as the firemen were pouring water on the gift shop roof, the fire had broken through into the main building, blowing out the windows that had been covered with black pitch since World War II and hidden by four Barberini tapestries. Flames started shooting across the interior space, and almost instantly ate away the top halves of two of the tapestries. At one point, Cummings told him, he'd heard a Cathedral official tell the fire chief that if the fire reached the Baptistry it would spread from there to all the heavily carved chapels and they could lose the whole building.

In the end, though, the fire had been bested, the roar and flames finally subsiding, then silenced, leaving behind a gigantic mess of water, charred wood and smoke. At that point the great bronze doors in the Portal of Paradise, the Cathedral's main entrance, had been opened to vent the smoke, and, thanks to a city truck used to pump out subway tunnels, which someone from the mayor's office had had the presence of mind to summon, the vast lake began to be sucked out of the building.

It was a cruel accident of history, Ken reflected, that one of the carved pillars in the Portal depicted a modern version of the Apocalypse as described by St. John: the Trade Center collapsing along with the rest of New York City. He'd heard one of the other staff commenting just before their meeting last night that conspiracy buffs were already claiming that the beautifully carved pillar, completed only a few years before, foretold the fall of the Twin Towers.

Ken looked at the clock: 8:25. He must have dropped off again. After a few seconds, he swung his feet clear of the bedclothes and onto the small rug to the right of the bed. Padding into the bathroom, he looked into the mirror and was startled to see a pair of bloodshot eyes that he hardly recognized as his own.

Grimacing, he turned on the shower and stepped in, the smell of smoke rising from his hair and even his skin as the water hit it.

In his mind, he kept hearing the words of the hymn in last Sunday's service: Grant us courage, grant us wisdom, for the facing of this hour. But his thoughts were still jumbled, unfocused. Yesterday had brought back all the terror of the September 11 attack, and the stomach-churning realization after that event, which he'd witnessed from just outside a subway stop at the corner of 14th Street and 7th Avenue, that despite all of his faith and training he had been just another frantic person wondering whether the next moment would be his last. He'd tried to overcome that fear by action, volunteering at Ground Zero to be a counselor to the families and the rescue workers who day and night streamed into St. Paul's Chapel. But the fear was always still there, always just below the surface.

He realized that when he spoke with the children, fear was what he needed to talk about, admitting his own fear and helping them with theirs. He resolved to keep the focus on the fact that while the world was sometimes a frightening place, there were many people whose job it was to take care of them. It might not be much, but it was the best he could do.

By the time Ken had dressed and eaten a bowl of cereal and said his daily office, it was nearly ten o'clock. But before sitting down to prepare for the afternoon, he decided to revisit the interior of the Cathedral to see how the cleanup was going. He walked across the path in front of Cathedral House, up the side steps and into the church's dark interior. The smoke still hung heavy in the air, but amazingly, all the water that had been there yesterday had disappeared. Across from him, he could see that workmen had already erected a scaffolding in front of the six empty windows and that the Barberini tapestries were now laid out in shreds on the floor. He marveled to think that he had never even realized that the windows were there.

As he watched the workers sawing great chunks of plywood to fill in the empty spaces, he wondered to himself how the Cathedral had looked in 1911 at the time of its dedication, when the great nave stretching for two or three city blocks was yet to be built, and the stained-glass windows and the Great Rose window had not yet been designed. How different it must have been, he thought, to have sunlight streaming through clear-glass windows into what he had known only as a dark, medieval vastness.

As he stood there, one of the workers, a heavy-set man of about forty dressed in work boots and a denim shirt over a t-shirt, walked up to him. Taking note of his clerical collar, the man asked, "Do you work here?"

"Yes," Ken said. "I'm the school chaplain and I also help out with services."

"I found this while we were clearing the bits of burnt wood and glass from around the windows," the man said, introducing himself as Jimmy Tessoro, one of the crew leaders. He pulled out of his pocket a small gold locket, badly discolored in a way that suggested that it, too, had been in a fire. "It was wrapped in a scrap of paper that had been pushed into a crack in the cement around that lower window on the left—it looked as though someone had deliberately chiseled out some of the cement to make the crack wide enough," Tessoro explained. "My guess is that whoever did it probably put a little putty in front of it to cover the opening but that the heat loosened the putty and caused it to drop away."

Ken took the locket in his hand. "Open it up," Tessoro said. Inside were two very small pictures: on the left, a young man who looked to be in his mid-twenties, on the right a young woman of about the same age with dark hair. It was hard to see much beyond the fact that both wore serious expressions: the young man with regular features and an intelligent but unremarkable face; the young woman, dressed in a high-necked white blouse with long sleeves, vaguely exotic looking owing to her curly hair—not beautiful but compelling. "They look like they don't belong together, but yet they do, don't you think?" Tessoro said, startling Ken by putting his own thoughts into words. "Turn it over."

On the back, Ken read the inscription, barely visible: "To Ana from Will, Christmas 1910."

6

"I guess this place has acquired a few secrets in the last ninety years," Tessoro said with a friendly laugh. "Maybe you can figure out this one." With that, he walked back across to where the other men were working.

Ken turned the locket over again in his hand, opened and closed the clasp a few times, puzzling over how it had come to be where it was. He looked again at the pictures. Was the young woman Ana? Or could these be Ana's parents? No, impossible. People of that era didn't put pictures of their parents in lockets, they put pictures of their sweethearts. But were these two sweethearts? And if they were, why was the locket here, instead of handed down by Ana to her daughter?

And surely it would not have been Ana who would have hidden it here; it was unlikely that any young woman of that era would have had the nerve or skill to chisel a hole in the wall of the Cathedral and fill it up again. No, it had to have been the young man. But why would he have gone to so much trouble to hide it here? If they'd been sweethearts and she had jilted him and handed back the locket why wouldn't he have just thrown it away? Or if she had died, why wouldn't her family have wanted it as a keepsake?

Slipping it in his pocket, Ken left by the way he had come. As he retraced his steps he tried to imagine what it would have been like to be young in 1910. It was, he knew, a time of great disparities of wealth, just like now, when Fifth Avenue was lined with mansions while immigrant families lived eight to a room in tenements on the Lower East Side and African-Americans were squeezed into equally appalling hovels in the Tenderloin and St. Juan Hill.

But in some ways, he mused, there were more stirrings of change in 1910 than in 2001. For one thing, there was the growing number of unions. For another, there was the founding of the NAACP. And, as he knew from a Princeton history class, there was the progressive movement, which, while it generally avoided issues of race, had helped lead to the civil rights movement (or so his professor had argued) in which his parents had participated.

Might the young white couple in the locket have been part of those battles? Could they perhaps have been brought together by them? What had that young man longed for, what had he dreamed of, and did any of his dreams come true?

Suddenly aware that he was beginning to construct a narrative to fit the worn photographs in a way that was reminiscent of his failed college efforts at fiction, Ken laughed at himself as he rubbed the locket between his fingers. Just like Aladdin and the lamp, he thought. If I rub it long enough, maybe the genie will appear and tell me the story.

CHAPTER ONE

"*W*ill Ingalls."

Will looked up, startled, from the New Testament page he was scanning in response to Professor Taylor's question to the class about the Trinity. Taylor was looking at him, holding a note that had just been handed to him by a secretary in the Dean's office.

"Mr. Ingalls, the Dean asks that you see him in his office at the end of class, before lunch." Then, a hint of mischief in his voice, Taylor added, "Maybe he wants to query you on those socialist deviations you've been encouraging among your classmates."

Will managed a small smile, but he was immediately filled with concern. Like many of the other students at General Theological Seminary, Will was an active participant in debates over the rights of workers, and he frequently referred to the ideas of Britain's Fabian socialists on issues like the need for a minimum wage. But as Professor Taylor knew well, he was hardly a revolutionary. Much as he sometimes wished he could be more like Samuel Gompers and the other fiery orators he read about in Pulitzer's *World*, he recognized that he was, by nature, most comfortable presenting his arguments as a sensible outgrowth of the new 20th Century's embrace of progressive thought. But Professor Taylor, one of the few younger faculty at the seminary and the only one Will regarded as intellectually curious, enjoyed jousting occasionally with Will in these debates and referring to him as "our radical friend."

For the rest of the class Will was only half listening as he tried to fathom what Dean Robbins could possibly want with him. Will had spoken to Robbins no more than once or twice at receptions during his time at the seminary and had heard him speak in public only a few times.

Will could not think of any academic trouble he could be in, so could it be his "deviations" as Professor Taylor called them? Hard to imagine, and yet he knew that the increasing militancy of workers in New York City as well as in the rest of the country was of growing concern to some of the church's leading supporters like J.P. Morgan, so it was not out of the question. Then, too, there was the matter of his occasionally making disparaging remarks about the quality of the faculty, and his insistence that he be allowed, under the seminary's recently-changed rules, to take a class at Columbia University in place of one at General.

He had chosen "Social and Religious Movements in America," a graduate-level course taught by a distinguished history professor who'd written several books on the subject, and already he felt confident that the long trip uptown every week was going to be worth it. Not just the professor, but also the students, were engaged with the material at a deeper level than anything he'd encountered at the seminary.

So what was it: Would he be accused of holding dangerous political views, or would the charge be lack of suitable respect for the faculty, or was it something else altogether? And what if he was to be ordered to withdraw from the seminary—what then?

When the bell rang, Will picked up his books and hurried out of the classroom, emerging from Sherred Hall into the bright sunlight of the mid-October day. Barely taking in the scene that had so delighted him in his first months at General—the graceful red brick structures surrounding the well-kept lawn, the old trees and the inviting benches, all creating a sense of peace in the middle of the noisy city—he quickly crossed to Jarvis Hall, which housed the administrative offices. There, he explained to the dour young man who served as the Dean's assistant that he had been summoned.

A minute later, Will was standing in front of the Dean's desk. "Please sit down," Robbins said, his face pale from the illness that was slowly sapping his strength, but his voice and manner still strong.

"The Bishop called me a few days ago asking whether I could recommend someone from the final-year class to assist him," the Dean began, wasting no time. "Bishop Greer has never been enthusiastic about the construction of the Cathedral of St. John the Divine—it was Bishop Potter who pushed that project so energetically until his death—but he assumed the burden with a good will and committed himself to finishing the sanctuary and eastern end by 1911. That deadline is now only a few months away, with the dedication scheduled to take place just before Easter."

As it dawned on Will that he didn't appear to be in any trouble, his expression shifted from nervousness to curiosity. "There are two problems: money and a certain amount of laxity or perhaps incompetence among the builders," Dean Robbins went on, seemingly unaware of the effect of his remarks. "The Bishop wants a young man who can help him with both—how, I'll let him explain. But I immediately thought of you as the ideal candidate. Your most important credential, I'll be frank, is your connection to Reverend Phillips Brooks of Boston, which I recalled from your application. He was your mother's cousin, is that right?" Will nodded. "Well, he was also the man the Bishop continues to admire more than any other he's ever known—a man who moved freely among the best of society but also cared deeply about the poor."

Will silently questioned that characterization. It wasn't that he disliked Brooks—not that he remembered him well, having been only a boy when Brooks died. Indeed, from what his mother and others had told him he admired Brooks for his powerful oratory and his influence on civic affairs. Many people had told him that Brooks was the greatest churchman of his time. But Will felt that

Brooks was something of a "type": the preacher who prods the consciences of his congregation to a point where they all contribute to help the poor but not to a point where they feel obliged to do anything significant about the conditions that created the poor in the first place.

"As I understand it," the Dean continued, "the job would involve an afternoon or two a week plus assisting him in occasional fund-raising efforts. He proposes that the remuneration for this be $400 for the year, payable in two installments at the end of Michaelmas term and at the end of Easter term. Are you interested?"

Will, still adjusting to this unexpected turn of events, at first could only answer with a positive nod of his head. Not only had his fears been baseless, but the job would mean he could return the tuition money his mother had advanced him from a small inheritance and still have a bit left over to live on after graduation if he hadn't yet got a job.

"Yes, I'm definitely interested," he finally said, stammering slightly. "More than interested, actually, quite enthusiastic."

"Good," said the Dean. "You're to appear at the Bishop's office this afternoon at four o'clock for an interview, which I expect will be more or less a formality, as I've already discussed you with him and his response was positive."

Robbins indicated the meeting was over, but as Will got up to leave, he added, "Just one more thing, Ingalls. The Bishop wants potential donors to appreciate that he's in touch with modern ideas, and your work at University Settlement House and your interest in Walter Rauschenbusch and the social gospel and that sort of thing—don't look surprised; I've asked around among your professors before recommending you—are all to the good in that regard. But my advice is not to push that too far; as much as anything the Bishop wants you as his aide-de-camp in order to show that young men from the best families are still choosing the church and finding a way to be 'modern' without being anarchists or revolutionaries. Do I make myself clear?"

Will nodded. So he was to be part of the Bishop's sales pitch:

give to the Cathedral and assure yourself at the same time that the church will be in the good hands of men who won't upset the world you've created. Very well, he understood the game.

But it was with a troubled heart that he left the Dean's office and made his way to the Chapel of the Good Shepherd as the bells for the noon service began to ring. Slowly climbing the smooth marble steps and walking through the arched rood screen, with its carved angels and ornate bronze gates, he slipped into one of the choir stalls and knelt down, letting the quietness of the place, and the soft improvisations of Mr. Goodhue, the organist, wash over him.

Left to his own devices, Mr. Goodhue found it impossible to play even the simplest hymn for more than a few minutes before going off on a tangent of discovery. Will liked that about Goodhue, an elderly man whom he had got to know a bit the year before when he sang for a semester in the choir. Despite having been the chapel organist for the past thirty years, Mr. Goodhue seemed to take every day as a fresh challenge, always seeking to find something new in the familiar. "It's what keeps me young," he would say, before launching into a Bach fugue that might end with a ragtime flourish if there weren't any senior faculty around.

All through the service, Will kept turning over Dean Robbins' comments in his mind. Apart from the money that came with the job, he was attracted by the chance to gain some knowledge of how things operated at the top of the church hierarchy.

But he was stung by the realization that the Dean, and very likely the rest of the faculty, perceived him as a "safe" choice. Everything in him rebelled at the thought. Couldn't they see that while he was deeply committed to his faith, he was no less committed to making the church an instrument of change? And that while he might not be a radical in the same way as the union men responsible for the *Los Angeles Times* dynamiting a few days ago, he understood and sympathized with their goals?

He felt certain that no one on the faculty had any doubts about his vocation to the priesthood. Ever since he'd been a young boy he'd felt drawn to the mysteries of faith—the Trinity, above all—

and had loved to spend time by himself "just being," as he'd explained more than once to an inquiring adult. All through his youth he had roamed the fields that surrounded his upstate New York hometown, happy with his own company and thoughts. Over time, the idea of becoming a priest had become more and more appealing, and all through his seminary training he had never wavered in that decision.

But perhaps, he admitted to himself, the faculty might not appreciate the depth of his commitment to radical change because he had never provided much real evidence of it. True, beginning at Amherst, and continuing through his time at seminary, he and his friends had invited speakers to the campus, collected money for housing projects in the slums, and met with labor activists. But those were hardly radical actions. Moreover, he was aware that he had arrived at his political views by intellectual means, not practical experiences. Even his half-formed plan to work among the urban poor in New York as Rauschenbusch had done was, at least for the moment, just talk.

How much, really, did the struggle mean to him, and how much was he ready to sacrifice? His immediate answer was "everything." But if that were the case, he asked himself, why hadn't he shown it more clearly already? Why did he feel happier praying by himself in the chapel than imagining himself walking with strikers on a picket line?

As Will bowed his head for the final blessing, he vowed: *I don't know how yet, but I'm going to make a difference.* After a pause he added, *And please let me get the job with the Bishop.*

CHAPTER TWO

*A*s Will walked out of the chapel, he fell into step with Hugh Prescott, who lived next to him in Dehon Hall and was his closest friend at the seminary.

"You look distracted, Will. Is something troubling you?" Hugh asked as they headed for the refectory. Will told him about the possible job with the Bishop and Hugh whistled. "Not bad." After a pause, he added, "I admit, I'm wildly jealous. You'll no doubt be hobnobbing with the cream of New York society—to say nothing of the most powerful men in the Episcopal Church. Just don't tell the Bishop that we're all turning into rosary-carrying socialists thanks to you and the crazy ideas you picked up in London."

Will laughed, though Hugh's words brought back a memory of the fear he'd felt upon being called to the Dean's office. "Please don't say anything to anyone because he may take one look at me and decide he's not interested," he said.

"Not much chance of that, Will. You look about as respectable as"—Hugh grinned—"as any backwoodsman from Greenville, New York, can be expected to."

They kept up the banter through a lunch of meatloaf and overcooked string beans but toward the end of the meal Will turned serious.

"Hugh," he said, "I want to ask you a question and I want you to be truthful. Do you think I'm just full of talk about workers' rights and the social gospel or do you think I'm capable of doing something important to change things?"

Hugh looked at Will quizzically. "Does this have something to do with the job offer?"

Will nodded.

Hugh, whose round face and open manner disguised a keen intellect combined with common sense, considered the question for a minute or two before giving his reply.

"Do I think you're capable of doing something important? Absolutely," Hugh said. "You're probably the smartest person I know. But do I have any idea what that will be—or even *if* it will be? No. You seem to me to have a lot of contradictions. You like the idea of influencing public opinion, but I don't think you really like the idea of being a public person. And although you talk about working among the poor, I just don't see you as being comfortable in that kind of life."

Will nodded glumly, his eyes on his plate.

"But that's not a bad thing," Hugh hastily added. "There's plenty of work behind the scenes that's important, too. Movements need leaders, but they also need supporters—people who write essays and head committees and convince the people in power to do what needs to be done."

Will nodded again. It wasn't what he wanted to hear, but he knew Hugh had touched on the truth.

With that, the two of them rose from the table and then parted as Hugh headed off to the library and Will returned to his room to change into a clean shirt and prepare for the interview with the Bishop.

What did he know of Bishop Greer? Already well into his sixties, the Bishop was said to be an excellent administrator and shrewd judge of character. Although his detractors, including some of Will's seminary acquaintances, criticized Greer as moving too easily among the city's financial titans like Morgan, even they admitted to admiring Greer for his talents and his long-time commitment to raising money for colored education in the South. Nor did he give only lip service to serving all the inhabitants of the city; Greer was famous for holding regular office hours to which any resident, high or low, was welcome.

So it was with a sense of the importance of striking the right note in his meeting that Will re-read a church magazine account of an address on poverty the Bishop had given a month before and leafed through a diocesan history that recounted Bishop Potter's efforts to get the Cathedral construction underway.

By a little after three o'clock, having earlier left a message with the office of his Columbia professor to explain why he would be absent at the weekly seminar, Will decided to leave for the interview. He had plenty of time, he calculated, to walk from the seminary to the Bishop's house on Gramercy Square, where the Bishop maintained an office. Donning his jacket, he fingered his tie and looked into the mirror to make sure that it was straight.

The young man looking back at him had a presentable face, saved from ordinariness by grey-blue eyes that, as one young woman had once told him, made her understand the saying that the eyes are the windows of the soul. Compelling, with dark pupils that one felt looked in as well as out, they conveyed not just intelligence but some deep source of inner quiet that made even much older men search them for a sign of approval.

All this, of course, was lost on Will, whose only thought as he ran his hand over his fine, light-brown hair was that he was glad that his ears didn't stick out like those of two of his cousins and their father.

It was a perfect afternoon—warm and sunny, but without the haze and humidity of high summer. He walked out from Dehon Hall onto Twenty-First Street, feeling in his pocket as he went to be sure he had his key. The seminary buildings themselves formed a single, impregnable wall around an entire city block, their backs to the surrounding streets and their fronts opening onto the close, as the interior grounds were called.

Along the street, attractive brownstone houses, some with small front gardens and most with iron railings, stretched in both directions. Their front stoops, as always, were swept clean, and in a few cases, window boxes of still-blooming geraniums and marigolds brightened their otherwise sober exteriors. The street was lined with trees on both sides, which even in hot weather gave it a feeling of being a cool and inviting place.

At Ninth Avenue, however, the tranquil scene shifted abruptly to one of city hustle and bustle. Overhead, the noise of the trains on the elevated line often made conversation impossible, while at street level shops of all kinds catered to the needs of neighborhood residents and seminary students.

Deliberately trying to keep his mind off the upcoming interview, Will crossed the street and made a short detour north in order to pass by a small bookstore where he had several times stopped to admire a volume of early Hudson River School paintings. He knew that the book, open to a scene of Kaaterskill Falls, was too expensive for his budget, but as he'd seen on the several occasions on which he'd gone in and turned over the pages, the quality of the reproductions was excellent. Staring at the book again through the shop window, he thought about the fact that while the Hudson River artists' approach seemed dated now—too much part of the 1800s when nearly a whole decade of the 1900s had already passed—there was something in their perception of Nature as a reflection of God's glory that spoke to him in a way that the modern artists he had grown to admire during his time in England did not.

After a few minutes, Will resumed his walk, only to pause again a block later to contemplate a Brownie camera in the display window of a photographer's studio. On an impulse, he went inside.

"I'm just looking, at least for the moment," he told the clerk who came up to him as he picked up a camera from the counter.

The clerk insisted on showing him how the camera worked, opening the back to demonstrate how the film spooled from one side to the other. "All this for only two dollars," the clerk said. "We sell the film, too, and you can bring back the films to us for developing."

Will shook his head in amazement. Two dollars: even an ordinary clerk or teacher—or seminary student—could afford one.

"They're selling like hotcakes," the clerk said. Then, practically bursting with enthusiasm, he added, "It's another example of why this country is the greatest in the world!"

Will smiled, then put the camera down reluctantly. "Thank you," he said, "I'll definitely think about it."

As he walked out he suddenly realized to his chagrin that the prospect of the job was leading him to think about all the ways he could spend money. This was not the proper attitude for a seminarian—or a social reformer—he told himself sternly. He resolved to stop window-shopping and instead focus on the new buildings going up around him.

Everywhere you looked, he thought to himself, New York was heading for the sky. You could almost feel the confidence and swagger of the city as it tore down its graceful old two- and three-story buildings without a second thought to make way for bold new creations of thirty, forty and even fifty stories.

At the intersection where Broadway overtakes Fifth Avenue to begin its long trek up the West Side to northern Manhattan, Will stopped to take in the view of the Fuller Building that rose grandly above the trams and other vehicles that thronged the streets around it. Completed only eight years before, it had already acquitted a nickname: the Flatiron, because of its triangular shape, which Will had also seen referred to as a "stingy piece of pie."

Just a few months earlier, Will had gone to a photographic exhibit where he'd seen two hauntingly beautiful images of the building, one taken by Alfred Stieglitz and one by Edward Steichen. The first showed the building on a winter day, rising above the snowy trees and benches of Madison Park. The second had been taken on a rainy evening, the building looming up through the mist as a top-hatted man in the foreground strode southward through the park. Will loved paintings, but there was something in those pictures that had made him feel that photography was going to be the medium of this new century.

On the top of the building, Will knew, was an observation deck and restaurant that were said to offer wonderful views of the city and to be very popular with tourists. "One day," he thought to himself, forgetting his resolve not to think about how to spend money, "if I get this job with the Bishop I'm going to go there to celebrate." Then, ruefully, he added, "All I need is a girl to go with me."

It wasn't that he'd have any problem finding a girl who'd be more than happy to be asked. But ever since college, when there had been one young woman at Smith—a quiet, dark-haired girl with a passion for literature who'd broken his heart when she'd dropped him to go back to Chicago to marry her high school sweetheart—there had been no one special.

Finally, finding no other reason for delay, and having gone over the points he intended to make in his interview at least a dozen times, he arrived fifteen minutes early at the Bishop's house. Although the diocese maintained offices in an old mansion on Lafayette Street, Bishop Greer preferred to do much of his work at home, a large and imposing structure at the southwest corner of Gramercy Park. When Will arrived, there were still two people in the anteroom, one whom he recognized as a member of the City Council, the other a somewhat shabby looking man clutching what looked to be a court document. Within twenty minutes, however, during which Will glanced at the headlines on several newspapers that were sitting on a side table—"Experts Warn of New Problems with Panama Canal Construction"; "President Taft set for Chicago Trip"—both had been dealt with and the Bishop's secretary ushered Will in.

Greer was dressed, as Will knew he would be, not in clerical garb but in a suit and tie, in this case an outlandishly red one that confirmed the reports Will had heard that Greer was color-blind. Like many of his generation, Will knew, Greer was uncomfortable with the Anglo-Catholic practices that had been gaining in popularity—clerical collars, vestments, candles, incense—and preferred to stick to older, plainer, habits.

"Sit down, Mr. Ingalls," the Bishop said brusquely, laying aside a sheaf of papers on his desk and gesturing to a chair directly in front of him. Will did as he was told.

"Tell me a little about yourself," Greer said, turning his

attention to Will. "What brought you to General Theological?"

Will took a deep breath, not wanting to rush the points he'd been rehearsing to himself.

"Well, sir, there are quite a few clergymen in my family on my mother's side, and so I've always been around theological discussions that I found of great interest," Will began. "During college I read all of *Lux Mundi*, as well as the work of men like Professor Charles Briggs who have engaged with the issue of Higher Criticism. But I never wanted to enter the church just because it was an obvious path. That's why I went to England for two years, to study art and to take time to think about my future."

Unable to gauge how his remarks were being received, Will plunged on. "I stayed with my aunt and her husband, who is also a clergyman, and it was through him that I met a number of young clerics working in the settlement house movement in London. It was through my involvement with them that I began to see that life in the church could be both intellectually and spiritually engaging and at the same time devoted to improving the lives of the poor."

"Yes, yes," Greer said with an impatient wave of his hand, "all very interesting"—in a way that suggested he wasn't very interested at all. "And what about this role I perceive for you as my assistant?"

Will instantly knew that he had come across as trying too hard. Deciding that frankness would serve him better, he made a quick decision to put Dean Robbins' briefing to good use.

"Sir, I know that the Cathedral isn't something that greatly interests you," Will said. "But I understand your feeling that there's a need to get it finished so that you can move forward on other projects. And without trying to suggest that I know more than I do, I believe that owing to my art training, which included a class devoted to architectural principles, I could adequately gauge how well the construction is proceeding."

"You're right, Mr. Ingalls," the Bishop said, his face relaxing a bit. "This Cathedral is something of a millstone around my neck. Fortunately, many of the leading families of the city, the Astors and Vanderbilts among them, have been supportive of the idea. But money remains a problem. At this moment we need at least a hundred thousand dollars, and possibly more, in order to complete just those areas that are to be dedicated in the spring. For that reason, I'll be embarking on a series of meetings and talks over the next three or four months that will, I hope, keep enough money flowing in to complete the work."

After a pause during which he seemed to be considering just how much he wanted to take Will into his confidence, the Bishop added, "There's something else that causes me sleepless nights, and that is the endless bickering that goes on between members of the various committees overseeing aspects of the Cathedral and Grant LaFarge, the architect, who since his partner's death has been proceeding alone. Some of the members are now having second thoughts about Heins & LaFarge's Romanesque design, and keep pressing for more of a Gothic appearance. LaFarge quite rightly takes offense, and so there are meetings and more meetings.

"I don't pretend to know much about architecture, but I do know something about running an organization, and I know that there can only be one boss," the Bishop continued. "LaFarge, poor fellow, has at least twenty of them. This isn't something you'll be able to do much about, but I would hope that you could at least befriend LaFarge to a point where he keeps his focus on the Cathedral over the next few months, rather than becoming so annoyed by the interference that he turns his attention to his other projects."

"It would be an honor," Will said. "I actually met LaFarge once—he's quite good friends with Mr. Roosevelt, whom my mother knows slightly, and she and I were once invited to a dinner at the governor's mansion in Albany where Mr. LaFarge was present. I was only in high school at the time, and he certainly wouldn't remember me, but he made a great impression on me."

Bishop Greer, clearly impressed at the anecdote, asked, "And what about your father? You didn't mention him."

"My father died some years ago," Will said. "He was quite a bit older than my mother and I was only seven when he died, of complications from wounds he'd received at Shiloh. I hardly remember him, to be honest."

"He must have been a brave man," the Bishop said. Then, after a pause, he indicated by rising from his chair that the interview was at an end. "I assume that Dean Robbins has informed you of the proposed financial terms of the job, and that they're acceptable?" he asked as they moved toward the door.

"Yes, very acceptable," Will said.

"Good, then we have an agreement," Greer said, as the two walked through the visitors' waiting area. "My assistant, Mr. Moore, has now left for the day, but I would ask that you be in touch with him about further details. He'll be the one who's in regular contact with you. But I want you to come each Friday at this time to give me a report in person on where things stand at the Cathedral, and what problems you've observed. We'll also see each other as often as once or twice a week when there's a meeting at which I think your presence would be helpful."

"Thank you for this opportunity," Will said, as the Bishop held open the door to the street.

As soon as Will turned the corner, he paused to catch his breath, suddenly aware of how tense he'd been, then resumed walking toward Madison Park. Although it was now nearly dark and he could feel a chill of autumn in the air, he sat down on a park bench to think over the interview.

He hadn't expected to like Greer as much as he had—more than anything for his straightforward manner. True, he might be a bit too impressed by social standing, but he was also clearly capable and hard-working.

Wincing slightly at the thought of what his seminary classmates might have said if they'd watched his clumsy efforts to "sell" himself, Will consoled himself with the thought that at least he'd got the job. He felt a little daunted—especially as he still had no clear idea of how even to begin, and Greer had said almost nothing about what he expected him to do—but he also felt excited. And he was pleased at the chance to get to know LaFarge and, perhaps, other members of his firm—men who'd found a way to combine art and science in the form of beautiful and useful creations.

Finally, as the chill found its way through his jacket, Will stood up and began to walk briskly toward the seminary. It would be time for dinner when he got back, and it had been a long day.

CHAPTER THREE

he next day was Wednesday, Will's busiest day of classes: Dogmatic Theology and Patristic Greek in the morning, then Moral Theology and Old Testament in the afternoon. It wasn't until after his last class finished at four o'clock that he had a chance to go to Hoffman Hall to use the one telephone available to students. There, he called James Moore, the Bishop's secretary, who told him that he'd arranged for Will to meet Grant LaFarge on Friday morning.

"He'll be at his office at the building site by ten o'clock," Moore said. "It's in the old orphans' asylum building, on the second floor." Then, continuing in the somewhat abrupt tone Will would come to know well, Moore added, "You'll also be accompanying the Bishop to a dinner Friday night honoring Lyall Adams Randolph at the Metropolitan Club. Randolph is a banker and, more to the point for our purposes, a leading Episcopal layman who is on the fabric committee of the Cathedral. Be sure you're here at the Bishop's house by six."

Will assured him he would be, then rushed back to his room to leave his books. This was the evening of the debate between the all-male University Settlement House and the all-female College Settlement House, both run by volunteers from institutions of higher learning. He'd promised to be there by six-thirty to help the two debaters representing University House run through their arguments one last time.

Will had been a volunteer at University Settlement House for over a year now. One of his Amherst friends, who had come there to live after graduation, had proposed that Will take on the once-a-week public speaking course after another college friend who'd been teaching it left to go to medical school.

Will enjoyed the class, which had grown from ten members when he arrived to fifteen. Many of the students had been through several English proficiency classes already, and some—especially the ones who'd been in New York for several years—were eager to discuss politics rather than just engage in classroom practice of the language.

The idea for the debate had come about because of his friendship with Lizzy Sperling, who'd gone to Mt. Holyoke with one of his Boston cousins and was now living at College Settlement House, where she taught hygiene and English and ran a reading circle. Lizzy was full of fun but also interested in social reform, and early on Will had wondered whether they might become more than friends. But somehow, on both sides, the attraction was always intellectual, nothing more, and so, without ever discussing it, they'd settled into a comfortable relationship that suited them both just fine.

One day, discussing their shared desire to provide their students with fresh stimulation, Will and Lizzy decided to stage a debate in which each settlement house would provide one affirmative and one negative speaker. Inspired in part by the continuing news reports of scandalous conditions in tenement properties owned by the very wealthy Trinity Church, they came up with the idea of focusing on the role of religion in improving social conditions. Many of the young people who came to the two settlement houses were Jews and Italian Catholics who lived in those Trinity tenements.

It took Will over an hour to get to University Settlement, making him late to the pre-debate meeting. At this time of day, the streets of the Lower East Side were choked with people coming home from work or doing last-minute shopping for their evening meal, and he had to make his way around pushcarts, piles of pungent trash, and knots of elderly men. On some blocks old wooden buildings were still mixed in with brick ones, almost all of them poorly maintained. In the park at Rivington Street, screaming boys raced around on the packed dirt that had once presumably been a lawn, enjoying a few minutes of freedom before full darkness descended.

Even though Will had made this same trip for over a year now, he never ceased to be amazed by how many children there were in the neighborhood. Where did they all sleep at night? Why were they always in the street, it seemed, instead of in their homes? And why didn't their parents see that the best way to improve their lives was to cut down on the number of children they had, so that there would be fewer mouths to feed and more time to spend with the children they had?

Not for the first time, he reflected on how little he knew of the ordinary inhabitants of this neighborhood. The young men who came to his class were those who aspired to something better—putting it bluntly, he acknowledged to himself, to becoming more like him. The others—the group of men always talking together outside a small synagogue, the Italian women who smelled of garlic as he passed them in the street—seemed indifferent to his presence and in fact often looked at him with hostility.

A few more minutes' walk brought him within sight of the University Settlement building, which stood out from the tenements surrounding it by virtue of its graceful architecture. Six stories high, constructed of red brick with white stone facings, it featured an entrance framed by pillars and made grander by the three steps up to the main door.

By the time Will got to the classroom where he'd agreed to meet his two debaters, Aaron Cohen, a Russian who worked in the garment factory, and Anton Diaconu, who'd been a teacher in his native Romania but who here helped out a fellow Romanian in a second-hand bookstore, he found they'd already left for College Settlement, where the debate was to be held. Annoyed with himself for being late, he hurried the three blocks there.

The Locket

College Settlement wasn't nearly as impressive as University Settlement, being only three stories high and so narrow it could only accommodate three street-level windows. But like its more elegant companion, it exuded an air of gentility.

Will found Cohen and Diaconu remarkably calm, both consulting with their team-mates from College Settlement while the middling-sized room rapidly filled with people. One of the College Settlement speakers was clearly Italian, a large-boned young woman with olive skin and black hair. The other one was slight—no more than five feet, if that, Will judged—with dark hair done up in a bun and an earnest manner.

"Sorry I'm late," Will greeted the two young men and Lizzy, who had just joined the group, and turned to the two young women. The Italian one was named Cecilia Raggaza, and the other introduced herself as Ana Markowicz. "Actually," she said, with the slightest hint of an accent that Will took to be Polish, "my name is Chana"—saying the word in a way that sounded almost like Hannah—"but when I came to this country the teachers could not pronounce it, so I became Ana."

Will responded with a smile, oddly pleased to know this small fact. "And I'm really William, but I much prefer to be known as Will," he said.

By now, almost all the sixty or so seats in the room were filled, so Will found a spot near the back, next to several of his students who had come to cheer on their classmates. Almost as soon as he'd sat down, Lizzy called the meeting to order and introduced herself and Will, who stood up briefly in acknowledgement.

"Thank you all for coming," she told the room. "We're very happy tonight to be joined by our friends from University Settlement. For those of you who are first-time visitors to College Settlement, we're nearly as old as University Settlement, having been begun by a few college women from Wellesley. Our goal is the same as that of University: to share the benefits of the education and experiences we've had with people who haven't been as fortunate"—here Will winced slightly, recognizing that while Lizzy meant well, the phrase came across as condescending—"and together to build a better future."

Taking a breath, Lizzy went on, "Our debate topic tonight is: 'Resolved, religion in America is a force for social progress.' Each debater will speak for eight minutes and then, after all have been heard, one speaker from each side will have four minutes to rebut. We're going to make a slight change from the usual debating format: we'll have both affirmative speeches first, and then both negative speeches. At the end of the rebuttals, the audience will vote to decide the winner. Since University Settlement are the visitors, they'll start."

Looking at the paper in her hand, Lizzy then introduced the four debaters and invited Anton Diaconu to speak for the motion.

Diaconu was a bit nervous, Will could see, but he grasped the lectern forcefully and managed a small smile as he began to speak.

"One of the first books I read in English," he said, "was published three years ago, in 1907, just at a time when my English had become good enough that I could read for meaning, without having to look up a word in every sentence." A murmur of understanding ran through the audience. "It was written by an American clergyman named Walter Rauschenbusch, and it's called *Christianity and the Social Gospel.*

"I'd like to quote just one sentence from that book—a very long one, so I'll read only part of it—because I believe it sums up the main points. It goes like this: 'If the luxury of unearned wealth no longer made us all feverish with covetousness and a simpler life became the fashion; if our time and strength were not used up either in getting a bare living or in amassing unusable wealth and we had more leisure for the higher pursuits of the mind and the soul—then there might be a chance to live such a life of gentleness and brotherly kindness and tranquility of heart as Jesus desired for men.'"

Looking up at the audience, Diaconu said, "These are the words of a man who has worked to bring the Kingdom of God to earth. When Rauschenbusch left New York City, where he'd been working, to return to his home in Rochester, he chaired many committees dedicated to improving the city's education, health and housing. Even his critics have described Rochester's reform movement as one of the most progressive in the nation."

Will began to relax. As Diaconu continued, describing other events such as the success of a church-sponsored mediation board in ending several strikes, he grew more confident that Diaconu's dry and academic approach was succeeding, drawing its strength from facts rather than a showy presentation. By the time he ended, Will felt sure Diaconu had made an effective case.

Following Diaconu, Cecilia Ragazza, also speaking for the affirmative, took to the floor. It was a painful eight minutes. The Italian girl appeared so flustered that it was hard to pay attention to her points. Mainly, as far as Will could tell, her argument rested on the kindness shown to her family by the nuns who had taught her for eight years. As she described it, they'd helped out her family when her parents' grocery store in Little Italy had been burned out in a fire, and had taken her on as a cook in the parochial school they ran after her mother died. This, she seemed to be saying, proved that religion was a positive thing.

Next came University's speaker for the negative, Aaron Cohen, who strode to the lectern with one hand in his pocket in a manner that suggested he was a practiced public speaker. Cohen was probably the best student in Will's class, combining well-thought out positions with a forceful and confident style. Yet there was something about him, some bit of showiness, that Will found at times off-putting. Cohen had responded politely to Will's suggestions as he prepared for the debate, but Will got the impression that he didn't particularly feel the need of any advice.

And just as Will had feared, Cohen's delivery tonight was if anything more self-important than usual. "The history of religion in this country, from the Puritans onward, has been one of ignorance, backwardness and sophistry," he began, thus, Will felt, instantly alienating many in the audience who were uncomfortable with such a sweeping indictment—and, perhaps, with the use of words they didn't understand.

Cohen went on to denounce the Spencerians like Bishop

William Lawrence, who used Darwin's theories to prove that wealth is a reward for morality, and to ridicule the authors of the new set of essays called The Fundamentals, which preached the Bible's inerrancy. Nor did the Catholics and Jews get off any better than the Protestants. "The well-fed bishops, who enjoy all the comforts of this world, exhort their ill-fed and ill-clothed flock every Sunday to keep their eyes on the hereafter," Cohen said mockingly, "while the rabbis are too busy studying the Torah to notice that their children have no shoes."

There was more in this vein, cleverly-phrased and well-delivered, but Will found himself growing concerned. By being so unrelentingly negative, he felt sure, Cohen was causing his listeners to wonder what he was leaving out. And there was also the matter of his somewhat pompous style. Still, Will consoled himself, Cohen, like Diaconu, was giving a solid performance, thus ensuring that the audience—which he knew from looking around included at least one University Settlement House trustee—would take away a good impression.

Finally, it was the turn of the second College Settlement speaker, Ana Markowicz. As she rose from her chair, Will found himself hoping she'd do well, if only for Lizzy's sake. When she got to the lectern, only her head was visible, prompting a brief delay while a small stool was quickly found and put into place.

Ana stepped gravely onto the stool, and stood solemnly surveying the audience. "I am a working girl," she began simply, "and I believe that is up to us workers to save ourselves."

She paused briefly, then continued, "I was on the picket line last winter during the waist makers strike and to this day I bear the marks of the beatings I received. There were no priests on that picket line, nor ministers nor rabbis either. Only us girls, freezing to death and being kicked and beaten by the company goons."

Again, she looked hard at the audience. For a second or two, Will felt sure, she was looking straight at him. Then, she continued, "Mr. J.P. Morgan may be donating money on Sunday to help the poor, but on Monday through Saturday he and his friends are letting the police crack our skulls if we so much as ask for a raise. I cannot help but think that it is *because* he goes to church and donates money on Sunday that Mr. J.P. Morgan feels not the slightest need during the rest of the week to consider why the poor need his donations—or indeed whether they are human beings at all."

The audience was leaning forward, fully engaged now, because Ana was speaking about things they understood. For most of them, the world of Wall Street was as far away as Arabia, but in the past year or two, since the shirtwaist factory girls had led the way, many of them had experienced, as Ana had, the whack of a billy club and the insults of the goons.

"I am not only a worker but I am also an anarchist," Ana continued. "I don't condemn religion—there are, no doubt, good men whose belief in God spurs them to work toward a better society—but anarchism liberates man from the belief that he must surrender to some higher being and cannot think and act for himself. Anarchism says that within every man is his own salvation."

Now, Will felt, Ana was on dangerous ground: just the word anarchism was enough to make many people uneasy if not downright alarmed. Yet she was carrying the audience with her. "Anarchism stands for a social order based on the free grouping of individuals for the purpose of producing real wealth," she continued, a bit stiltedly but nonetheless with careful attention to language. "An order that will guarantee to every human being free access to the earth and full enjoyment of the necessities of life."

Then, after elaborating on this theme for a few minutes, Ana took off in a different direction. "Consider the story of the militant abolitionist John Brown," she said. "If it weren't for Brown and his comrades—taking direct action rather than preaching pious sermons—America would still trade in the flesh of the black man. Trade unionism, too, is the result of workers standing up and standing together. Had trade unionists waited for the religious leaders of this city or this country to lead the way, we would still be waiting. Instead, we are marching"—and here her voice grew louder— "not toward some imaginary kingdom but toward a heaven right here on earth."

And with that final flourish, Ana nodded politely to the audience and returned, amidst spontaneous applause, to her seat.

For all practical purposes, Will knew, the contest was already over. Diaconu did a credible job of rebutting Cohen's historical references, noting that while Darwin had indeed inspired a cohort of clergy who argued that the poor had only themselves to blame, it was that same Darwin who'd led to the flourishing of 'higher criticism,' which reinterpreted the Bible in a figurative rather than a literal manner. But he was far less successful in arguing against Ana's view of a world in which man's own reasoning and actions had replaced an indifferent God.

In contrast, Ana made short work of Cecilia's presentation, noting, not unkindly, that individual cases, whether positive or negative, don't prove a thesis. She accorded Diaconu's arguments a more respectful treatment, but maintained that while Walter Rauschenberg may have prompted the wealthy of Rochester to treat the poor more humanely, he did so as a member of the elite "helping" the poor, rather than as one who believed in the right, and the ability, of the poor to help themselves. Will silently disagreed, thinking that if Ana had actually read Rauschenbusch carefully, she couldn't dismiss him so easily.

But his was clearly a minority view. When it came time for the voting, the applause for the team of Ana and Aaron Cohen was twice as loud, and lasted at least twice as long, as the applause for their opponents.

And with that, the event was over. Lizzy thanked the debaters and invited them and the audience to enjoy the refreshments that had been laid out in an adjoining room. Then, linking her arm through Cecilia's, she walked toward the inner door.

Will hung back, chatting with several young men from University Settlement. But finally, as the crowd in the room thinned, he, too, moved toward the room with the refreshments. After accepting a cup of tea from one of Lizzy's friends, he gazed around the room until he spotted Ana standing off to one side near the window. She was talking animatedly with Aaron Cohen, and

Will found himself, much to his surprise, feeling jealous. What could she possibly see in that know-it-all?

He strode over to the two and made a small mock bow to Ana. "Congratulations," he said with a grin. "You were so persuasive in your remarks that I'm considering leaving the seminary and becoming a union organizer."

Ana responded with a look of earnest surprise, softened by a small laugh as she realized that Will was making a joke. "Really, I don't think that you'd make a very good organizer," she said, picking up on his light tone. "You would probably use too many fancy words, just like this fellow here"—pointing to Cohen.

"Oh, I doubt that," Will said. "My mother is an English teacher, and she always drilled it into my head that the best words are the simple ones that came from the Anglo-Saxons, not the fancy ones that the Normans brought over to England from France."

"Then what does your mother think of your becoming a clergyman?" Ana asked. "Surely clergymen are expected to give sermons full of long words and long sentences."

Now it was Will's turn to laugh, but with the slightest hint that Ana had touched a nerve. "That will never be me," he said. "I'm not even sure I want to give sermons. I think I might be more interested in writing books or teaching than serving in a parish. At least half the people who come to church on Sunday don't even want to be there in the first place, and probably most of the rest are thinking about what's for dinner."

As Will and Ana continued to banter, Cohen, sensing he was being cut out of the conversation, moved away to join a group of friends. Before long, that group left, and as if by a prearranged signal, others started to follow. Soon, only a handful of people were left and Will, glancing up at the clock on the wall, saw that it was already after nine o'clock.

"I must be going," Ana said, following his gaze. "I have to be at work by eight in the morning. If we're late by even one minute, they refuse to let us in and we miss a day's pay."

Will, without stopping to think, responded, "But surely it's not safe for a young woman to walk the streets around here after dark? Let me see you home."

"Oh, I assure you I'm quite safe," said Ana sharply, clearly offended by Will's implied criticism of her neighborhood. "I've lived here since I was a little girl. And my house is only three blocks away."

Will instantly rushed to make amends. "I didn't mean to suggest that this area is any more dangerous than where I live," he said quickly. But realizing that he was only compounding his error, he continued, "Or maybe the truth is that I did, in which case I apologize. The real reason I want to walk you home is that I'd like to have a chance to talk a bit more."

Ana, obviously disarmed by his candor, responded with a small laugh. "Well, perhaps it is quite dark tonight," she said. "If you would just wait a few minutes, I'll get my coat and say goodbye to Miss Sperling. I'll meet you outside the front door."

Will nodded, then turned and made his way out through the room where the debate had been held to the front entrance. Standing in the glow of a street lamp, Will turned up the collar of his light jacket and studied a leaflet he'd picked up in the entrance hall that listed several forthcoming events.

He'd hardly had time to scan it when Ana came out, looking slightly flushed. Will couldn't help noticing how small she was, wrapped in a worn-looking gray coat that seemed a size or two too large for her.

Now, out here on the street, the easy conversation of the evening gave way to awkwardness. "My house is just down Eldridge Street," Ana said, gesturing as she spoke. "It won't take us more than two or three minutes to walk there."

But Will knew he didn't want the evening to be over so soon. "If you wouldn't mind," he said, "I'd welcome a chance to get a bit of fresh air. Let's walk to Delancey and over toward the bridge. You can tell me a bit about the neighborhood. To be honest, I've been coming here for over a year but I've never really had a proper tour of the place, and I tend to just come, teach my class, and go back to the seminary."

Ana looked at him closely. "Perhaps just a half-hour," she said. "My aunt will be waiting up for me, and it's true what I said about the factory. We start at eight o'clock sharp, and I must be there when the door opens."

And with that they began walking the block to Delancey, the sidewalks now much emptier than when Will had arrived. Those still out at this hour tended to look a bit harder, he noticed, as he and Ana rounded the corner and started heading east.

"Tell me what I should know about Delancey Street," Will said, as they passed closed shops, their awnings tightly rolled up and their windows emptied of anything of value. In some shops, he could see, crowded together, rough wooden bins that during the day were rolled out in front of the shops and filled with goods to attract passers-by.

Ana smiled. "Well, I don't think there is anything you *should* know," she said, regaining the bantering tone of their earlier conversation. "This one," she said, pointing at the Yiddish lettering on the window, "is a bakery. You can see the places where they put plates of bread and cakes because there's no dust where the plates generally are." Two shops down, she pointed to another set of letters and said, "And this one is a butcher. But you can tell that for yourself because of the smell! Even though they wash everything down when they finish for the day, there's always some smell that remains."

"And do you do your shopping here?" Will asked.

"Sometimes," Ana said. "But usually my aunt likes to buy what we need from the shops near where she works on Orchard Street. Many of the people around there come from the same town she and my uncle came from in Poland. My parents came from there, too. They died in a typhoid epidemic when I was only six years old, which is how I came to live here. At first after they died I stayed with my grandmother in Poland but after a year my uncle arranged for a couple who were emigrating to bring me along with them, and as soon as I got here my uncle and aunt adopted me."

It took Will a minute or two to absorb this information.

"I'm very sorry to hear about your parents," Will said finally.

"But I'm glad you came here."

"Thank you," Ana said. "Sometimes I feel sad that I hardly knew my parents but it was all so long ago that I don't think about it much."

They walked on in silence for another few minutes.

"And what about your uncle, where does he work?" Will asked.

"My uncle is dead, too," Ana said. "He died six years ago. He was a printer at the *Forward*"—then, seeing his puzzled look, adding, "the newspaper for Jewish people."

Will, unable to think of any appropriate further expression of sympathy, said nothing. But after a minute or two he stopped and turned to Ana. "Please forgive me for knowing so little about what goes on here," he said. "I'm embarrassed and a little ashamed that I didn't even know the name of the newspaper. It's as though I'm in a foreign country: I don't know the language, I don't know the geography, and I don't even know what people eat for dinner."

Ana laughed, disarmed again by Will's readiness to admit fault. "Maybe not so different from you," she said. "Potatoes. Always potatoes. And cabbage. And for Shabbat, maybe a chicken."

By now they had walked as far as Pitt Street, where they turned back. As Ana had said, her house was only a short way from the Settlement House. It was a nondescript brick tenement distinguished only by a pot of zinnias perched on the windowsill of the first-floor apartment. Seeing Will look at them as they approached, Ana smiled. "The flowers are thanks to our neighbor Mrs. Simkovic. She barely has enough money to feed her children but she says she can't live without something beautiful in her life. For me, I'd rather have something practical."

"Like what?" Will asked.

"Oh, I don't know. Maybe a thick scarf for the winter."

"I think it would be nice to have both," Will said.

As Ana turned to say good-bye, Will started to shake hands, then added quickly, "I noticed in the list of upcoming events at College Settlement that there's an outing planned for next Sunday afternoon at Central Park. If you're planning to go, perhaps I could meet you at the settlement house and we could go together."

Ana considered this for a moment or two. "Well," she said slowly, "I usually help my aunt with the cleaning and cooking for the week because that's the only day we're free." Then, obviously intrigued, she went on, "But maybe she wouldn't mind just this once. It's not so far away, is it? I've never been there myself."

Never been to Central Park? How could a person live in New York City and never have been to Central Park? With an involuntary shake of his head that betrayed his amazement, Will assured her that it was an easy trip and that he'd be glad to act as her guide. Having agreed to meet at one o'clock, they shook hands again. "Thank you for the tour," Will said. "On Sunday I'll try to return the favor."

He waited until she'd climbed the tenement steps and closed the front door, then turned to begin the long trip back uptown. Anyone whom he'd passed on the way down would have noticed nothing different in the way he walked or carried himself, but perhaps a truly observant person would have seen just the slightest hint of a smile that passed now and then over his face.

CHAPTER FOUR

W hen Will woke up on Friday morning, the first thing he thought of was that it was only two more days until he would see Ana. Since Wednesday night she'd been much on his mind.

He kept picturing her, and how small she was, and how it had been all he could do to keep from insisting she take his arm as they walked along Delancey Street in the dark. It was clear she didn't feel she needed his protection—or anyone else's—but still he'd longed to display some kind of caring for the tiny figure in the too-large coat.

He liked the way she spoke so carefully, and the way some of her words showed just a trace of an accent. And he liked the way her face lit up when she felt strongly about something—even when that something was a remark of his that she didn't agree with.

Of course, he told himself, what he was feeling was nothing more than eagerness to learn more about the Lower East Side and the plight of workers like Ana who lived there.

But he knew perfectly well that there was more to it than that.

He was still thinking about Ana when he emerged from the seminary onto Ninth Avenue, where he stopped for a minute to decide whether to take the Ninth Avenue elevated train or the subway to Morningside Heights to meet Grant LaFarge. The el entrance was practically in front of the seminary's main door, but the trains were noisy and during rush hour there were sometimes delays since all of the trains had to slow to a crawl as they navigated the wide turn high above Morningside Park.

In the end, he opted for the subway, on the grounds that it would provide a useful opportunity to take a close look at some of the design elements that LaFarge and his business partner had created for the subway platforms and entrances. He loved the decorative station tiles that gave a hint of each Manhattan neighborhood's attractions—a sailing sloop at South Ferry, a stockade at Wall Street, and, at One Hundred and Sixteenth Street, the Columbia University seal showing a seated female imparting knowledge to children. And he loved even more the graceful glass and wrought iron entrance kiosks that made him think of Paris and the walks he'd taken there on trips to the Continent during his time in England.

He supposed that LaFarge's artistic sensibilities had been shaped in large part by his father, who, Will knew, came from a distinguished family of French Catholics who had settled in New York many years before. The elder LaFarge was a highly-regarded painter and creator of gorgeously colored stained-glass windows, some of which Will had seen at Trinity Church in Boston and at St. Paul's in New York. Will had also read with interest an essay the elder LaFarge had written on Japanese art. The essay had surprised him with the freshness of its observations since he thought of LaFarge as somewhat old-fashioned by comparison with artists whose work he'd seen in Paris like Duchamp and Cezanne.

It must be hard, he thought, to be the son of someone so famous and to always know that the world was comparing your accomplishments with his. Maybe that was why Grant LaFarge seemed so driven. He and his business partner, George Heins, not content with having won the competition for the design of the Cathedral while they were still in their thirties, had taken on project after project: the Bronx Zoo, the subway, plus numerous churches and private homes up and down the East Coast. And, besides all that, LaFarge had found time to go exploring with Teddy Roosevelt, study Spanish, and go out with the local fishermen in Rhode Island where he had a summer home—all bits of information Will had picked up through acquaintances he and LaFarge shared.

Still, LaFarge's life was hardly without problems, Will knew. Ever since Heins had died unexpectedly three years before, LaFarge, who had always been the artistic member of the team, had had to assume Heins' role as day-to-day manager as well. And Will had heard that LaFarge had a somewhat loveless marriage and an explosive temper, hardly a good thing in someone who had to deal with an army of suppliers and workmen.

Will was still reflecting on these snippets of gossip, interspersed with thoughts of Ana, when he suddenly realized that the train was pulling into his station. Jumping to his feet, he got to the door even before it opened and was soon part of a small crowd of people pushing their way up the stairs to the street.

Once outside, he spent a few seconds orienting himself—Will never could understand why, but he always had trouble figuring out in which direction he was facing when he emerged from the subway—and started up Broadway. He noticed that a new advertisement for Sloan's Liniment had been painted on the side of a building across the street, and that just in front of the building was a peddler's horse and cart selling fruit. Meanwhile, an automobile was slowly making its way down Broadway and was about to pass the horse and cart. Funny, he thought, how subways, horses, trolleys and automobiles were now all contending for dominance in the city. If anyone was looking for an example of how the world was changing faster than anyone could keep up with, this scene was a perfect one.

After passing a stationer's, a cobbler's, and a greengrocer's with its awning permanently lowered, Will turned onto One Hundred and Eleventh Street and headed toward Amsterdam Avenue. It always surprised him how these few blocks seemed so unrelated to the great university nearby; to anyone who didn't know differently, this was just another neighborhood of middle-class apartment buildings, most of them recently completed and vying to stand out from their nearly identical neighbors.

He particularly liked this street, which despite being so close to the hubbub of Broadway was an oasis of quiet, with graceful trees lining both sides of the block. Whereas on Broadway the city seemed to be moving at a snail's pace to remove the detritus of the subway construction of a few years before, on these side streets new buildings were no sooner up than the owners rushed to remove all signs of construction and to place small planters of boxwood by the entrances. Within a short time, tenants had moved in, curtains had been hung, and flowerboxes had appeared outside the street-level windows. Here on One Hundred and Eleventh Street, the evidence of upward aspirations was particularly notable in the names chiseled in stone above the entrances: Kendal Court, Criterion Arms, and, in acknowledgement of the city's Dutch heritage, the De Peyster.

Idly, Will wondered whether Ana had ever been to this part of town, and what she'd thought of it if she had. Probably, if she'd never been to Central Park, she had never been here either. Maybe one day he could show it to her.

The view from Amsterdam Avenue into the Cathedral grounds was somewhat bleak, Will thought. The completed portion of the Cathedral was impressive owing to its immense size, but the unfinished walls that would one day give way to the nave and the transepts were right now just large expanses of stone. Around the building was open ground, punctuated here and there by bits of machinery, pools of water left over from the rain earlier in the week, and piles of rubble. Far back toward the property's southern boundary, he could just make out the top of St. Faith's House, a training school for Church deaconesses, which was well on its way to completion.

As he crossed the street and walked through the entrance to the grounds, he could see on his left the orphans' asylum building that the Bishop's secretary had referred to; it now provided space for LaFarge's offices as well as for the choir school and assorted Cathedral-related activities. The building, constructed in the middle of the last century and designed to resemble a small Greek temple, looked incongruous and out of proportion, Will thought, situated as it was next to the Cathedral's massive bulk. How long would it be, he wondered, before it was torn down.

Farther back, Will saw a roughly-built shed from which he could hear slight clinks that indicated that the stone carvers were at work. Strange, he thought to himself, as soon as a visitor was just a few yards inside, the noises of the city rapidly faded away and one could actually hear such tiny sounds.

Relying on the directions he'd been given by the Bishop's secretary, he climbed the stairs of the asylum building and walked through the only open door in sight. The room was filled with draftsmen's tables, some with drawings tacked above them, others covered with bits of marble of varying colors and the occasional small, carved figure or flower that Will assumed was meant as an experiment before its larger counterpart was undertaken. There was dust on the floor and on the tables and the general sense was one of unkempt confusion.

Some way along the right-hand wall of the room was another open door, and, seeing no one in the large room, Will walked toward it. As he entered, he saw the man he assumed to be LaFarge sitting behind a desk that was cluttered with papers and more bits of marble.

"Mr. LaFarge?" he inquired.

LaFarge nodded an assent. Will introduced himself and LaFarge, after saying that he'd been informed of Will's visit, indicated that Will should take the only chair in sight, from which LaFarge first had to remove a heavy binder. As he sat down, Will observed that Grant LaFarge looked a lot like a picture he'd seen of LaFarge's father: lean, dark-haired, with a long, attractive face. But in Grant LaFarge's case, the attractiveness was lessened by a harried expression that looked as though it was habitual.

"So, as though I don't have enough bosses already, you're going to be another one," LaFarge commented flatly. "Or is it more that you're meant to be a spy?"

Will, taken aback, protested weakly that he was neither. "In fact," he said, "Bishop Greer has a great deal of sympathy for your position. He sees my main role as reporting back to him what your problems are and letting you know what he's doing about them. He's aware that you've already got far too many bosses as it is."

LaFarge sighed. "You have no idea," he said, waving a letter in the air which he'd apparently just been reading when Will came in. "Listen to this, from Ernest Flagg, an architect I've never even heard of, who took it upon himself to write to the chairman of the trustees, who of course thought he really must send the letter on to me: 'The choir area as it stands is not worthy of what the Cathedral ought to be.' Quite a useful observation, don't you think?"

LaFarge sighed again, rather melodramatically. "This is what we've been putting up with even before the first spade was in the ground more than fifteen years ago," he said. "Do you know the history?"

Without waiting for Will's response, LaFarge went on, "Some trustees were unhappy when we won the competition because they wanted something more Gothic. That would have been Huss & Buck—they were among the four finalists—but their design was unimaginative to say the least. Potter and Robinson's was also Gothic, but Potter was related to Bishop Potter, who was the Bishop at the time, so that more or less left him out; no one wanted to be accused of nepotism, least of all Bishop Potter. And then there was Wood; well, the less said of that one the better. So there it stood: deadlock, with us as no one's favorite but in the end the only ones left standing."

Will tried to look sympathetic, although he himself leaned more toward Gothic than the dominant Byzantine and Romanesque elements in Heins & LaFarge's design.

"No changes we made were ever enough," LaFarge went on. "We agreed to add some Gothic touches before the final decision was made, but as soon as the contract was signed there were requests for yet more. We lengthened the windows to look more Gothic. We redesigned the towers. We increased the length of the building.

"The final straw was when they told us we had to realign the building from north-south to east-west 'in accord with tradition,' so they said. Why hadn't they thought of that earlier? Now instead of the facade facing the city from atop the Morningside escarpment, it faces a row of apartment buildings!" LaFarge gave an annoyed shake of his head. "Why we didn't just say no and quit at that point I'll never understand. I suppose it was because we were young and hungry and we thought we could live with the changes and that once we got going on the construction they would leave us alone to get on with the job. How wrong we were!"

Will wasn't sure how to respond—or even why LaFarge was telling him all this—so he said nothing. But then, deciding he couldn't act too sympathetic lest LaFarge take him for an uncritical ally, he said, "Well, I do sympathize, and so does Bishop Greer. But the Bishop says that the consecration absolutely must go on as planned on April 19 and so we've all got to ignore everything else and just focus on getting ready for that date."

LaFarge looked at Will intently, clearly aware that Will was implying that he wasn't doing enough of either, then sat back in his chair, his exasperation seemingly spent. "Easier said than done," he said grimly. Then, standing up, he announced, "Well, let's see how things are going."

With that he swept past Will and down the stairs, Will trailing behind. Once out of the building, they walked a short distance to a rickety iron staircase and entered the Cathedral by a small side door.

Inside, it took Will's eyes a minute to adjust. Even though all the windows, both on the sides of the crossing and behind the altar, were clear glass, on a cloudy day like this one the vast interior space was shrouded in gloom. Slowly, however, Will made out the dominant features: the eight soaring columns—so huge, he remembered reading, that even in two pieces they'd required six days each to be hauled from a dock at West One Hundred Thirty-Fifth Street to the Cathedral site; the intricately carved wooden choir stalls, on which craftsmen were still working; and, most stunning of all, the spectacular saucer dome covered with tiny glowing tiles above the crossing.

Will knew that the dome was intended as only a temporary measure until the crossing tower was built, but his immediate reaction was that it was so beautiful that he hoped it would never be removed. Perhaps, he thought with surprise, he'd been wrong to think that Gothic architecture was most suited to raising man's eyes to heaven; this dome led to thoughts to the vault of the universe as it appeared on a starry summer night.

"It's beautiful," he said simply to LaFarge.

LaFarge nodded a thank-you. "I'm glad you see the glory," he said. "As the architect I appreciate that. But as the 'chief contractor' right now all I can see are the hundreds of things that have yet to be done and all the problems—like the leaking steam pipes and the delays in the delivery of the organ."

Over the next hour LaFarge took Will on an inspection tour that, among other things, included a quick tour of the ambulatory behind the main altar which contained spaces for seven chapels, only two of which were intended to be ready for consecration in April.

"The seven is deliberate," LaFarge said. "We've tried to incorporate the numerology of Revelations in as many ways as we can; for example, there are also seven eastern clerestory windows." Will nodded, recalling how many of the cathedrals he'd seen in Europe also employed the seven concept to reflect St. John's vision of the seven seals, seven trumpets and so on. It was appropriate, Will supposed, for the Cathedral to be named for the writer of the final book of the New Testament, for wasn't America meant to be the New Jerusalem of John's imagining?

Will's instant favorite among the chapels was St. Saviour's, or the Belmont Chapel as LaFarge referred to it because it had been given by August Belmont in memory of his wife. Located directly behind the main altar, it had been designed personally by LaFarge, using the English Decorated Gothic style. But it included icons and sculptures of Eastern Church doctors and saints—St.Polycarp, St. Athanasius and St. John Chrysostom among them—in honor of the Christian communities of the East.

What first caught Will's eye was not these sculptures,

however, but the twenty stone angels flanking the entrance, each wearing a different expression and intended to represent the heavenly choir. Will remembered, looking at them, that he'd read that they had been created by a sculptor named Gutzon Borglum, who had caused a minor controversy by depicting them as females, contrary to the male tradition extending back to Michael and Gabriel. Will was also amused by the small faces on the two side walls: on the left, an unhappy-looking fellow with a cleft chin, on the right a bearded figure with downcast eyes.

St. Saviour's was, in all ways, a visual delight, from the orange and black marble behind the white Carrara altar to the soft green marble around the edges of the floor and the blues and dark blues used in the stained-glass window. The window, LaFarge explained, was the work of the highly regarded Hardman firm of Birmingham, England. The large central panel showed the Transfiguration, with the transfigured Lord flanked by Moses holding the Ten Commandments and Elijah holding the receptacle of the scrolls. LaFarge told him that the pavement stone was from France.

Will also admired the four vaguely Egyptian-looking pedestals, the wrought iron candle stand, and the black wrought iron screen at the entrance, which, LaFarge told him, was modeled after one in Orvieto, Italy. Above the delicate gates were two golden angels holding a wreath at the foot of the cross. "Lovely," Will said with unforced admiration.

As they finished up, LaFarge paused to give Will a description of what the nave would look like once it was built and how it would add a graceful outside line to the Cathedral's now stubby east end. "But our nave, while creating a dignified approach to the sanctuary, won't be the main seating area," he explained. "Instead, the crossing will play that role, much as it does in Trinity Church in Boston. That guarantees that the largest possible number of people will be able to both see and hear the service."

Will nodded again in understanding, having more than once undergone the experience in a European cathedral of being present at a service but, relegated to some side aisle or to the far back of the nave, coming away with no idea of what had actually gone on.

As they came out of the building by the same door they had come in, Will glanced at his watch and saw that it was already noon. He wanted to spend the afternoon at Low Library doing some reading for his Columbia course—he had the time because the Bishop's secretary had told him not to come by since he'd be seeing the Bishop that evening—so he suggested to LaFarge that rather than return to LaFarge's office, they part company there.

Explaining that his hope was to stop in once or twice a week to see how things were going, he asked LaFarge for permission to wander around, even when LaFarge wasn't on the site, in order to be able to report back to Bishop Greer what progress he had observed. LaFarge agreed, and mentioned the names of several on-site bosses he could talk to.

"I try to be here as much as I can," LaFarge said, "but as you know our firm has several other projects that I oversee from our main office downtown. If there's something you need to ask me about urgently, you can always find me there." As they shook hands, LaFarge added, far too casually to make it sound anything but casual, "By the way, have you heard anything about a move to replace my firm with Ralph Cram?"

Will looked surprised. "No, nothing," he said.

They said good-bye and Will returned as he'd come, onto Amsterdam Avenue.

After a quick lunch at a noisy neighborhood cafe, Will turned into the Columbia campus and was immediately struck by the contrast with the Cathedral. Here, all was red brick and white facing marble—almost cozy after the somber granite of the Cathedral. He loved in particular the fact that the Columbia architects had chosen Catskill brick, made near where he'd grown up, for the paving as well as for many of the buildings. And perhaps because the sun had started to come out, the plaza in front of the library, which repeated the red and white color scheme, seemed a wonderfully warm and human-scale place.

He decided to sit for a few minutes on one of the stone

benches, to give him time to consider what he would say to Bishop Greer about his meeting. LaFarge had been friendly enough, after the first chilly exchange, and the work in the Cathedral seemed to be going on with decent speed. And certainly the Cathedral itself, though so far yet from finished, promised to be as imposing as its supporters could wish.

But...what? Looking around him at the streams of cheerful students, struck by how at ease they seemed in their surroundings, he couldn't help wondering why the Cathedral was being built at all. Somehow its granite solidity seemed out of keeping with the sense of modernity, the sense of energy and innovation, that were the hallmarks of the city which it aimed to serve. Maybe when it was first conceived, half a century before, there had been a feeling that America had to prove to Europe that it was more than a brash upstart. Now, however, America was rapidly establishing itself as the world's great new center of power, with New York City as its financial and cultural capital. It didn't need a new Episcopal Cathedral to prove anything.

But it had one, Will soberly concluded, and it was his job to help make sure it was ready for April.

With that, he bounded up the wide stairs and into the library reading room. There, for the next two hours, he concentrated on the Second Great Awakening, allowing himself only occasionally to daydream for a minute or two about Ana and the Sunday outing ahead.

CHAPTER FIVE

our o'clock found Will back in his room at the seminary, where he lay down for a brief rest before the evening's activities. Just as he was dozing off, he heard a knock on the door and his friend Hugh's voice asking if he could come in.

Will called out that the door was unlocked, then swung his feet onto the floor.

"You look worn out, Will," Hugh said. "I know you've been out all day because I didn't see you at noon services or at lunch. Is the new job with the Bishop even more exhausting than a debate in the refectory over the latest article by Lincoln Steffens expressing outrage about something or someone, somewhere in the country?"

Will laughed, then sat leaning back on the wall behind his bed while Hugh took the chair by Will's desk. "I'm not even done for the day yet," he said, explaining his evening engagement with the Bishop.

For the next half hour, he told Hugh about his meeting with LaFarge and how he'd come away wondering about the whole Cathedral project. The church was changing, they agreed, and the country, too, and it was hard to know what the future might hold. Hugh had always expected to seek out a parish in a small town somewhere in western New Jersey, where he came from, and where his father and an uncle were both ministers, but living in the city had made him wonder whether that was what he really wanted. The issues of whether or not to allow bright-colored stoles or to have earlier Sunday services seemed pretty unimportant, he'd said more than once after arriving back from a visit home, compared with debating the rights of workers and enjoying the excitement of city life.

To Hugh, Will, with his Boston relatives and years in London, represented the height of sophistication. But to Will, Hugh had an equally strong appeal, as the embodiment of the small-town good manners and good sense he remembered as a boy. Yes, conversations in Greenville were generally limited to the health of a farmer's dairy herd or the new road being built to Albany, but there was something deeply satisfying about looking around the church where he'd been baptized and seeing people he'd known all his life. Hugh was a reminder of all that, as well as an agreeable companion whose insights were sometimes all the more thought-provoking for being expressed in simple, unaffected language.

And so perhaps for these reasons, or perhaps for other, more undefinable ones, the two had been friends since the week they arrived at the seminary. Hugh had been engaged for two years and planned to get married right after graduation, and he'd already asked Will to serve as his best man.

At quarter to five, glancing at the clock, Will announced that he was throwing Hugh out so that he could wash up and get into his dinner jacket and still have time to get over to the Bishop's house. "Okay," said Hugh good-naturedly, heading for the door, "but try to bring some dessert back for me."

By ten minutes before six, Will was ringing the bell at Bishop Greer's door, which was opened by a maid who showed Will to the parlor. A few minutes later, Bishop Greer came in and nodded to Will.

"The car should be outside by now," Greer said, "so we'll just go out the way you came in."

The same maid appeared and held the door open for the two men. Greer strode the few steps to where a chauffeur was holding open the back door of a large black automobile that Will recognized as a Packard. Seeing Will admiringly taking it in, Greer curtly explained as they settled into the back seat, "I don't want you to think my salary is enough to pay for and maintain an automobile like this one, never mind the driver. One of my former parishioners at St. Bartholomew's gave me the car as a parting present, when I became Bishop, and he pays the driver's salary."

Will was quick to explain away his surprise. "It's true I was impressed, sir," he said, "but I wasn't being critical. In fact, I was thinking that by using an automobile you're showing the world that you're ready to embrace new ways of doing things."

Greer visibly relaxed. "I agree with you that some people make it a point of honor to reject anything they regard as 'modern,'" he said, "when in fact they're just concerned about looking foolish because they don't understand it. The reality is that having this vehicle makes me much more efficient: Every weekend I have to travel out of town to conduct confirmations or other services and now, thanks to this automobile, I don't have to worry about trains and being met and all that sort of thing; I just show up."

Pausing, he added, "Although I must say, it breaks down with some regularity. Fortunately, the chauffeur is an excellent mechanic as well."

They sat in silence for a minute or two as the car made its way uptown. Then Greer asked abruptly, "So, what did you think of LaFarge?"

"I think much of what he has done is brilliant," Will said, glad that he'd taken time to prepare his response. "I was prepared not to like the Cathedral very much but in fact I like it quite a lot, especially some of the smaller details like the angel carvings. However, LaFarge strikes me as someone who is so confident of his own judgment that he's not likely to take criticism—of which I gathered there's been a considerable amount—with grace."

Greer nodded grimly. "Exactly my conclusion. If you can just keep his shoulder to the wheel until April...well, whatever happens after the consecration is of no concern to me right now."

Will immediately thought about the question LaFarge had put

to him as they parted. "Sir, LaFarge asked me point blank if I knew anything of plans to replace him as architect, and I told him I didn't."

"Then let's talk no more of this matter," Greer said firmly. "It's best that you avoid idle chatter and speculation."

As Greer finished his sentence, the car pulled up in front of the Metropolitan Club. Designed less than twenty years before by Stanford White, the club had been much praised for its simple, elegant design. Will had been there a couple of times with college classmates whose fathers belonged, but it had been several years since his last visit and he marveled again as they made their way through the entrance and up the grand staircase at how White had produced something so graceful despite its enormous size.

The dinner was being held in one of the club's largest rooms, set with tables for eight, which Will quickly calculated meant that getting on for two hundred guests were expected. Lyall Randolph had been the vice-chairman of one of the city's largest banks, and the bank's trustees, having passed him over a couple years before for the chairmanship, were clearly intent on doing their best to make up for it with a grand send-off. It was also, of course, an opportunity for their executives and their best customers to renew acquaintances and perhaps to pave the way for a little future business.

At one end of the room, a bar had been set up and already a few small knots of attendees were gathered there exchanging greetings and small talk. For the Bishop, this was a work event, and he plunged briskly into it, engaging with one group after another and introducing Will as a seminarian who was helping him out on various matters.

The men all cordially welcomed Will and a few asked him questions about his studies, but mainly they were interested in each other and Will was content to listen to their conversations. At some point he realized the Bishop had left the group they'd both been a part of, but this came as no surprise. The Bishop's main goal at such events was to raise money, whether for the diocese or the Cathedral or one of the many good causes supported by the church, and he needed to work fast to shake as many hands as possible before the formal proceedings began.

When the call came to take their seats, Will found himself at a table near the back of the room, seated between a lawyer who worked for the bank's outside counsel and a manager in a manufacturing company that was a long-time bank client. Will could tell from the introductions that most of the men at the table were relatively junior in their firms, making him think wryly that they were probably all there only because they were protégés of senior men.

The talk soon turned to politics, not surprising given that the mid-term Congressional elections as well as the election for New York State governor were coming up in less than a month. Thanks to what many saw as the meddling of Teddy Roosevelt, back from his post-presidential safari in East Africa, Henry Stimson was to be the Republicans' gubernatorial candidate, a choice that had made many members of the state party, who saw Stimson as far too radical for their tastes, deeply unhappy.

"Roosevelt spent too long out there in that African sun," offered one of Will's table mates. "It just cooked his brains."

"It's not that, it's just that he wants to give President Taft and his New York State cronies heartburn and show them he's still boss," said another.

"All I know from my colleagues in our Buffalo and Albany offices is that the Democratic congressional contenders are turning out huge crowds upstate," said the lawyer. "And I hear the same from the lawyers in our office in Trenton. They think this Democratic fellow Woodrow Wilson is likely to win the New Jersey governorship."

A brief moment of gloomy silence ensued.

"Maybe that would be quite a good thing," Will said deliberately, addressing the table in general. "It seems to me that Wilson is a reformer who's aware of the need to attend to the needs of the poor, not just the wealthy men who live in his state and commute to Wall Street. I've read some of his remarks on the need for workmen's compensation and his arguments seem very well thought out."

The other young men, startled, stared at Will.

"Did you say you're a seminarian?" one asked.

In response to Will's nod of assent he added in a condescending tone, "Well, that would explain how you know nothing about politics or economics."

Will felt his face flush with anger, even though he'd known what reaction he was inviting when he made his remarks. But before he could reply, the evening's master of ceremonies announced that the speeches were about to begin. Will turned his chair half-way to face the head table, where he saw the Bishop sitting next to the guest of honor. On his other side, Will realized, was J.P. Morgan, whom he'd never met but whose bulbous nose, cruelly red and mottled from acne rosacea, made him unmistakable.

The speeches were predictable: a few brief and relatively witty, plus several that went on too long about the supposedly excellent qualities of the honoree. Among the latter was one given by a well-fed looking colleague of Randolph's who maintained that the United States' new position as a major world power was in no small part thanks to the caliber of businessmen like Lyall Randolph—men of good breeding and education who had nevertheless risen strictly on their own merits. Glancing around the room, Will saw several heads nod in agreement.

The Bishop was last. After paying tribute to Randolph's work on the Cathedral fabric committee, he segued into a short exposition of the importance of the Cathedral to the entire city, not just the Episcopal or the Protestant community, and expressed the hope that those present would consider a donation to complete the first phase of construction. He ended his remarks with a benediction.

Everyone stood up and said their good-byes, then started heading out of the room. Will held back, waiting for the Bishop, who was making his way out in the company of Morgan, with whom he appeared to be in deep conversation. Suddenly the Bishop noticed Will and summoned him over.

"This is my assistant, Will Ingalls," he said by way of introduction. "He's in his final year at the seminary, related to Phillips Brooks, a fine young man who is a volunteer at University Settlement as well as an outstanding scholar. I've asked him to be my eyes and ears at the Cathedral over the next few months until the consecration."

Morgan looked directly at Will with his famously piercing eyes. "You know that I'm one of the Cathedral's major donors," he said. "And I'm concerned as to whether the money is being well-spent. I've asked LaFarge several times to give me a report on how things are going but he has always begged off with a claim that he's too busy." Morgan's tone conveyed his annoyance that anyone would dare to treat him in such a high-handed way. "Mr. LaFarge can thank the Bishop, who seems to regard his continued presence as essential to getting the Cathedral prepared for the consecration, for the fact that I haven't moved to replace him."

The issue of LaFarge's replacement again. Will knew now that it was more than idle talk. But he acted as though he hadn't registered what Morgan had said, instead making a comment to the effect that from what he'd seen earlier in the day, the work was going on well.

"Tell me what you like most about what you've seen," Morgan demanded.

"The dome," Will answered. "The craftsmanship is extraordinary. Rafael Guastavino and his son have both shown themselves to be brilliant engineers as well as artists." Then, seeing Morgan's look of interest, he added, "We think of art as objects, or paintings, but art can also be taking a simple need, like a ceiling, and creating something of true beauty."

Morgan gave him an appraising look. "And what causes you to speak with such authority? Do you regard yourself as an artist?"

"Not at all," Will said. "At least not in a professional way. I've studied art, and tried my hand at painting, but I came to realize that my role in life is to be what I call an appreciator, an informed appreciator."

Morgan nodded. "That is precisely how I see myself," he said.

"One day you must come to my house and I'll show you some of the things I've collected over the years."

"I'd like that very much," Will said, and with that Morgan bade them good-night and strode out ahead of them.

Will and the Bishop said nothing more until they were again seated in the Bishop's car and heading back downtown.

"Mr. Ingalls," the Bishop said as they passed Forty-Second Street, "I believe you've just earned your first half-year's pay."

CHAPTER SIX

ill spent all of Saturday in the library, only emerging for noon prayers and lunch. He'd missed his Friday Dogmatic Theology class but he could get the notes for that from Hugh. As he could tell already, passing that class would just be a matter of repeating everything the professor had said—or for that matter, what the professor had written in the required textbook. He also had a Greek passage from one of the church fathers to translate, but that would be reasonably simple.

Of more concern was coming up with a topic for the paper he was required to write for his Columbia seminar. He was supposed to submit his idea at the next class, but after going over his notes and studying the readings for the semester, and then sitting staring into space for nearly an hour, he still hadn't come up with anything.

But then, on the way to evensong, it came to him: He'd always been fascinated by the Shakers, who had several communities in Massachusetts and upstate New York, two of which he'd visited with his mother. He found their religious practices strange, but he admired the way they'd created communities in which all goods were held in common and each member was expected to freely contribute his labor. The amazing thing was that they'd succeeded as well as they had, not just for a few years but for decades. He decided that he'd propose that he look at the Shakers in terms of their efforts to create a worldly utopia as an integral aspect of their spiritual beliefs.

Relieved to have the issue finally resolved, he walked into the chapel with a light step.

After dinner, Will and Hugh spent a couple hours talking with friends in Hugh's room until Will, pleading exhaustion, said goodnight to the group and turned in early. As he drifted off, he thought about Ana and the fiery speech she'd given at the debate.

The next morning, he woke up startled by the fact that the sun was pouring through his window and the bells were already ringing nine o'clock. Sunday service wasn't until eleven, but the refectory stopped serving breakfast at ten, so he quickly got up and washed. After a plate of toast and eggs and two cups of strong coffee, he felt ready for the day.

There was just time to write to his mother, something he did every Sunday, before the morning service. He had a lot to tell her this week: the job with the Bishop, meeting J.P. Morgan, and his idea for the class paper, and it was five minutes before eleven when he slipped the sheets of paper into an envelope, put on a two-cent stamp, and quickly wrote out the address. He could put the letter in the outgoing mail basket on his way out.

Guiltily, he acknowledged to himself that the reason he hadn't written anything about the debate at College Settlement, whose planning he'd described at length in an earlier letter, was because doing so would involve mentioning Ana. Not sure what his feelings were, or perhaps because he knew all too well what they were, he preferred to wait a little longer before saying anything. "I will in my next letter," he promised himself.

As he slipped into a pew just as the bells began to chime, Mr. Goodhue launched into the opening hymn. It was one of Will's favorites, "Guide me, Oh, thou Great Jehovah," which Will had first heard in England when it was still very new, and he sang it with enthusiasm.

Fortunately, the service was unusually short, just a little over an hour, which gave him time to rush back to his room, change into an informal jacket, and jump on the el, all by quarter past twelve. At the other end he bought a large, soft pretzel from a street vendor and ate it hungrily as he hurried to College Settlement, arriving there just in time to hear Lizzy say, "Well, I think we'd better get started," to a group of about fifteen young people who were milling around in front of the building.

"Sorry I'm a bit late," Will said to a surprised Lizzy, who hadn't known of his plans to join them. Glancing around, he saw Ana, looking even smaller than he remembered her, on the edge of the group. She was wearing a white shirtwaist but with a pretty red and blue shawl thrown over her shoulders, and her somewhat wild and curly hair, rather than being pinned up in a bun as it had been the night of the debate, was loosely gathered at the nape of her neck with a black ribbon.

"We're glad you could join us," Lizzy said in response, looking at him quizzically as she led off toward the nearest streetcar. As soon as he could do so without looking obvious, Will managed to fall in next to Ana and they exchanged pleasantries as the group made their way to Central Park. Ana seemed relaxed despite her lack of familiarity with midtown, and Will was struck by her confident manner.

"For someone who claims not to have seen much of the city, you seem quite the opposite of fearful," he observed.

"Oh, that's because Miss Sperling is in charge," Ana said. "She seems to know everything there is to know about New York. Sometimes she talks about places she's been to—museums and libraries and concerts—and she describes them so well that I can almost imagine I've been there myself. She says she wants to be a writer and I think she'll be a very good one."

Strange, Will thought, I didn't even know Lizzy was interested in being a writer. That must be something that had developed since college, since he never remembered her talking about it then. Well, they'd both had a lot of experiences since their college days; after all, hadn't he still been thinking at that time that he might become an artist?

When they reached Central Park, Lizzy gathered them

together and suggested they pick a spot at which to meet at four o'clock. There, they could rest and eat the small cakes she'd brought along before heading back. After a bit of discussion, in which Ana took no part, they agreed on a grassy outcrop not far from where they were standing. Turning to Will, Ana said with an earnest expression, "I hope you don't mind if I stay with you since I don't know my way around?"

"I insist on it," Will responded more gravely than he intended. "After all, I promised you a tour in exchange for the one you gave me the other night."

At first, the group more or less stayed together, stopping at the zoo to inspect the monkeys in their cages and to marvel at Hattie, the elephant, whose arrival six years before had been front-page news. But slowly people wandered off in twos and threes as they moved deeper into the park, some drawn to the paths and lawns and others to the pool for model boats or the reservoir.

Will suggested to Ana that they head northwest, toward the lake, which they did, speaking little until they came to the edge of the water and found a bench where they sat down.

"This is all so beautiful," Ana said, waving toward the lake and the trees, just starting to turn color, on the other side. "It's so hard to believe that all of this space exists in the same city where a family of ten people often share two rooms."

"But anyone can come here," Will objected. "It doesn't cost anything, or at least not anything more than the cost of the el or the subway."

"For a lot of families, a nickel each is too much," Ana said, a testiness in her tone. "It might mean the difference between having a meal or not. And even if they can afford it, most people in my neighborhood would say that places like this are not meant for them, they're meant for the real New Yorkers."

"And who might those be?" Will asked, a slight edge creeping into his voice.

"They mean the people who speak good English," Ana said, her tone matching his own. "People who were born here."

Will was silent for a moment. "Well, I think people have to get over those feelings," he said. "If they act like they belong here that's how they'll be treated."

Ana looked at him almost pityingly. "Do you really believe that?" she asked. "Do you think that I can go into Lord & Taylor and be waited on, just like some lady from Fifth Avenue? They know who we are and they want us to stay in our place, which is in the tenements far away from where they are. Jewish people are regarded as not even white, and they treat us almost as badly as they treat the colored people."

Will was silent again. "You may be right," he said. "But I think you're too ready to assume the worst about people you don't even know."

"I'm not saying everyone is like that," Ana responded, her voice rising and her careful diction beginning to falter. "There are some rich people like Mr. J.P. Morgan's daughter Anne who have been a great help to working girls. They put up bail for us when we were arrested and some of them even came to see us on the picket lines. That's more than a lot of the men in the unions have done—most of them don't even want us girls to *have* a union. But still, I get the feeling that the rich women are doing what they do because it makes them feel good and it doesn't cost them anything apart from a few dollars that they won't even miss."

Will felt stung by Ana's comments. Wasn't he part of the group Ana was referring to, even if he wasn't rich like Anne Morgan? To someone like Ana he probably did seem rich; he certainly had never had to share a room in his life, except with cousins when they were all on summer vacations in Maine, or even imagined what it would be like not to have enough to eat. And if he was to be honest with himself, what was he sacrificing by working at University Settlement House other than a few hours of his time, in return for which he got to feel virtuous?

For the next few minutes, Will and Ana sat there saying nothing as Will went back over the conversation, trying to figure out how things had so quickly gone wrong. His immediate reaction was to suggest that they walk back to where they were to meet the others. Then, as soon as he could, he'd make his apologies and leave. He and Ana were unlikely ever to run into each other by chance, and he could just regard what had happened as an unfortunate experience and forget it.

But something made him not want to leave things there.

"Ana," he said, "I admired how you spoke at the debate and it made me want to know you better. I know I could learn a lot from you about many things that interest me and trouble me about the way this city operates." Then, taking a quick gulp, he added, "And I also think you look very pretty today."

Ana, clearly taken aback, started to laugh. "Well, a minute ago I thought we would never see each other again," she said. "And now you're giving me compliments."

They sat in silence again for a minute or two. Then, in a quiet voice from which the harshness of a few minutes before had drained out, Ana began to speak. "I have spent many years learning hard lessons about how the world works," she said, looking not at Will but at the lake in front of them. "I come from a world where you have to be tough to survive, and never admit to any weakness. And I've become used to people—especially the girls in the shops where I've worked—looking to me as someone who always has an opinion about what to do and about who is to blame for our problems.

"But I've been thinking since we met the other night that maybe I don't know as much as I think I do. I've experienced a lot of life, but you've thought about issues and read about them in a way that I haven't. And you aren't afraid to admit that you've made a mistake, which I find very strange but yet at the same time I admire it."

Pausing, she added, "I don't know if we can be close friends but at least let's not be enemies."

Will was silent, taking in what she had said. Then, smiling, he said, "I agree."

With that they both stood up and started walking again, this time down through the center of the park. In a few minutes they began to hear the sound of a calliope, and Ana looked at Will questioningly.

"It's the carousel," Will explained. "Have you ever been on one?"

"No," Ana said, "but I have seen pictures."

"Well, no time like the present," Will said, his gaiety a bit forced but a sense of relief in his voice that they'd managed to return to the bantering tone that they'd already established.

A few minutes brought them to the carousel, whose brilliantly painted horses bobbed up and down to the sound of the music. There was only a short line, and the carousel was already slowing down, so within a few more minutes Will had bought their tickets and they were seated side by side on their horses, grasping the poles in front of them.

Ana looked a bit frightened as the carousel started up, but within a minute she was laughing and turning this way and that as she gazed first at the clown faces painted on the inner part of the carousel and then at the park swirling around them.

When the carousel stopped Ana gave Will a happy smile as he helped her down from her horse. "Thank you very much," she said. "That was the most fun I've had in a long time."

"You're very welcome," Will said. "And thank you for coming today. I've enjoyed it."

As they headed back toward the meeting place, Ana suddenly stopped and said, "Have you ever heard Emma Goldman speak?"

"No," said Will. "I've always wanted to, but I was worried I'd feel out of place or that people wouldn't want me there."

"Ah!" said Ana. "Now you see what I was talking about! But let's not go back to that subject again. The reason I asked is that she is giving a talk at Cooper Union next Friday night and I'm planning to go. I think she's a wonderful speaker, and of course I agree with almost everything she says. If you'd like to go, perhaps we could meet there. It's at eight o'clock."

"I'd like that very much," said Will. So it was agreed: they would meet at quarter to eight just outside the entrance.

By the time they got back to where the group had arranged to meet it was already almost four, and nearly everyone was there.

Without saying anything, Ana and Will deliberately parted ways as they approached; Ana went to sit with two other young women and Will took a place by Lizzy's side.

Munching one of Lizzy's cakes, he braced himself for what he knew was coming.

"So, I see that you and Ana have become good friends," Lizzy said in a teasing voice.

"That's all, just good friends," Will said, trying to sound nonchalant. "I liked what she said at the debate and I wanted to talk more about it."

Lizzy looked at him searchingly. "Be careful, Will," she said lightly, but with a warning tone in her voice. "Ana is an impressive young woman—probably the most impressive I've met in my time at the settlement. She thinks for herself and she's open to new ideas without feeling a need to reject her past, as so many of the others do. She approaches the books we read in our Sunday evening group without preconceptions about what she should like or shouldn't like, and she expresses her opinions in wonderfully clear terms. But I know I don't have to tell you that she comes from a very different world than we do. I wouldn't want her to get hurt, and I wouldn't want you to get hurt either."

"I understand what you're saying," Will said. "And please don't worry; I promise to be careful."

He proceeded to fill Lizzy in quickly on his meeting with J.P. Morgan and mentioned how Ana had told him that Anne Morgan was one of the women who were helping the girls who were trying to get better working conditions.

"Oh yes," said Lizzy. "Anne Morgan is quite serious about what she's doing and she's helped out a lot, not just with money but also by talking to some of the powerful people who are in a position to actually do something about the disgraceful conditions the girls have to contend with."

Then, after a pause, she added, "Did you know that she and her father are completely estranged? It's not just her politics but also"—here Lizzy stopped, searching for the right words—"her personal arrangements."

"What do you mean?" Will asked.

"Well, she's friends, and I mean more than friends, with two women who were already a scandal because of their relationship. One is an actress and the other is a theatrical agent."

"Oh my goodness, I hadn't heard about that," said Will, coloring visibly. "I'm afraid you're much better informed than I am about many things. I just sit there in the seminary reading dead texts written by church fathers who couldn't even speak Greek very well."

Lizzy laughed. "It's amazing what you hear at 'the best' dinner parties in New York City," she observed dryly.

Will glanced at his watch and saw that it was getting on for five o'clock. He apologized to Lizzy and the group for not accompanying them back downtown but explained that he wanted to be at the seminary for evening services at six. Everyone waved to him as he set off out of the park.

After evensong, he met up with Hugh outside and they headed off to the refectory. Sunday nights were always quiet, and the meal was a simple one, so by seven-thirty they were finished and at slightly loose ends.

"How about a walk in the neighborhood?" Will asked. Hugh agreed, and with that they set off toward the river, chatting about their classes and their professors and about Hugh's efforts to resolve his career dilemma.

"I have an idea," said Will. "I've been thinking about signing up for the weekend retreat at Holy Cross monastery in West Park in mid-November. I saw the announcement on the bulletin board near the mailroom a few days ago. Why don't you come, too? It would be a good chance to get away from here for a couple of days, and maybe get to know Father Huntington, the Superior, a bit."

Hugh reflected on the idea for a minute. "I've never done such a thing," he said. "My uncle has no use for Father Huntington, even if Huntington is supposed to be a great thinker, and he says Huntington's ideas about contemplation and celibacy are all Papish nonsense. He says that all a good Episcopalian needs is to go to church on Sunday and read the Saint James version of the Bible."

"Your uncle may be right," Will responded. "But I've never done such a thing either and I'm curious what it's like. I'm also curious about what led Huntington to embrace the monastic life, after so many years of living in the worst parts of the city and being so active in political reform efforts."

"Wasn't he a big supporter of Henry George's single tax movement that argued that natural resources should belong to everyone?" Hugh asked.

"Yes," Will said. "I remember reading about how Huntington campaigned for Henry George when George ran unsuccessfully for mayor of New York. I don't know if it was in that election or another one—I think George ran at least twice—but I know that in one of them, George polled more votes than Teddy Roosevelt, who didn't win either. Then Huntington gave it all up and moved to West Park."

"I'll think about it and let you know in a couple days," Hugh said, in a tone that was sufficiently vague as to suggest what his answer would be. With that, they turned back into the seminary grounds and climbed the stairs to their rooms.

CHAPTER SEVEN

he rest of the week sped by, marked by the usual routine of chapel and classes. Will daydreamed about Ana from time to time, but knowing that he was going to see her on Friday somehow made it easier to cope with the many demands on his time. He did spend a few minutes in the library reading about Poland in the Encyclopedia Britannica. And one night he re-read a chapter in one of his first-year textbooks that discussed theological and historical connections between the Old Testament and the New Testament, searching for possible points of similarity between Ana's Jewish beliefs and his own.

Will made only one visit to Morningside Heights, to attend his Tuesday afternoon seminar, and after it was over he stopped by the Cathedral grounds only to find LaFarge not around. Eager to acquire some bit of news he could report to the Bishop, he wandered around the former orphanage building, hearing as he did so the voices of the choirboys at practice. He knew that the choir school occupied half of the building, and that the headmaster, Canon Ernest Voorhis, had been the one who had started it a decade or more earlier.

As he was reflecting on what changes that decade must have brought, around the corner came a figure whom he immediately concluded, based on the man's air of authority, must be Voorhis himself. Greeting him, Will introduced himself and explained his role.

"Welcome to the Cathedral, or perhaps I should say, the madhouse," Voorhis responded amiably. "You know this used to be an orphans' asylum. These days I think of it as an asylum of a different sort."

Will laughed and asked Voorhis what it had been like living with chaos for so many years.

"In fact, at the beginning it was relatively quiet," Voorhis responded. "When I first came here, there was a very old willow tree that stood at the southwest corner of this building. An old French woman had for years cut small branches from this tree in the autumn for basket weaving.

"I also remember the dense jungle of small trees and bushes that existed along Amsterdam Avenue from One Hundred and Tenth to One Hundred and Thirteenth Street, into which surplus rocks that had been blasted from the excavations had been dumped pell-mell. In the midst of this jungle a strange individual used to sleep at night, having constructed a kind of Indian shelter of boughs to which he returned nightly in the warm weather. His covering and mattress consisted of newspapers. After his primitive abode was discovered, he seemed to think the region had become too civilized for his taste and departed. That must have been sometime in late 1902."

"Were the grounds ever in better shape than they are now?" Will asked.

At this, Voorhis grew visibly agitated. "The whole grounds were once very lovely," he said. "I remember visiting when the orphans were here—as you may know, the building dates back to the middle of the last century—and there were beautiful rose bushes and flowering shrubs in front of the building. But around 1900 an appropriation was made for 'improvements' and Heins and LaFarge spent the money on ploughing up the entire lawn between the old hall and the cliff on One Hundred and Tenth Street. All the roses and shrubs were ploughed under. When the choir school opened in 1901 it was impossible to walk anywhere, owing to the furrows, and the boys had no place to play. Finally, at my request, the furrows were harrowed and raked smooth in the southwest corner and grass was seeded so that we could have a small lawn for games of ball and cadet drill."

Will nodded sympathetically. "Well, based on what I hear from the practice room, the boys have been getting plenty of exercise; they sing with considerable energy," he said.

Voorhis looked pleased. "Yes," he said. "I think the school has come along well and the boys will be ready in April to give a good accounting of themselves. Right now, they sing at the services in the crypt but we haven't let them appear anywhere else as we want to be sure they're first-class before they make their debut, as it were."

Eager to bring the conversation back to the Cathedral itself, Will asked Voorhis what had impressed him most about the construction, watching it as he had at close range.

"Oh, without doubt the care taken by the stone masons," Voorhis said. "Every stone that was laid in both the choir and the transept was cut to exact measure, and every stone, large and small, bears the private mark of the mason who cut the stone. This custom dates back to the Middle Ages. The granite stones for the buttresses were not just selected and laid as best might be, but each one had its own particular place for which it had been cut."

Voorhis reflected a moment. "I've also been impressed with the finishing work," he said. "The red marble of the Ambulatory was highly polished by hand. The work was done by a French mason. His polishing instrument was a piece of the same stone, which he used with water, rubbing over the surface until the polish was satisfactory. I often wondered at the man's patience."

Will nodded in agreement, then thanked Voorhis for his time and said he hoped they'd meet again.

Voorhis gave Will a serious look. "I didn't much care for Heins and I don't care for LaFarge either," he said. "But I believe they set a standard of excellence in their work here, and I'm sorry more people don't recognize how fine an addition to the city this Cathedral will be. I hope in your role of assisting the Bishop in his fund-raising you'll be able to convey that."

Pausing a moment, he went on, "My greatest concern is that the lack of money is going to be a constant problem, one that may plague not just the finishing of this first phase but also those phases yet to come. Apart from a few Lutherans and Baptists, it's only Episcopalians who've been supplying the necessary money for the Cathedral. The others don't see it as having much if anything to do with them, and I must say, with reluctance, that I see their point." With a little ironic smile he added, "And even when it comes to the Episcopalians, I wonder whether the current contributors have a sufficient number of loving children who will want to memorialize them in the form of a stained-glass window or communion rail that the Cathedral can count on a steady flow of funds from the next generation."

Mulling Voorhis' words on his way home, Will realized they rang true. Even Bishop Greer, although he always talked about the Cathedral as an institution for the whole city, seemed to take it as a given that all the liturgy would be traditionally Episcopalian. Perhaps, Will thought, he could use Voorhis' comment as a way of hinting to the Bishop that it might be an idea to try to present the Cathedral as more welcoming to the non-Episcopalian world.

Will began his Friday report to the Bishop by repeating Voorhis' comments about the excellence of the masons' work. He also mentioned having noticed some signs of a cleanup of the grounds underway, which, given the oncoming winter, was a welcome development. It was conceivable that there would be snow on the ground until shortly before the dedication, and even if the grounds couldn't be turned into a lawn, at least if the piles of earth and rubble near the Cathedral could be moved or at any rate smoothed over it would make for a more pleasing approach.

The Bishop listened with only half an ear, Will felt, then apologized for keeping their appointment short because of a Columbia trustees' meeting he had to attend. Will, with so little of substance to report, was secretly relieved.

"I'll want you along at two events next week," the Bishop told him as he got up to go. "Moore can give you the details."

"Sir, there's one other thing Canon Voorhis mentioned that I thought was worth relating," Will said quickly, "and that is his concern that mainly it's only Episcopalians who are donating to the Cathedral, even though it's meant to benefit the whole city. It occurs to me that perhaps the Cathedral could attempt something along the lines of what Dean Robbins has done at the seminary and announce plans for a series of guest sermons or lectures by great thinkers of all denominations. That would certainly give the Cathedral a great deal of positive attention."

Will would have said more but the glare on Bishop Greer's face stopped him short.

"Mr. Ingalls," said the Bishop icily, "when I need your advice on how to do my job I'll ask for it. Perhaps my positive comments of a few days ago on your handling of yourself at the Metropolitan Club dinner have caused you to presume an unwarranted intimacy. If you consider for one minute how such an initiative would be received by leading Episcopalians like Mr. Morgan, let alone whether I myself think it would be appropriate, which I do not, you'll appreciate how foolish your idea is."

Pausing to let his words sink in, he added, "Let us say no more about it, and I'll mark this conversation down to the enthusiasms of youth."

With that, the Bishop dropped his glance to the papers on his desk and Will, stung by his remarks, hurried out of the room.

Later, over dinner with Hugh, Will described what had happened.

"I don't think he'll fire me," Will concluded glumly. "But he was certainly angry."

Hugh was silent for a moment. "I guess we're all living in a sheltered environment here in the seminary," he said finally. "We may think that the faculty are old-fashioned, but they're enlightened compared with most of the rest of the world—at least the Episcopal world. Your idea doesn't seem outrageous to me, but in the Bishop's circles it probably would be seen as radical."

Will listened thoughtfully. "You're completely right," he said. "I think I was too impressed with my new importance"—he gave a rueful laugh—"which was really self-importance, I can see now."

He sat there staring into his empty plate.

Then, shrugging, he added, "But still, perhaps it's a good thing that I made it clear that if the Bishop wants someone who has modern ideas to help him sell the Cathedral, he has to accept that those ideas won't always be the same as his own."

Hugh laughed, clearly impressed, just as Ana had been, with Will's ability to acknowledge his mistakes, and relieved that Will hadn't taken his comments amiss. "I hope you're right," he said. "I don't want your job to end before you've had a chance to see the inside of a few more of New York's finer institutions and report back to the rest of us what the high and mighty have for dinner."

As they made their way out of the refectory Hugh suggested they take a walk, but Will begged off, explaining that he was going to a lecture at Cooper Union.

"Who's talking?" Hugh asked.

Will hesitated. "Emma Goldman."

"Why on earth are you going to hear Emma Goldman?" asked Hugh. "You know what she's going to say, and you know the police will probably come in and break it up and you're likely to get your head bashed in for your troubles."

"I hope not," Will said. "It's only an event to mark the one-year anniversary of some Spanish anarchist's death by firing squad. Nothing likely to rouse the American rabble too much. As for why, I've always wanted to see her in action, and someone I met through my settlement work"—Will kept the identity of the 'someone' decidedly vague—"invited me to go."

"Well for heaven's sake be careful," Hugh said. "I don't want to have to come and bail you out of jail at midnight."

Will assured Hugh with mock gravity that he wouldn't call him from jail until the morning and, after grabbing a warm jacket and a scarf, since the weather had turned cool, set off.

When he got to Cooper Union, a grand old Italianate brownstone building whose Great Hall had been the scene of an important address by Abraham Lincoln on slavery, his first thought after seeing the large crowd outside was that perhaps he wouldn't be able to find Ana. But he quickly spotted her, dressed in that same coat he remembered from the evening of the debate. Greeting each other, they quickly moved inside and were lucky enough to find two seats together.

Goldman was the last to speak, after several others had eulogized Francisco Ferrer as a fighter for justice and an international hero. This gave Will time to observe Goldman as she sat with the other notables on the stage, feet planted firmly and wearing an alert expression despite the fact that she must have endured hundreds if not thousands of sessions much the same as this one.

When she rose to speak, Will couldn't help thinking how physically unprepossessing she was. Stout, and stern in appearance, she looked like a Russian peasant, Will thought, than a world-travelled firebrand. Yet her presence was commanding, and, as she spoke, Will began to understand why she'd amassed not just political followers but a string of male admirers as well.

Knowing that English was her second or possibly even her third language, Will was impressed by her fluency and even more by her frequent literary or philosophical references. At one point, she quoted Ralph Waldo Emerson speaking of the soul as "the one thing of value" that every man contains within him. But more than anything, it was her passion that carried the audience along.

Ana, for her part, was completely rapt, Will observed, when he glanced over at her. Sitting slightly forward in her chair, her face tilted upward, she wore an expression of intense concentration.

Now Goldman was building to a climax. "The killing of Francisco Ferrer was not the first crime committed by the Spanish government and the Catholic Church," she proclaimed. "The history of these institutions is one long stream of fire and blood."

Pausing for dramatic effect, she went on, "Francisco Ferrer needed no lying priests to give him courage, nor did he upbraid a phantom for forsaking him. The consciousness that his executioners represented a dying age, and that his was the living truth, sustained him in the last heroic moments!"

With that, the audience burst into applause as Goldman, face impassive, returned to her seat. Will applauded, too. After the applause had died down and people began to leave, he turned to Ana and asked if she had time for a cup of tea or coffee before heading home. She quickly agreed, and Will suggested a small place he'd noticed on the way there. After they'd settled themselves at a table, he asked Ana what it was about Goldman that she found so appealing.

"For me the main thing is that she speaks so eloquently," Ana answered in her slightly formal style, which Will had come to realize was the result of speaking Yiddish or perhaps Polish at home and learning English only in school. "She is a political activist but she is also a learned person. I would like to model myself on her, trying to make up for with my reading what I didn't have a chance to learn during my school days."

"Tell me about what happened with that," said Will.

"There's not really much to say," Ana responded. "My uncle died unexpectedly, of a heart attack. He was only 48. He was a skilled printer, and made a good salary, but he had no savings, and my aunt had not been working since I came to live with them. I had just started my last year of high school, and was expecting to go on to college—Hunter College, which is a college for women, is free for anyone living in the city who can pass the entrance test—but there was no help for it; I had to leave school and get a job.

"My aunt got work, too, in the small shop of someone she knew from Poland, but our two salaries together didn't come to more than half of what my uncle made. So we moved into one room together and rented the other one to two sisters, and that is how we continue to live. At first I was very bitter about losing out on the chance for more schooling, but so many people have a harder time than we do that I feel I should be grateful for what we have. And thanks to the schooling I did have, I understand many things other workers don't and can speak up for them."

She added with a laugh, "Of course, I've also been fired several times because of that but I seem always to be able to find another job because I'm quick and capable, and besides, even if bosses have been warned about me I'm so small that they find it hard to believe that I can be dangerous."

Will smiled. "Tell me about your uncle," he said.

"He was a wonderful man," Ana said, an unaccustomed softness in her voice. "He only had a few years of schooling himself, but he had learned his trade in Poland and he was very good at it. He and my aunt had left Poland before I was born because my uncle decided that there was no future there for Jews and he wanted to try his luck in the New World.

"He read books all the time and he liked to talk about books and politics with his friends. And in fact, some of the writers at the *Forward* trusted his judgment so much that they used to ask him to read what they'd written before they gave it to the editor. When I was about twelve he began taking me with him to hear lectures and to listen to the debates afterward between him and his friends about what had been said. That was my real education."

She paused. "My uncle wanted me to be a teacher, or maybe a professor. He even paid for me to have elocution lessons so that I would sound 'like an American' as he put it. He thought that in this country everything was possible."

"Was your uncle religious?" Will asked.

"Not in the way you mean," Ana answered. "Of course we always went to High Holiday services, and we always had Shabbat dinner, but we didn't pray or go to services every week the way you Christians do. And I can't remember ever discussing with my uncle or any of his friends what they believed about God, or whether they believed in God at all. When my uncle and his friends talked, it was about politics, or what was in the *Forward,* or about the unions. I think for Jewish people being Jewish is who we are, not about how often we go to the synagogue."

"And your aunt?"

"She was happy to go along with whatever my uncle wanted," Ana said. "She's a good woman, very friendly to everyone, but not very educated. She and my uncle never had any children of their own, but it was my uncle who wanted to have me come to

America after my parents died. He'd been very close to my mother, who was his sister. My aunt has always been very kind to me but sometimes I get the feeling that she thinks it's time I got married, even though I don't know how she would be able to pay the rent without my salary to help."

"Do you have plans to get married any time soon?" Will asked evenly, trying to conceal the unexpected stab of jealousy that Ana's words had produced.

"Not soon and maybe not ever," Ana replied, seemingly unaware of his reaction. "I think that the work I'm doing trying to build the union is more important than having a family, and I don't see how I could do both. In any case I'm already twenty-two, which some people think is quite old, so maybe no one would want me anyway."

Will laughed. "I'm twenty-six, and I don't think twenty-two is old at all. I must admit it's sobering, though, to think that I haven't even started my career and you've already been working for six years."

"Well, you have a family and plenty of money," Ana said. "You probably don't have to work at all."

"That's not true," Will said. "My father was the principal of a school but he died when I was seven. My mother was a teacher at his school—that was how they met—and she still teaches there. Her family has some money, but it's in no way a fortune. I received a small inheritance from an aunt of my mother's but I used up most of that while I was in England and I need to start working just as soon as I finish the seminary."

"Oh," said Ana. "Knowing you're not rich makes me like you even more." And then she laughed, slightly embarrassed at what her words had revealed. "I just mean that you're not quite as bad as Mr. J.P. Morgan!"

As they came out of the cafe, Will said casually, "Well, I don't know of any more scheduled events at University Settlement or College Settlement but I think it's my turn to propose an outing. Have you ever been to the Statue of Liberty? I've never been, even though I've lived in New York for more than a year."

Ana said she hadn't ever been either, so they agreed to meet the following week, on Sunday afternoon.

"Thank you again for inviting me to the lecture," Will said. "I'm very glad to have heard Goldman speak. Whatever one may think of her politics, she's very good at what she does."

Ana insisted she didn't need an escort home, so they shook hands somewhat awkwardly and said good-night. By the time he got back to the seminary, Will had already come up with a mental list of other places he might take Ana, after the Statue of Liberty.

CHAPTER EIGHT

ill again spent Saturday in the library, but his thoughts turned often to the previous evening—both Emma Goldman's speech and the conversation afterward with Ana. What, he mused, did he really know about the lives of workers or the ideas that moved them? Yes, he'd read a lot, as Ana said, but reading wasn't the same as experiencing. Listening to Goldman, observing the crowd and its reaction to her speech, he felt that he'd learned more about the attractions of anarchism in one evening than through ten books on the subject.

By four o'clock he decided to give up for the day and returned to his room, where he threw himself on the bed and took up the novel he'd started two weeks ago but had hardly read a page of since. It was called *The House of Mirth,* and it had come out a few years before. But Will, whose tastes ran more toward biography and history than fiction, had only recently bought a copy, after being informed in articles by New York critics that Mrs. Edith Wharton was one of the leading novelists of the day.

But whether this was true or not, Will thought to himself as he sighed and put down the book for the third or fourth time, she hadn't captured his attention with this overwrought tale of a young woman of limited means but high ambitions. The main problem, it seemed to him, was that it portrayed a world that was already gone, or nearly so. Young women these days weren't bound by the same limits as their grandmothers and mothers had been, making Lily, the main character—Will wasn't sure the word 'heroine' applied—seem more irritating than tragic. Moreover, he didn't like the character of Selden: he was altogether too restrained for Will's taste...perhaps, he admitted, a little too much like himself.

After one final attempt, Will sat up, closed the book, and, walking over to his bookcase, stuck it in between two other books on an upper shelf. "Enough," he said, aloud. It wasn't like him to give up on any book, but he decided it was alright to make this one an exception.

Hugh was away, visiting some relatives on Long Island, so Will walked over to the refectory on his own. Once there, he joined a table of several other men from his year and they talked for an hour or more after they'd finished eating until the staff indicated that they'd like them to leave by starting to wipe all the tables and to sweep under them.

Reluctantly, Will returned to his room, where he busied himself with some reading for his 'Social Movements' seminar until he concluded it was time to get ready for the party at George Bellows' house to which he'd been invited.

He'd met Bellows a few months earlier, at the opening of an exhibition at Alfred Stieglitz's "291" gallery, which focused mainly on photography but which had also become a haven for modernists of all types. Several of Bellows' paintings were included in the show, and Will had been instantly drawn to them because of their arresting subject matter—fighters engaged in ferocious combat at a small-time boxing club—and the painter's direct and powerful style.

It was while he'd been studying one of them that Bellows had come up to him and said, "Pretty great, don't you think?" and then, with a laugh, introduced himself. Only two or three years older than Will, Bellows was just beginning to make his mark with paintings that captured all aspects of urban life. His love of the city, at both high levels and low, and his genuine delight in scenes that others might find either too ugly or too ordinary, like construction sites or municipal workers shoveling snow, marked him as someone ready to break with the past and show things as they really were.

Will and Bellows immediately hit it off, despite their very different lives, and in the months that followed they occasionally got together to attend some new show and compare opinions on what they were seeing. For the most part, their tastes were similar, with the exception that Will sometimes felt Bellows was ready to like anything as long as it was likely to be regarded as outrageous.

Bellows was forever inviting Will to parties, which he and his wife gave for any reason or none at all, and while Will had only attended a few of them, he'd always came away having had a good time. These parties drew a mix of artists, activists and writers that reflected Bellows' own wide interests, and tonight proved no exception.

As soon as he walked into the house, which was close to Gramercy Park, Will spotted Robert Henri, the well-known art teacher who numbered Bellows among his former students. With him was Gertrude Vanderbilt Whitney, a prominent art patron who was also, in her own right, an accomplished sculptor. In another corner was John Sloane, a somewhat older painter but no less radical in his art and his politics than Bellows, talking with Bellows' attractive wife.

As Will was contemplating the scene and trying to decide what group to join, he heard a familiar voice say, "Hello there, Will Ingalls, it's been awhile." Will, instantly recognizing the voice, turned to greet Upton Sinclair, whom he'd met before Sinclair had moved to a commune near Philadelphia the previous spring.

Sinclair had been brought up an Episcopalian, and even now, having given up on organized religion and become an ardent social reformer—his novel *The Jungle*, about conditions in the Chicago stockyards, had been a huge success—he still held Christianity in high regard. He and Will had met at a reception after a talk by Walter Rauschenbusch, and found they shared an enthusiasm for Rauschenbusch's social gospel philosophy.

"How's life in the woods?" Will asked Sinclair, smiling.

"Colder and wetter with every day that passes," Sinclair responded. "I may have to take refuge in a good hotel for the winter."

With that he pulled forward the man standing next to him, whom he introduced to Will as his friend and fellow writer Ray Stannard Baker. Will immediately recognized Baker as the author of an article defending Trinity Church which Baker had written after the church's exposure as a slum landlord.

Perhaps to compensate, Baker had gone on to write a book called *The Spiritual Unrest*, about Trinity Church and the shortcomings of the Protestant churches in general. Will had read when it came out the year before. He told Baker how surprised he'd been by Baker's Trinity defense, but how much he'd liked *The Spiritual Unrest*, in particular Baker's point that all the old-line churches were losing members because they didn't have any urgent message.

"I especially remember what you said about the lack of young men entering the ministry," Will said, after explaining that he himself was a seminarian. "You said that young men 'with ideals,' as you put it, feel little inspiration or vision within the churches."

"Yes," said Baker, "and I'd be interested in knowing your position given that you made that choice."

"I think you're right that there is, in general, a lack of vision about what the church ought to be in the modern world," Will said. "But for me, that very problem of vision is part of what draws me to the ministry; I want to help the church, which I do believe is trying its best, to find its way."

Baker nodded, but seemed unpersuaded about the church's ability or desire to lead, prompting Will to continue.

"Much of the confusion, or lack of vision, is, I think, a reflection of a broader uncertainty about where we're heading as a society and what we want to become," he said. "What, for example, is the church's proper response to Darwin's theory of evolution and survival of the fittest? If Darwin is right, does that mean that as Professor Summer of Yale—an ordained Episcopal priest, as you may know—argues, any efforts at social reform are useless?"

Now Will, perhaps helped along by the large glass of wine he'd grabbed from a table nearby and consumed as they talked, was getting quite animated. "And furthermore," he went on, "as you point out in the book, there are now one million Jews living in New York, along with thousands of people from every country of Eastern Europe. How does a church that since colonial days has spoken to a relatively homogenous society find the means of addressing a very different audience?"

Baker nodded his head, obviously surprised by Will's depth of knowledge of his work. "Well, as you know from reading the book, I've offered some ideas as to what might be done," he responded. "And I'd like you to know, if you don't already, that like your friend Sinclair here, I consider myself a man of faith. In fact, I'd say that virtually all of us 'muckrakers,' as Roosevelt called us, are inspired by some form of religious impulse. But while we hope to see a new sense of social mission from the churches, we feel that at best they're moving at a snail's pace. The Episcopalians have without question been in the lead on this, at least here in New York, but that's not saying a great deal."

"Hear, hear," said a voice behind him.

"Steffens!" Upton Sinclair exclaimed. "What are you doing here?"

"I'm just in town for two days," Lincoln Steffens responded. "Trying to drum up some interest in my muckraking of Greenwich, Connecticut with the help of a young chap named Walter Lippmann. But I heard there was a party tonight and couldn't miss an opportunity to mingle with New York's finest thinkers and artists."

Then, with a mocking grin, he went on, "But why is Baker ruining a good evening with talk about the church? It's only Jesus Christ, not the churches, who can save this country. I've been working on a series of articles about the life of Jesus that, if I can complete them properly, will be the biggest thing I've ever done. I want to show how Christ could solve the problems of the cities and their corrupt administrations."

Seeing Will looking surprised, he added, "I don't know who you are young man, but I can tell you that I've been contending all my life, and always with God."

Will quickly introduced himself, then said that until this evening he'd had no idea that so many of the writers he admired were also serious Christians. "Yes, to be sure, Christians," Steffens responded, "but not churchgoers. There's a big difference."

With that, Steffens moved off to greet other friends, and Sinclair and Baker did the same, leaving Will on his own. Walking over to the makeshift bar, he encountered Bellows, who was now acting as bartender, and told him what had occurred.

Bellows looked as surprised as Will had been. "I had no idea who Baker even was when Sinclair introduced him," he said. "I didn't realize that I had so many actively Christian friends. Well, I guess the next thing is that someone will be passing a collection plate!"

Will laughed, then moved off to talk to John Sloane and Robert Henri, who were absorbed in a conversation about the latest outrage, as they saw it, at the National Academy of Design. As far as Will could make out it had something to do with whether or not a recent teaching appointment had been made on the basis of connections rather than talent.

"I don't want to talk about art school politics," Will objected, "I want to talk about art."

"My dear Ingalls," said Sloane, in his most avuncular tone, "art is what we do; politics is what we talk about."

"And speaking about politics," said a young man who had just joined the group and was clearly determined to inject himself into the conversation even though he had no idea what they'd been talking about, "has any of you seen the latest edition of *The Nation*? It appears that a magazine that once was required reading for progressives is losing its edge. The piece I'm referring to claims that Americans don't like radicals of any kind. I can't believe that Garrison would have ever allowed such a thing."

"You're right," Will said, "I saw that, too, and was surprised. But at least the editors remain steadfast in their support of rights for colored people. They've been routinely arguing that the unions must open up to allow colored people to join, and they've been denouncing union leaders like Samuel Gompers who oppose it."

"True," said Sloane. "Let's just hope they continue to stand firm on that one. At least now there's going to be a magazine devoted to colored issues. A week or so ago I met the new publicity director of the National Association for the Advancement of Colored People, which has moved its office to New York. Very impressive fellow, by the name of W.E.B. DuBois. He told me he plans to start a magazine, the first issue of which will be out in a few weeks."

The others murmured their support of the idea, and the conversation moved on to other topics: the recent deaths of Mark Twain and Julia Ward Howe; the bombing of the *Los Angeles Times* building, almost certainly by anarchists who had yet to be apprehended; the demands by Civil War veterans for larger pensions.

Someone commented on a recent article in *McClure's* about salesgirls at the big department stores who made only $4 to $10 a week. "No better pay than the shirtwaist makers, and they have to stand on their feet all day," the man commented. Another remarked on the campaign by Columbia students to end the university's ban on smoking. "If the faculty can smoke in their offices I don't see why students can't smoke in their rooms," he observed.

The talk then turned to politics: whether Roosevelt would run in '12 against Taft for the Republican nomination, how soon the country was likely to move to the direct election of US Senators, and the upcoming elections. "I predict the Democrats will win big at both the national and state level," said one middle-aged man whom Will had been introduced to at an earlier gathering as a theater owner and supporter of progressive causes. "People are tired of the high cost of living, tired of high tariffs, and tired of machine politics. Roosevelt is still trying to be both radical and conservative but his time has run out and so has that of the

Republicans."

By now it was nearly midnight, and Will had just decided it was time to leave when a sudden hush fell over the room. Looking toward the doorway, Will saw, walking in and escorted by Bellows, none other than Emma Goldman herself. Will had been aware that Bellows and Sloane both knew Goldman, but it was still a surprise to see, at such close quarters, the woman whom he'd seen from afar just a night ago.

Goldman greeted various friends and then, spotting Sloane, came over to say hello. Sloan introduced the others in the group, including Will, and she chatted with Sloane for a bit about some drawings he'd agreed to do for a magazine she was planning.

She also mentioned a recent visit she'd made to Jack London and his wife at their rural home not far from San Francisco. "What a beautiful place it is, and for that matter, all of California," she said. "I wanted him to attend a lecture I was giving on Francisco Ferrer, but he responded to my note of invitation with one of his own saying, 'I would not go to a meeting even if God Almighty were to speak there,'" Goldman said, laughing. "He said that the only time he attends a lecture is when he is doing the talking."

Instead, London had invited her to his farm, Goldman recalled, speaking with a warmth that had not been on display during her lecture. "What a good comrade he was," she remarked, "all concern and affection. We argued about our political differences, of course, but Jack has nothing of the rancor I've so often found in the socialists I've debated with. But then, Jack London is an artist first, a creative spirit to whom freedom is the breath of life."

Will wished he could think of something insightful to say, but wisely contented himself with trying to look engaged as the others chatted about London and other mutual friends. Finally, after Goldman had moved on, Will expressed his thanks for the party to Bellows' wife—George was still escorting Goldman around the room—and made his way outside.

There was a chilliness in the air that spoke of colder days to come, and Will wrapped his scarf firmly around his neck before starting the walk back to the seminary. Despite the cold, he was glad to have a chance to observe New York on a Saturday night. He loved the city at times like this, when everyone seemed to be out enjoying themselves and the sounds of laughter were everywhere.

Heading toward Gramercy Park, he passed the National Arts Club just as a crowd of formally dressed people was walking out the front door. Will had only been inside the club once, for an exhibit of Bellows' paintings, but he'd been captivated by the rich interior, with its dark paneled walls and profusion of paintings and sculptures. He remembered hearing someone say at that event that the club had been the home of Samuel Tilden, a New York State governor who'd made a run for President that was doomed by a rigged election. At least, Will mused, Tilden had the solace of returning to this glorious house, surrounded by his books and his collection of original manuscripts.

From the Arts Club it was only another minute or two to Broadway. Will turned north, gazing as he walked at the crowd of automobiles and carriages stretching all the way to Forty-Second Street. The blaze of electric lights, Will had read, was causing people to start referring to Broadway as the Great White Way. Will knew that at one time the center of the theater district had been much farther downtown, and he wondered idly how far it would progress northward in his lifetime. Maybe the Cathedral would find itself surrounded by theaters and 'dens of iniquity!'

Suddenly feeling tired by all the noise, Will turned west toward the seminary. The side streets at first offered as varied a profusion of restaurants and night clubs as did Broadway, but the level of accompanying chatter and street traffic quickly diminished. There was so much to think about: Baker's comments, of course, and Steffens', too. Who would have guessed that these men of the world shared such a serious interest in religious concerns? Or that Lincoln Steffens was working on a series of articles about Jesus Christ?

But the real high point, Will thought, had been meeting Emma Goldman. If that didn't impress Ana, nothing would!

The Locket

CHAPTER NINE

unday afternoon found Will at University Settlement for a meeting of the volunteers who lived there and the ones like him who came just to help with specific programs. The purpose of the meeting was to make plans for the next few months. On the way down, he kept wishing that he'd suggested to Ana that they see each other after his meeting, even if only briefly, but it was too late now to do anything about it.

By three o'clock about twenty-five young men were seated in folding chairs that had been set up in a circle in the main room and the head resident, a slightly older Harvard graduate called Frank Hastings, had called the meeting to order.

After Hastings' summary of what had happened since their last meeting, including the departure of two volunteers and the arrival of two new ones, Hastings explained to the meeting that one of the full-time volunteers, Henry Dowling, had a proposal he'd like to put to the group.

Dowling, who'd been at the Settlement for almost four years, stood up and began to read from some notes he'd prepared. Over his time at the settlement, Dowling said, he'd been struck by two things: one, how seriously the volunteers took their work, and two, how little fundamental change had occurred as a result.

"Yes, we've all had experiences of a young man coming back to thank us for helping him to improve his English or find housing or prepare for a job interview," he said, looking around the room.

"But the reality is that wages have barely increased in the time I've been here, many families are still living in worse conditions than the livestock on even a moderately well-run farm, and children are still dying of diseases that are not so much the result of germs as of poverty. The time has come for us to actively press for more government involvement: factory safety inspections, tenement laws requiring proper sanitation and ventilation, adequate health services for the poor."

"How do you propose to do that?" asked one of the volunteers.

"Politics," said Dowling. "Facts *and* politics. In the past we and other groups have done a number of excellent reports on things like housing and health. But we haven't done a good job of persuading public officials to introduce legislation to deal with the problems. And not only do we have to do a better job on that, but we've also got to get involved in the campaigns of politicians who support our views."

"But is that really our role?" asked another volunteer. "I'm comfortable as a teacher. But I believe, as my father says, that the less government the better. I agree with you that conditions aren't getting noticeably better. But laws—and unions, too, for that matter—are coercive. Can't we instead work harder to convince the tenement owners to improve their properties and the factory owners to improve conditions for their workers? Cooperation, rather than coercion, is surely a better way to go."

For the next forty-five minutes the discussion continued, with some arguing for Dowling's approach and others suggesting actions ranging from community meetings to letter-writing campaigns. Several people noted that many settlement house groups, not only those in New York, had been marshalling facts and writing reports for years but the results hadn't been particularly dramatic.

Will said little. He believed Dowling was right—that government was the only way to deal with problems too big for any volunteer effort to address. But he wasn't completely convinced that active campaigning for new laws by groups like the settlement house workers was going to make a significant difference. Somehow, he thought to himself, in order for real change to occur, citizens as a whole had to come to believe that it was wrong for a society to exist in which a few had so much and the many had so little. Right now, there wasn't enough moral outrage, enough sense of moral obligation. That was where the churches came in.

He tried to make that point late in the discussion, but most of the others had given up on organized religion and there was little sympathy for his position. "Look, Ingalls," said one, "the churches—all of them—have had plenty of chances to push for reform. But think about who their biggest donors are and you quickly understand that they're never going to push very hard. Yes, they support reform, but do they truly lead? Never!"

In the end, it was agreed that Dowling would head up a new project, with the help of two other volunteers, to canvass a ten-block area around the Settlement to determine how closely the tenement owners adhered to the weak laws on ventilation and sanitation that were already on the books. Then, if the results were as bad as Dowling expected them to be, the group could decide on how best to press the case for change, including possibly working for candidates in the next city council elections.

Somewhat reluctantly, given all his other commitments, but feeling he needed to show his colleagues—and, he admitted to himself, Ana—that he believed in more than just talking about problems, Will agreed to be one of Dowling's assistants and to join him on his first canvassing visit a few days later.

"If Dix is elected governor of New York next month," Dowling remarked as the meeting came to a close, "and if the Democrats gain control of the House, then I believe we'll have the best chance in years, in New York State and nationally, to make some real advances. We need to be ready to act at both levels."

By the time Will got back to the seminary, it was nearly time for evensong. Hugh had returned and he and Will spent half an hour talking about their weekends before walking together to the chapel. Hugh, predictably, was hugely impressed by Will's report of meeting Lincoln Steffens, less so by his description of meeting

Emma Goldman. "Steffens is famous as a writer and reformer," he observed, "whereas she's just famous for being a troublemaker."

In the chapel, listening to Mr. Goodhue's soft organ playing in the few minutes before the service began, Will was aware that his head was so full of conversations and arguments and impressions that he was unable to concentrate on prayer. It was as though the weekend had jammed together all the different parts of his life and left him with a confused jumble, not the least of which were his feelings about Ana.

Had he really been telling the whole truth when he told Baker that his aim in going into the ministry was to help the church find its voice—or was he taking the easy way out with regard to a career? And why, if he wanted to be a minister, was he so much more interested in his Social Movements seminar at Columbia than in his classes at the seminary on church doctrine? And why, when it came to Ana, was he so unable to stop thinking about her?

Around and around his thoughts swirled as he went through the motions of giving the responses to the collects and reciting the Apostles' Creed. Even the Nunc Dimittis failed to move him as it usually did. It was only as he sat listening to Mr. Goodhue's organ improvisation after the service was over, and watching the stained-glass windows rapidly lose their color, that Will finally felt a quietness beginning to steal over him. He remembered how it was in a moment of that same quietness, in the chapel of Queens' College at Cambridge, where he'd gone to visit an Amherst friend who was studying there, that he'd decided to apply to the seminary.

For all of his interest in social issues and intellectual debates, it was the quiet of the church, and the beauty of the services, that most moved him. He sometimes wondered whether he would have been happy as a medieval monk, drawing illustrations for a Book of Hours when he wasn't engaged in chanting the psalms or meditating on the holy mysteries.

When the organ piece ended, he and Hugh and the few other people still left in the chapel applauded politely. Then, in silence, they filed out onto the familiar paths of the seminary grounds under the darkening sky.

As they emerged, Will suddenly decided that he couldn't go a whole week without seeing Ana. Making a feeble excuse to Hugh that he'd forgotten an appointment with a college friend who was in town, he ate a quick cold supper at the refectory and hurried to College Settlement House. He knew that Lizzy Sperling's reading circle met from 7 to 8, and when he got there he asked the receptionist at the front desk if they had finished yet. She said they hadn't, and gestured to a small room just off the main hall. There, through an open door, he saw Lizzy and a group of about ten young women, among them Ana, talking intently.

The receptionist, recognizing him as a friend of Lizzy's and assuming he was there to meet her, urged him to take a seat in the small parlor. But Will, not wanting to have to explain himself to Lizzy, said that he preferred to enjoy some fresh air while waiting for the group to finish and went outside.

No more than five minutes later the front door opened and the young women in the group came out together, chatting and laughing. Will, who was standing just to the side of the door, watched the group pass him and then, feeling a bit foolish, called out Ana's name.

Startled, Ana looked up, then flushed with confusion mixed with pleasure as she saw him.

"Good evening," Will said. "If your companions can spare you, and you have a few minutes, may I have a word with you?"

The other young women, most of whom had been on the Central Park outing, smiled knowingly. One went so far as to give Ana's arm a surreptitious poke as they all murmured that it was of course fine with them for Ana to stay behind.

Will gestured in the opposite direction and took a few steps. Ana, after hesitating, followed.

"I'm not quite sure why I'm here," Will said as they fell into step. "But I was wondering whether we could just have a cup of coffee. So many things have happened this weekend that I wanted to tell you about them now, rather than wait a whole week."

Ana looked up at him inquiringly. "I hope nothing bad," she

said.

"Oh, no, quite the contrary," Will said, as they walked into a small café and took a seat at a table near the back. Will proceeded to tell Ana about the event the night before, including his conversations with Lincoln Steffens and Steffens' friends and the brief encounter with Goldman. Ana showed little interest in Steffens but wanted to know everything Goldman: what she was wearing, exactly what she said about Jack London and the new magazine, and how she was received by the other guests.

"How I wish I could have been there!" she said excitedly, hanging on every word. "To think that you were as close to her as we are now!"

Will felt a pang of remorse. Why hadn't he asked Ana to go to the party with him? He was sure George Bellows wouldn't have minded. Even though he hadn't known Goldman would be there, it would certainly have been a chance to introduce Ana to some interesting people from the world Goldman inhabited.

He told himself it was because he didn't know Ana very well yet, but that wasn't the whole answer. He knew that the sight of him and Ana together would have raised some eyebrows and led to later questions that he wasn't ready to answer.

So instead of responding to Ana's comment, he changed the subject to the afternoon discussion at University Settlement and asked Ana what she thought of the residents' plan.

Ana listened impatiently as he described how they intended to document the conditions in the neighborhood and then use the results to demand change.

Finally, she burst out, "All of us who live here know already how bad the situation is. And we've already been studied enough by people who've been to college. What we need is not more 'help' of the kind you and your friends want to give but the kind *we* want: money for organizing, support for our unions, and help in electing people of *our* choosing to office who will get rid of the corrupt police and enforce the laws that already are in place but never paid any attention to."

Will felt a moment's irritation with her for not even giving him a chance to fully lay out the scheme before criticizing it. But he recognized that there was truth in what she said. The settlement movement had been going on for two decades already but as Dowling himself had said, there wasn't nearly as much to show for it as there should be.

But he and his friends could hardly be blamed, Will felt. Most of them had jobs or were in graduate school; they weren't full-time social reformers. Moreover, they didn't all share the same opinions about their role. As the afternoon discussion had shown, there was a lot of opposition to the idea of becoming politically active and working for specific candidates.

Will tried to explain some of this to Ana but she wasn't interested. "What I know is that change comes from the streets, not from someone making a high-sounding speech or doing a study," she said. "I'm not saying that the only way is revolution. But I do believe that action—whether it's strikes or marches on City Hall—is what gets results."

As they talked, Will kept thinking about how pretty Ana looked when her cheeks flushed from the intensity of what she was feeling. He longed to see her laugh in the way she had during the carousel ride in Central Park but he knew already that such moments were rare. And he also knew that it was Ana's very intensity that he found so appealing.

Looking at her with a grin, he said, "Comrade, I don't think we will come to any conclusions tonight. But I look forward to many more conversations."

Ana managed a smile, though it was a small and somewhat reluctant one, and stood up from the table. "I like that plan," she said.

CHAPTER TEN

he first event of the week that Will attended with Bishop Greer was another dinner, this one on Tuesday night at the Waldorf-Astoria. A fund-raiser for the Metropolitan Museum of Art, it was a much bigger affair than the dinner of the week before and included among the guests a large number of wealthy New Yorkers whom the Bishop had targeted as possible donors. Will was relieved to find that the Bishop either had forgotten about their Friday exchange or had chosen to ignore it.

To Will, the hotel, on Fifth Avenue between Thirty-Third and Thirty-Fourth Streets, represented all that he didn't like about modern New York. There was too much of everything—too many palms, too many overly-decorated public rooms, too many rich factory owners from Detroit or Buffalo trying to appear to be locals, and too many social-climbing locals trying to appear to be members of the city's elite.

But there was no question that the Waldorf-Astoria was 'the' hotel for major gatherings, if for no other reason than its capacity to handle large numbers of diners at once. Will stayed at the Bishop's side during the pre-dinner cocktails, and found himself impressed both with Greer's large number of acquaintances and with his ability to quickly steer any conversation to the issue of the Cathedral and its need for funds. Several times he turned to Will to ask Will's impressions of LaFarge's design, the progress of the construction, or the quality of the work being done. Greer no doubt was getting other reports as well as his, Will realized, but what he wanted from Will was for him to convey a fresh sense of excitement about the project.

The dinner itself was predictably long and boring. Will saw J.P. Morgan seated on the dais, along with two members of the Vanderbilt family, two Rockefellers, and the mayor, but on this occasion there was no opportunity to talk to the great man. By the time the speeches were over, Morgan had slipped out, as had a number of other guests, leaving the Bishop to deliver his brief benediction to a half-empty room.

"Never mind," said Greer, when Will commented on the deserted state of the banqueting room as they rode back downtown in the Packard. "I sat next to August Belmont, who's been one of our most generous contributors, and he agreed to give another $5,000 for general expenses."

Will silently compared that amount with a newly ordained clergyman's $1,500 a year salary and wondered what it would be like to have so much money that you could just decide on the spur of the minute to give $5,000 of it away.

The second event, on Thursday afternoon, was far more interesting. It was a tea at the Colony Club, which Will had heard much about but never seen for himself. A large and graceful building on Madison Avenue designed by Stanford White, the club had been started a few years before to be the women's equivalent of the city's many clubs for men. As Will, accompanied by a woman who'd been assigned to greet him, ascended a staircase to the Louis XV assembly room, he gazed with admiration at the simple white interiors. He knew that the club had a marble swimming pool and wished he could work up the nerve to ask to see it, but given that normally men weren't even allowed above the first floor, he thought he'd better be satisfied with these glimpses of the public rooms.

He met Bishop Greer, deep in conversation with Mrs. Daisy Harriman, one of the club's founders, standing just inside the door. Will realized with a small jolt of surprise that he and Bishop

Greer were the only two men in the room. The Bishop's secretary had explained to Will that Bishop Greer had been asked to talk about the Episcopal Church's efforts on behalf of the city's poor, and warned Will that he would probably be asked to say a few words about his work at University Settlement.

The room was full—Will estimated that there were well over a hundred women present—and there was a considerable buzz of conversation until Mrs. Harriman led him and the Bishop to the front of the room, a signal for everyone to take their seats. She and the Bishop sat to the left and right of a small table and she indicated to Will that he should take a seat in the front row.

After being introduced, Bishop Greer began with thanks for the invitation to address the group, noting that several members of the club were among those who had been good friends and strong supporters of the Cathedral for many years. From here, he launched into a brief discussion of the Episcopal diocese's growth in the city, from its beginnings at Trinity in Lower Manhattan to the Upper East Side and beyond, as it accompanied parishioners on their northward migration.

"But even though many of our older churches have closed for lack of congregants," Bishop Greer explained, "we haven't left the poor behind. We've opened missions throughout the city's slums where in addition to preaching the gospel we help young people to learn trades. We also engage in other activities such as sponsoring outings for mothers and children to allow them, at least briefly, to breathe fresh air. Working at times in collaboration with some of the settlement houses—many, incidentally, started by young Episcopalian graduates of our leading colleges and universities— we've tried to help the poor in their own neighborhoods, where they feel at home."

The Bishop spoke for about twenty minutes, after which he introduced Will and asked him to talk about his work at University Settlement. Will did so, briefly, describing how his experience at Toynbee Hall in London had convinced him of the importance of taking social programs into the heart of the slums. He described some of the students who had passed through his public speaking class, and made a point of mentioning the debate between University Settlement and College Settlement and the fact that the speech of a young woman from College Settlement had carried the day—which prompted a modest ripple of applause from the audience.

Mrs. Harriman then said that the Bishop would be happy to answer any questions, which produced an immediate show of several hands.

The first three questions had to do with the particulars of some of the church's work, but then a young woman stood up and said that at the risk of sounding impolite, she wondered whether the church's efforts among the poor weren't more a matter of salving consciences than a real commitment to improving conditions, starting with higher wages for workers.

Will could sense Bishop Greer's irritation, but the Bishop showed no signs of his feelings. "In fact," he said, "the church has been a leader in supporting labor's right to organize for many years, starting with the efforts of my predecessor, Bishop Potter. It was thanks in large measure to him that the Church Association for the Advancement of the Interests of Labor was set up. Starting almost twenty years ago Trinity Church has held an annual celebration called Labor Sunday and not long after that it established a Board of Arbitration to help settle strikes."

Seeing the young woman roll her eyes a bit, as though to ask what this all amounted to in practical terms, Greer added, "As one example of the diocese's commitment to fair labor practices, it was around that same time that the diocese made a decision to allocate church printing only to firms that paid union rates."

The next questioner, following the lead of the questioner before her, asked the Bishop whether he supported the Women's Trade Union League.

"I do, and as you know, many outstanding Episcopal women, and in fact some members of this club, are among the league's leaders," he responded. "I'm in full agreement with their support of the young women who belong to Local 25 of the ILGWU and who participated in the strike last year. As one of the league leaders noted, I recall, in a newspaper interview at the time, joining a union will help lead to the Americanization of these young workers."

Unfortunately, Will thought, the Bishop wasn't content to leave things there, going on to denounce as equally repugnant violence on the part of employers and violence on the part of unions. But he admired the Bishop's strong support of worker's rights, and felt he was making a persuasive case that the church was very much in favor of reform.

The final question was from a woman who, after explaining that she'd been a congregant at one of the Episcopal churches that had closed as the neighborhood around the church had changed, asked whether the Bishop felt it was appropriate for colored New Yorkers and whites to mix, whether in churches, unions or elsewhere.

The Bishop seemed caught off guard by the question, and began by explaining that he had been the head of the Church Institute for Negroes, a union of all schools for colored people in the South, since its inception. "To me the Institute is probably the single most important thing that I do," he said. "I believe that education is the most effective way to uplift colored people from their current state."

Seeming to recognize, however, that he hadn't addressed the questioner's central point, Greer paused and then went on, "There is a considerable divergence of opinion within the church as to how best to serve the colored population. It's well documented that urban colored people are for the most part unskilled, uneducated, and unwelcome in most churches and trade unions. Some clergy and laymen are in favor of forcing integration while others—a majority, I would say—believe that the best approach is to elevate them to a level where, in time, those among them who show themselves the equal of white people will in fact be treated that way."

Silently, Will disagreed. His mother, who had taught in one of the Freedmen's schools set up in the South after the Civil War, had driven home to him, with examples drawn from that experience, that it was foolish to believe that white people would treat Negroes as equals without being forced to. To accept equality meant to be ready to give up privilege, she always said, and very few white people were ready to do that.

Now, thinking back to the Sunday discussion at University Settlement, he realized, in a way that had eluded him then, that it was equally foolish to believe that people whose lives were built on cheap labor would ever treat poor people of whatever color decently—even if the churches became paragons of progressivism—unless they were similarly forced to. Moral outrage and moral obligation were all very well and good, but it took laws, and the enforcement of those laws, to change society.

But most of the audience at the Colony Club appeared to favor the Bishop's opinion. A murmur of approval greeted the Bishop's remarks, and with that, Mrs. Harriman closed the meeting. She thanked Bishop Greer and Will and urged everyone to stay afterward for more tea. Will, finding himself between two middle-aged women who insisted on escorting him to the tea table, did his best to be amiable, chatting with them and some of their friends about his work and future plans. Several announced that they intended to invite him for dinner, claiming that any number of young women they knew would be eager to meet him.

"I doubt that's true," Will said, smiling. "My experience suggests that most young ladies, when they hear that I'm going to be ordained, instantly picture themselves in a rural parsonage scraping by on a salary that is less than they're accustomed to spending on new dresses each year, and having to run the women's group besides." But, seeing one of them about to object, he added gallantly, "Nonetheless, I make it a policy never to turn down the offer of a meal."

As he excused himself from the group and turned to look for Bishop Greer, a tall woman with strong features came up and introduced herself. "I'm Anne Morgan," she said, "and I'm one of the women who helped the girls during the strike last year. I heard what the Bishop said about the Women's Trade Union League but I'd be curious to know what *you* think of it."

Will took a deep breath. A month ago he would probably have echoed Bishop Greer's comments, but now that he'd met Ana, he realized his perspective had changed. "I admire what the WTUL did," he said, "but I think that some of the young working women feel that while they appreciated the WTUL's help, you and the others in the WTUL got to go home after joining them on the picket line or bailing them out of jail, while they had to stay and freeze in the cold and get beaten by the company goons."

Anne Morgan nodded. "I completely understand," she said. "Who wouldn't feel that way? But I want you to know that for me this is not just a rich woman's hobby. I believe whole-heartedly in their cause and I intend to continue to do all I can to support them. If you have suggestions of how we in the WTUL might become more engaged in a way that truly aids the cause rather than one that just gets headlines, I'd very much like to hear them."

Will nodded. "To be honest I don't have any ideas myself, but if you'd ever like to sit down with a few of the young women who are most active in the movement, I'd be glad to try to help arrange that."

"That's a good idea," Anne Morgan responded. "Let me think about it. I assume that I can reach you through the seminary?"

"Yes," said Will. "If you call the main number someone will get a message to me."

Anne Morgan nodded and then was gone, leaving Will to say his good-byes to the Bishop and Mrs. Harriman. The Bishop pulled Will aside to say, in a friendly manner that indicated Will's performance had reinstated him in the Bishop's good graces, that he needn't come for his weekly meeting as there was some diocese business Greer had to attend to, but that his secretary would be in touch.

CHAPTER ELEVEN

The Bishop's unavailability on Friday was lucky for Will, as that was the day he had agreed to join Dowling in his canvassing effort and it would have been hard to get down to University Settlement by five o'clock, the time they'd agreed on. Dowling was already there when Will arrived, and together they went over the list of questions Dowling planned to ask residents. "I've decided that early evening is the best time to try to catch people with a few minutes to spare," Dowling explained; "If they work at a factory or shop they're home by then, or at least many of them are, and if they work at home they haven't sat down to dinner just yet."

By five-thirty they were standing in front of the first of the ten buildings on Dowling's list, on a block where every building looked virtually identical: five stories tall, made out of brick, narrow, and immediately butting up against its neighbors. Each floor, according to the city plans Dowling had consulted, contained four apartments of a little over 300 square feet each, some with two windows at the front and the others with two windows at the back. There were supposed to be two toilets on each hall and cold running water in each apartment.

"Ready?" Dowling asked. Will nodded. "Just remember, I'll take the lead but if it's noisy or there are problems, try to do what you can to distract the other family members while I talk to whoever can answer the questions. We'll start at the top and work our way down."

As they opened the sagging front door, both Dowling and Will instinctively recoiled from the strong smell of urine and human waste that assaulted them. Passing one of the water closets, Dowling looked in and quickly turned his face, grimacing at the sight of a clogged toilet that was responsible for the smell.

As they climbed the stairs to the top floor, similar smells, though not as bad, followed them, mixed with other odors that ranged from onions to disinfectant. Knocking on the first door, they found themselves face to face with a harried-looking woman with a baby in her arms and another small child just behind her. In the background, Will could see three or four other adults and two other children.

At least four adults and four children in this tiny space, Will thought with dismay. This whole apartment wasn't much bigger than his and Hugh's adjoining rooms at the seminary.

Dowling's explanation of the reason for their visit met with a blank and somewhat fearful stare, and the woman quickly turned around to appeal for help. At that point a girl of no more than ten or eleven came forward; in halting English she explained that her mother spoke only Polish and Yiddish, then added, at her mother's prompting, that their rent for the month had been paid.

Dowling quickly explained that their visit had nothing to do with the rent; they were only trying to find out whether the landlord was providing the services he was supposed to. Intimating that he and Will were there in some official capacity, he learned, with the girl's help, that there were actually ten people living in the three small rooms—a family of six and four boarders—and that at the moment the taps in the apartment weren't working so they had to fetch water from the sink in the hall or an outside spigot. One of the toilets on the hall was working; the other was not. For this they paid $10 a week, which was nearly as much as the father earned at a factory a few blocks away—hence the need for boarders. The four boarders and the mother worked sewing shirt collars during the day in the room that doubled as kitchen and factory. The girl and a younger brother were in school in the neighborhood.

While Dowling wrote down the details of what the girl was saying, Will had a chance to look around. It was clear that the mother was trying her best, but the task of making this a home was beyond anyone's ability. The walls were dirty and peeling, as was the linoleum in the kitchen area. Everywhere were bales of shirts and the family's belongings. The children looked wan and pinched, and one of them had a hacking cough.

How can people live like this? Will thought, then, ashamed, reminded himself that these people had no choice.

Over the next two hours, Will and Dowling made their way down, floor by floor, hearing much the same story with only slight variations as they went. By the time they'd finished, it was too late to start another building and in any case, they were both exhausted. In fact, they barely exchanged a word until they were back at University Settlement, sitting with cups of strong coffee in front of them.

Will was the first one to speak. "We had a copy of Jacob Riis' *How the Other Half Lives* in our house when I was growing up," Will said. "I used to look at the pictures and think that of course what they showed was by now completely changed. But what we just saw—it wasn't that much different."

Dowling nodded in agreement. "Reading about it or even looking at pictures isn't the same as seeing it first-hand," he said. "I've done some of this kind of work in the past, so I wasn't as shocked as you were. But there's no question that it's terrible."

After a minute or two of silence, Dowling spoke again. "You've given me an idea with your comments about the Riis book," he said. "We should take photographs to go with our report. Maybe you could do that while I ask the questions. Of course, pictures aren't the same as being there, but they're much more powerful than just words."

Will said he'd been thinking about buying a camera anyway, and would be glad to do as Dowling proposed. But still unable to shake the effect of what they had just seen, he returned to his earlier line of thought. "Here it is, 1910," he said, "twenty years after Riis' book, and we're living in a city whose poor could as easily be living in Calcutta or Shanghai as in New York, the largest city in what is supposedly the greatest and richest country on earth."

He and Dowling were silent again. Finally, Will said, "Just one thing: I think we shouldn't be so ambitious with our survey; if we complete one square block we'll be doing well. Even that will take weeks at the rate we're going."

Dowling nodded. With that, they drank up their coffee.

Will knew he'd missed dinner at the seminary but he didn't really feel hungry after what he'd seen. He read a bit after he got back and turned in early.

Sunday at one-thirty found him at the agreed-on meeting place with Ana. When she arrived, Will was pleased to see that she again was wearing her hair down and loosely tied in the back and had on the same shawl she'd worn on the outing to Central Park.

"Another beautiful day," she observed after they'd greeted each other. "There won't be many more of these."

They walked quickly to the landing where the Statue of Liberty ferry docked, and, after buying their tickets, stood in a line waiting for the ferry to depart. For the next two hours they gave themselves over to enjoying the experience as tourists might, climbing the stairs to the Statue's crown, exclaiming over the views of the harbor, and at length, back in Battery Park, throwing themselves exhausted on a bench.

"I liked the view but not enough to do that again," Ana said with a laugh.

"Yes, I agree," said Will. Then, recalling the poem written by Emma Lazarus and engraved on a plaque mounted on the inner wall of the statue's pedestal, he briefly described his experiences on Friday and concluded soberly, "Now I understand better what she was referring by 'the wretched refuse of your teeming shore.'"

"I don't like that line," said Ana, immediately turning serious. "It makes it sound as though the people coming here are not just poor but ignorant and dirty—all the things many Americans say about immigrants. My uncle and aunt were certainly not ignorant and dirty, and neither are many others. But that's the way Americans are encouraged to view them by the bosses who want the freedom to continue to oppress them."

"Oh Ana," sighed Will. "I spent Friday talking to people in what must be some of the worst tenements in the city but it didn't stop me from enjoying today. I'm beginning to understand the need to get personally engaged in reform rather than just talk about it, and that's partly thanks to you. But I wish I hadn't even mentioned what happened Friday because I'd like to continue to just be with you and forget politics for a little while."

"How can I do that, when there's so much injustice and unfairness?" Ana responded sharply. "I shouldn't even be here when I could be home helping my aunt or making myself useful at the union headquarters."

Will looked at her silently for a few seconds, then impulsively grabbed her shoulders, pulled her toward him, and kissed her with a passion that surprised even himself. Then, pulling away and laughing, but with a quaver in his voice, he said, "That's one way to silence a labor activist!"

Ana looked at him with a shocked expression. But he could tell that his action hadn't been unwelcome. "I've wanted you to do that since the first night we met," she said quietly. "But now that you have, I feel confused and a bit frightened."

She looked down, then met Will's gaze directly. "I like the way you're so open to learning new things," she said. "I also like the way you don't rush to react to things—like my comments when we were at Central Park. I too often speak before I think, whereas you always take your time."

She hesitated, then went on in a rush, "But how can we possibly be together?"

Will smiled. "Thank you for your compliments," he said, "but please let's not think about anything else right now except that we're happy. There'll be plenty of time later to wonder what to do."

The two of them sat there for many minutes, close but not

quite touching, as dusk fell and the electric lamps in the park came on. Will watched two sparrows on the path in front of them picking up the crumbs of a cake some child had no doubt dropped earlier in the afternoon. Neither one of them said anything, lost in their own thoughts and in each other.

Will's sense of contentment was, however, short-lived. No sooner had he walked into his room in Dehon Hall than Hugh knocked.

"Okay, Will, what's going on?" said Hugh as soon as he was in the door. "You always used to be around on Sundays but now you have better things to do. And you're acting mysterious in other ways, too, like suddenly taking an interest in Emma Goldman. The way I see it, you're either training to be an anarchist—or you've met a girl who already is one."

Will laughed to cover his embarrassment at being so easy to read, at least by a close friend like Hugh. "I plead not guilty to anarchism," he said. "And yes, there is a girl, but she's not really an anarchist in the way you mean, only a labor organizer."

Hugh looked at Will levelly, then said, "So you mean she's a Jew?"

"Not all labor organizers are Jews," said Will, "but yes, she is a Jew. Not a devout one, though; the only thing she believes in is the union."

Hugh shook his head in disbelief. "Of all people, Will Ingalls, you're the last one I would have guessed would have fallen in love with a Jew. Have you really stopped to think about what you're doing? You're running the risk that if you're found out—which you almost certainly will be—you won't be considered a suitable candidate for ordination. And even if you're not found out, what kind of a life can you imagine for yourself with someone who's not even a Christian?"

"Look, I'm not about to marry her," Will protested. "I only met her recently and I have no plans to propose."

But Hugh remained unpersuaded. "Will, I've known you now for over two years, and not once have you indicated any serious interest in a woman. But now, when I look at your face, I see the signs of a man who is in love."

Hugh paused. "I'm only saying this for your own good but I hope you'll reconsider," he said. "I hate to see you throw away the chance for a successful career. But it isn't just that. You've helped me to see that the church needs real leadership on matters of social justice and workers' rights and you could be one of those leaders. But you won't be at the rate you're going. This isn't a matter just of your own feelings but of how you can best serve the society you claim to be so interested in."

Hugh's words stung. Will knew he was right about the dangers of his relationship with Ana, but he was concerned even more by what Hugh had said about how he was putting his feelings ahead of his responsibilities.

Will looked down, unable to meet Hugh's gaze. "I really don't know what to do," he admitted. "I know I'm in love, even though I haven't told her yet. And I think she loves me, too. But I also know that I can't live without a spiritual life."

Finally looking up, he said, "Please don't judge me too harshly, Hugh. And please stand by me while I try to figure this out."

"Of course I will," said Hugh. "You're the best friend I've ever had or hope to have."

Standing up and moving toward the door, he added, "And just so you know, I still expect you to serve as my best man and she's welcome to come to the wedding."

CHAPTER TWELVE

*O*n Monday afternoon, finding himself with a few free hours and restlessly aware that he wouldn't be seeing Ana until the following Sunday, Will decided to check on progress at the Cathedral. Grant LaFarge wasn't in his office but when Will entered the Cathedral he saw him in consultation with the boss of one of the work crews. Waiting until the two had finished, Will stood watching one of the carvers as he worked on one of the twelve oak stall finials, putting the final touches on a figure whom Will didn't recognize.

"It's Tallis," said the carver, who introduced himself as Otto Jahnsen and explained that he'd asked to work on the finials because his hobby was playing in an Early Music group and he knew a lot about some of the composers. "He's right across from Palestrina, which seems appropriate, given they lived at almost the same time and created some of the most beautiful music ever written."

"Yes, I agree," said Will. "Elizabeth I was fortunate that Tallis' music didn't cause her subjects to demand a return to Rome on the grounds that if a Catholic like Tallis could produce such extraordinary music then he must have a direct connection to the Almighty."

Jahnsen laughed. "Better not let Bishop Greer hear you say that."

Will laughed, too. "Who else is here?" he asked. "I see Bach,

Handel and Purcell. And is that St. Cecilia?"

"Yes," Jahnsen said. "She managed to get included because she's the patron of sacred music."

Just at that minute Will noticed that LaFarge had finished with the crew boss and was turning as though to leave, so he hurried to catch up with him before LaFarge reached the door.

"I was just admiring the choir stall carvings," Will said by way of a greeting. "The whole of the choir design is very fine."

"The canopies are after those in one of the chapels in Westminster Abbey," LaFarge said in response. "We studied a great many cathedrals, as you can imagine, before we decided on each element here. It wasn't easy blending so many ideas and styles, but I think it worked out well."

LaFarge, clearly enjoying an opportunity to show off his work, added, "Have you looked at the choir pavement closely? It contains quite a number of types of marble: The red is Numidian, the black Belgian, and my favorite, the violet, is from Italy. We spent an inordinate amount of time choosing the colors and tile shapes, but I think the result is worth it."

Will agreed, then asked how the construction was going. At that, LaFarge's expression darkened. "The latest problem is the organ," he said. "We're supposed to be installing it in two weeks, but they haven't finished the necessary preparation work yet. That's what I was discussing with Carl Brachtman when you came in. He's simply got to get the men to work faster in order to be ready."

Will asked LaFarge to tell him about the organ. "It's been built by the Skinner Company," LaFarge said with enthusiasm. "It's quite a new company but I very much admire their work. Skinner is a risk-taker and loves new technology, and he's therefore a perfect candidate for the job of creating a true Twentieth Century instrument."

"Where will the pipes go?" Will asked.

"In the upper arches on both sides of the choir," LaFarge responded, gesturing to the spot. "All five thousand six-hundred and fifty of them. The console itself will be located in the gallery on the south choir screen."

Will nodded.

"I must be going," LaFarge said. "In addition to all my other problems, my father is ill and I'm worried that it may be serious. My brother, who's a Jesuit priest, is already here in the city but can't stay more than a day or two because of his other commitments and I want to talk with him about our father's condition."

Will expressed his sympathy and said good-bye, then turned back for one more look at the work underway. Behind the high altar, carvers were still working on the lovely and delicate white marble and plaster reredos, while in various corners workers were putting the finishing touches to the floor's tile borders. From overhead, banging and hammering indicated that LaFarge's words about the organ's imminent arrival had been heeded.

On his way out, Will caught the sounds of the choirboys as they returned to their classrooms from afternoon recess. The happy shouts of thirty-five boys provided a pleasant counterpoint to the serious work going on inside, and Will felt that the Cathedral had made a good decision in choosing to build a choir school on the Cathedral grounds. He understood that the school, blueprints for which had already been drawn up, was to go at the back of the property, where the large carving shed now stood. From there, he thought, the boys will be able to walk easily to the Cathedral even in bad weather, but they'll be just far enough away that they'll be out of its massive shadow—in more ways than one.

Why was it, he thought on his way back to the seminary, that his visits to the Cathedral always left him a bit subdued. Was it the knowledge of the unpleasant fighting between LaFarge and the trustees? Or perhaps the immensity of what was still left to be done before the building was complete? Or was it, simply, that the Cathedral's size made everything else, including his own life, seem puny by comparison?

Half an hour later, he was standing in front of the shop near the seminary where he'd seen the display of Brownie cameras. After studying the various models, he went in and, after some discussion, bought the one he'd seen in the window. The salesman, the same one who'd shown him the camera initially, and who clearly was an enthusiast, spent a good ten minutes showing him how to load the film and wind the camera. He also repeated that Will could bring the finished films back to the shop and they would arrange for the processing.

"Remember, if you open the camera before the film is finished you'll ruin at least some of the exposures," he warned him.

Will left the shop with one film in the camera and three in his pocket, and by the time he got back to his room he'd already almost finished the one in the camera because everywhere were scenes and people he wanted to capture. Looking through the lens, he had the excited feeling that he was seeing the world in a new way. It was, he realized, much the same feeling he'd had as a child when he first picked up a crayon and tried to capture not an actual horse or cow but the way he felt about the horse or the cow. Yes of course he could use the camera to document tenement life, but there was so much more he could do with it, too. Maybe not like Stieglitz or Steichen, or at least not right away, but perhaps his artist's training would come in useful as he gained experience.

And best of all, he thought, he could take a picture of Ana.

That evening found him on the East Side, where he'd been invited to a small dinner party by one of his mother's elderly aunts. The occasion was a visit by her brother Clarence, a lawyer who lived in California. Will had only met the brother a couple of times, but he'd liked him and looked forward to seeing him again.

His aunt, the widow of another successful lawyer, lived in a modestly grand house on Park Avenue, and Will was met at the door by a butler who showed him into the drawing room. Will kissed his aunt, an energetic woman of nearly eighty, with obvious affection, then shook hands with Clarence. Ruddy-faced and as full of energy as his sister, Clarence asked him how things were going and repeated the invitation he'd first made several years before for Will to visit him.

"California is the future," Clarence said. "I see that clearly every time I come back here. There, it doesn't matter if a thing has never been tried before, or whether you're descended from a blacksmith or a Pilgrim father, all that matters is that you have a good idea and a willingness to work."

"That may be true," Will responded, "but California is hardly immune to what's going on elsewhere. The recent bombing of the *Los Angeles Times* building made that pretty clear."

"True, true," said Clarence, "but I'm telling you, on the whole Californians are eager to just get on with things. And they see, in a way that people in New York and Boston and Philadelphia don't, that America's future is going to largely be across the Pacific. The Easterners still think Europe is all that matters. But while the Chinese and Japanese may not be powerhouses yet, they will be."

The two continued talking in this vein, including what the results of the previous week's elections might bring by way of changes in tariff policy and trade, until it was time for the meal. As predicted, the Democrats had made a clean sweep of New York State and also made big gains in Washington, including control of the House.

There were only twelve for dinner, but Will found himself placed between two people he didn't know, one a friend of his aunt's and the other a friend of her late husband. The latter turned out to be Henry Lewis Morris, another lawyer and one of the Cathedral's trustees. Morris already knew of Will's work for the Bishop and immediately asked him his opinion of the Cathedral's design. Will responded as he had to the Bishop, that while he'd been prepared not to like it, he had in fact found himself impressed.

Morris grunted. "I suppose it's all right for Catholics," he said. "But this is a Protestant cathedral and I believe it should be Gothic. Why the Heins & LaFarge design was chosen I have no idea. I wasn't a trustee then. All I know is that I don't like it."

After a pause, Morris asked him, "Do you know the work of Ralph Cram?" Will, on his guard, said he remembered hearing that Cram had been appointed the consulting architect at Princeton a few years before.

"Yes, and his firm also designed the buildings at West Point," Morris said. "He's the best architect around, for my money, and a strong believer in the Gothic tradition. I've talked to him and he says it's not too late to make adjustments to the Cathedral. I wish there was some way we could get him involved. A few of us trustees have been meeting informally about it, but we still haven't come up with a plan."

So that was it, Will thought. At least some of the trustees including Morris were keen to find a way to 'Gothicize' LaFarge's design, and Cram was angling to be the one to do it. LaFarge's suspicions were correct.

He said nothing to Morris, however, moving the conversation on to some of the buildings he'd particularly admired in England and from there to a discussion of church and city politics. When they shook hands at the end of the evening, he could tell that Morris regarded him as a young man 'to keep an eye on.'

But on his way home he thought again about the conversation with Hugh. He knew that Hugh was right: Will couldn't expect to rise in the world of people like Henry Morris if he continued his relationship with Ana. It wasn't just that she was Jewish, though that by itself was problem enough. But as Lizzy had pointed out, she was also from a completely different world.

He could 'visit' that world of sweatshops and tenements but he would never be comfortable there. And it was hard to imagine how happily or easily Ana would fare in his world of sailing in Maine and dinner parties on Park Avenue. Yes, she was bright, and came from a family that believed in books and ideas, but she didn't know the manners and customs of his world, and she didn't have the shared connections—the schools, the acquaintances, the family friends—that mattered there. However much he might try to shield her, she would feel, and be made to feel, completely out of place.

So there it was, it seemed: choose Ana, with all the difficulties that would bring for both of them, or choose the church and everything that represented his life to date.

Then, from somewhere in his memory of the evening's conversations, Clarence's comments about California came back to him. You could more or less reinvent yourself there, Clarence had said. And you could make your life what you wanted of it.

He's never before thought about living anywhere west of the Hudson River, but now he began to wonder what it would be like. He knew a lot more about England and Europe, he realized, than he did his own country. Kansas City—Denver—San Francisco: they were all just names to him; places he'd read about in histories of the Wild West but not places to which anyone he knew, with the exception of Clarence, had moved voluntarily.

Maybe he and Ana could go to California, he thought—before being taken aback by even imagining such a thing. He glanced at his watch, then down at the book he had opened on his lap, but it was no good: his brain insisted on returning to this startlingly new possibility. Perhaps he could teach—surely they must need teachers there, and Clarence could help him with some introductions. Maybe Ana could finish her schooling there, and even go to college. From what Clarence and Emma Goldman had said, California was a lovely place, full of oranges and redwood trees and an openness to new ideas.

But did he want to move to California? And did he really want to give up a career in the church?

And what about Ana? For her, her union was as important as the church was to him. Would she be willing to leave all of that for the unknown?

His final thought as he fell into a restless sleep that night was that there must be a way to avoid having to make a choice. If he just waited awhile, he tried to convince himself, everything would work out.

Hugh didn't raise the subject of Ana again, and by Wednesday, Will had almost talked himself into believing that he and Ana were, in fact, just good friends. But then, when to his surprise he saw Ana waiting for him after his University Settlement class, he knew that he'd been wrong. He felt a sick longing as she looked up at him, then indicated he should follow her around the corner to a dark patch of sidewalk.

"I need to talk to you," Ana began.

In response, Will blurted out, "I love you," having had no idea until that moment that he would make such a declaration.

Ana, clearly surprised, at first said nothing. "Thank you," she finally responded, her words sounding absurdly formal. An awkward pause followed.

Will drew back, a bit hurt.

"Have I done something wrong?" he asked.

"No, no, nothing," Ana said. Then, slowly, she said, "I was very happy to see you."

"But what?" asked Will.

"But I've been thinking a lot and I don't see how we can continue," Ana said. "It's not so bad for me, because I'm not devout and neither is my aunt, although she'd be very unhappy to know I'm keeping company with a non-Jew. But for you, religion means something—something beyond just going to church. I see it in the way you talk about certain books you've read, and what you say about liking to be alone in the chapel. You're a believer."

She paused. "But it's not just that. I know you're ambitious—in a good way, I mean, ambitious to make a difference in the world. But I can't imagine that your church, however eager it is to 'help' the poor immigrants, or to speak up for the unions"—here she gave a tight little laugh—"would like the idea of one of its ministers-to-be falling in love with a Jewess from the Lower East Side."

Will was silent. It was almost as though Ana had overheard his conversation with Hugh and was echoing everything Hugh had said.

"Ana," he said, "The one thing I know is that I love you and I want to be with you. I've never told anyone before that I loved her, and that's because I never did. But I know without any doubt that I love you."

Ana was silent and they stood both at a seeming loss as to what to do. "Listen to me," Ana finally said, rather unfeelingly, Will thought, especially considering what he'd just told her. "I think we shouldn't see each other for a little while—maybe a few weeks—and then see how we feel. I've had a few male friends in the past"—again, Will felt that same stab of jealousy he'd experienced when Ana had mentioned the possibility that her aunt was waiting for her to get married—"and I know that at first everything feels exciting and thrilling. But life isn't like that."

Will found himself irritated by her words. Ana was practical. She'd had to be. While he and his friends had had the luxury of taking time to 'find themselves' she'd been working and experiencing life. But that didn't mean he appreciated her telling him, in effect, that he was immature.

"I understand," he said stiffly. "You're no doubt correct. I'm sorry if I've been too forward. We both need to think about our futures. Why don't we agree that you'll get word to me through Lizzy if and when you'd like to meet again. In the meantime, as you suggest, we'll both just live our lives."

Then, trying to sound as though nothing serious had happened, he said, "By the way, I met Anne Morgan a few days ago and she said she's interested in learning more about how she could be useful to the organizing movement. I told her that if she'd like to meet with some of the young women involved, I might be able to help arrange it. If she contacts me, I'll leave a message for you with Lizzy."

"Thank you," Ana said, in a barely audible voice. "And now I must be going." Turning away, she crossed the street and almost immediately rounded a corner. For a moment, Will considered running after her, but he didn't. Even if she regarded him as immature, he thought to himself, at least he refused to be a complete fool.

Only now that she had gone did he allow himself to experience the full effect that her words had produced. He stepped into a doorway and took a few deep breaths.

Just a few days ago they'd been so happy. What had happened?

It was several minutes before Will felt calm enough to be able to start walking to the el. All the way to the seminary he went over and over what had just happened, trying to make sense of

Ana's behavior. He knew already how impetuous she could be, but it was clear in this case that she had thought through what she wanted to say. He could tell that she cared for him, so what had made her change so suddenly? Perhaps her union acquaintances were criticizing her for keeping company with someone they regarded as part of the bosses' class. She said she was concerned about *his* future, but maybe she was just as concerned about her own.

Still, he refused to see the situation as hopeless. He thought again about the conversation with Clarence and wished that he had had the chance to tell Ana his ideas about California. Maybe they were complete nonsense, but at least it was better to consider possibilities than to just say the situation was impossible. Why did Ana have to see everything in black and white?

Later, tossing and turning before going to sleep, he realized that it might be just as well that he hadn't mentioned California. For Ana, the prospect might be far more alarming than it was for him. At least he had the luxury of knowing that however far away he was, and however bad things might get financially or otherwise, he could always turn to his family for help. Ana didn't have anyone, as far as he knew, apart from her aunt.

So perhaps, he consoled himself, Ana didn't really want to break things off, it was just that she was frightened. What he needed to focus on was how to reassure her.

But first, he needed to be in God's grace.

The next morning, he checked to see if there were still any vacant places for the retreat at Holy Cross on the coming weekend. Fortunately, there was still one space. Hugh had already told him he'd decided he had too much work to be able to go, so Will put his name down. He wouldn't be able to leave until after his regular Friday meeting with the Bishop, but he'd still be there no later than nine. In the country, he thought to himself, that's practically the middle of the night.

CHAPTER THIRTEEN

*W*hen Will alighted at the West Park train station, he was immediately struck by how much colder it was here than in the city. Coming down the hill from the gatehouse into the Holy Cross Monastery property, he felt the cold wind whipping off the Hudson River even though he couldn't actually see the river in the dark.

A novice answered the door and, after Will had given his name, showed him to the room that would be his for the next two nights. Small and spare, furnished with only a bed, a small table and lamp, and a desk and chair, it nevertheless pleased Will in its clean simplicity. The shared bathing and lavatory facilities were down the hall.

The novice explained that compline had already ended, meaning that no talking was permitted, except by people with jobs like his, until the morning. Even then, the novice added, conversation would be limited to the group discussions with Father Huntington; meals would be taken in silence.

Will nodded, then asked how many men there were in the retreat group. "Fifteen," the novice answered. "Five each from two seminaries and five individuals who've come on their own."

He gave Will a small sheet of paper that outlined the program for the weekend, which started with matins at seven o'clock. "A bell will be rung in the corridor fifteen minutes before the service begins," the novice said. With that he bade Will good-night and left, quietly closing the door behind him.

Will walked to the room's only window, but could see nothing apart from a lone star, or perhaps a planet, emitting a tiny speck of light. Turning back toward the bed, he removed from his valise the two books he'd brought, along with a few items of clothing and his toiletries. As he entered the large communal bathroom he encountered another young man of about his age coming out. They nodded to each other in greeting.

Back in his room, Will looked around, wondering what to do next. He didn't feel like sleeping just yet, but he didn't feel like reading either. 'I should be praying,' he suddenly thought, and dropped to his knees by the bed. But the feeling that he was acting out a script, rather than engaging in a real activity, was impossible to shake off, and after a few minutes he gave up. Instead, he picked up the Bible that had been placed on the table next to the bed and opened it to the Gospel of John.

The first few lines of the gospel were, to Will's mind, the most beautiful, and the most profound, in the whole of the New Testament. "In the beginning was the Word, and the Word was with God, and the Word was God." What did that mean, "In the beginning was the word?" He had pondered it countless times, but had never come up with a satisfactory answer. It appealed to him as suggesting a presence that had nothing to do with an actual being, only an intellectual or spiritual reality. Or maybe not anything that could be described using words at all, but rather a truth that always was and will be, something not to strive to understand but simply to accept.

Slowly, Will felt his mind grow quiet, only to return to confusion as thoughts of Ana took over. Her abrupt departure troubled him. It was as though she'd wanted to make their parting as unpleasant as possible. Or maybe she'd been planning a more reasoned discussion but when it came down to it, the only way she knew how to do it was in a rough way.

But yet he loved her. Why? Partly for her bravery and fierce commitment to the union. Partly for her undisguised keenness on 'improving herself' as she might put it. But mostly, he admitted to himself, because he just did.

Sighing, Will climbed into bed and turned out the light. Starting in the morning, he promised himself, he'd put all thoughts of Ana aside and make the most of this chance to deepen his spiritual life.

Only moments later, or so it seemed, he heard the faint sound of the morning bell. Instantly awake, he hurriedly put his clothes on and visited the lavatory before descending to the chapel. Most of the dozen or so monks were already there, along with a scattering of the retreat participants. Over the next five minutes, the rest appeared, slipping quietly into the pews.

More silence.

Finally, one of the monks began the service, leading the chanting of psalms that was taken up first by the monks on one side of the altar, then the other. Relatively tuneless, unlike the Gregorian chant Will was more familiar with, it went on for many minutes until Will felt lulled into something that wasn't sleep but wasn't a state of being fully awake either.

Eventually, it ended, and a simple service of prayers followed. When it was over, no one moved until finally one of the monks stood up and blew out the two candles on the altar, the sign for the others to file silently out.

Back in his room, Will took off his clothes, picked up the towel that had been provided, and headed for the communal bathroom. There, he washed, brushed his teeth and shaved. Several other young men were doing the same things he was doing, but all kept their eyes averted. Once again in the room, he put on a fresh shirt and, after finishing dressing, made the bed and straightened up the room—not that there was much to straighten.

By now it was time to return to the chapel for the second service, the daily Mass, which was said by one of the monks who had now put on priestly vestments. Then, breakfast and a few minutes' walk down toward the river and back, and it was time for the first meeting of the retreat.

Will was happy that Father Huntington, rather than one of the other senior monks, was conducting the retreat. Huntington, who was now, Will knew, in his late fifties, began by welcoming them all to Holy Cross and encouraging them to make use of the grounds and the library while they were there. Tall and thin, patrician in his bearing and voice, Huntington was dressed, like all the monks, in a white habit with an attached cowl, and on his chest hung a large, simple crucifix. He explained that the theme of the weekend would be Christian meditation, with some talks on the role it played in early Christian life, and some suggestions on how to begin practicing it.

It was not, he said, the same as praying. Rather, it was an effort to both empty the mind of all distractions and to focus it on spiritual concerns. As a start, he suggested, he'd like to have each of them picture some event in the New Testament—for example, the scene of Jesus preaching to the multitudes from a boat—and to think only about that scene for the next few minutes. They could think about anything having to do with the boat and the message and the crowd, but nothing else. They could close their eyes or not, as they chose.

For the next ten minutes, all that could be heard in the room was breathing and an occasional cough. Will, unable to come up with anything better, took Huntington's suggestion and focused on the boat scene, trying to picture the colors and shape of the clothing the disciples wore and to smell the bodies of the large crowd. The longer he focused on the scene the more real it became to him—not just the details he'd made up but what Jesus was trying to teach the people through parables.

Just before noon, after two hours of lecture and discussion on the difference between meditation and prayer, they finished up and went to the chapel for diurnum. This was followed by lunch and then there was free time until four.

Will used the opportunity to take a walk shown on a small map in the reception area. It took him out of the seminary grounds and down a side road to an abandoned quarry. In the summer, Will thought, the quarry might be a pleasant place, with smooth rocks on which to sit and soak up the sun, but at this time of year there was little to see apart from some brush and broken bits of rock. The sky was gray but there was no rain until he was nearly back to the seminary, when small drops began to fall. Speeding up his pace, he got back just as the rain began in earnest.

For another hour they met with Father Huntington, during which Father Huntington talked about some of the less well-known Christian mystics and about some of the reading he'd done on Eastern mysticism. It was curious, he said, that although Christianity had had a strong mystical tradition for hundreds of years, today that tradition had virtually disappeared, at least in the Protestant denominations, and indeed anyone who brought up the subject was likely to be regarded with skepticism and sometimes even alarm.

Will found himself fascinated by Father Huntington's remarks. It made him think about how appealing he'd found the Transcendentalists during college and how surprised he'd been not long after coming to the seminary to read an essay that described the ways in which they'd been influenced by Eastern thought. Thoreau in particular had been greatly impressed with the Bhagavad Gita and the notion of the oneness of all beings, and all the Transcendentalists had emphasized the importance of contemplation and subjective insights as opposed to doctrine.

During college, he'd regarded Emerson as having made a mistake in giving up the pulpit. Surely, he thought, there was a way of combining modern ideas with old ones. But now he saw that perhaps Emerson had understood more clearly than he did that institutions, the modern Church included, didn't have much room for mystics or misfits.

Will's attention shifted back to Father Huntington just as Huntington was finishing up his remarks, after which it was time for vespers and then supper. At eight they gathered one more time in the chapel for compline, and then it was off to bed.

Will was so tired from the day's events that he was asleep by nine-thirty, and he slept until the bell awoke him at quarter to seven. Sunday morning was more or less a repeat of the day before, but at the end of the morning session Father Huntington told them that after lunch he would hold what he called 'office hours' when any of them could come to see him individually for thirty minutes. He passed around a sign-up sheet and Will put himself down for the three o'clock slot.

At the appointed time, Will was standing outside Father Huntington's office when the person before him emerged. He waited half a minute, then walked in the door, which had been left ajar. Greeting Father Huntington, he introduced himself and sat down in the chair in front of Huntington's desk.

"Thank you for this weekend," he began. "I've learned a lot about meditation, which I intend to incorporate into my daily practice."

"You're very welcome," said Huntington, "but I think that's not the reason that brought you here to the monastery."

"No," said Will. "And in fact there are so many reasons that brought me here I don't know where to start."

"Well, just pick one and we'll move on from there," said Huntington, the slightest hint of amusement in his voice.

"In a way they're all related," said Will, his usual self-possession for once deserting him. "I'm about to finish my seminary training and present myself for ordination but I don't really know if I want to be a clergyman, not just because I can't see myself as a church rector—I realized yesterday that I'm far more interested in exploring Christian mysticism than in baptizing babies—but also because I have so many questions about whether the church is the right place to work for social change. I don't have any doubts about my faith, but I have many doubts about the Church as an institution." Pausing, he added rapidly, "There's also something else, which is that I've fallen in love with a Jewish labor activist. She says it's impossible for us to make a life together, and my friends say the same, but I don't want to give her up."

"There's an awful lot of 'I' in what you've been saying," Huntington commented mildly. "What 'I' want and do not want, what 'I' think of the church and its role, what 'I' want in terms of a relationship."

He stopped there and let his words sink in.

"Perhaps," he went on, "you should fret less and listen more in order to hear what God is telling you He wants you to do."

Huntington paused again, then said, "I'm going to tell you a story. When I was your age I was so busy denouncing predatory capitalism and making speeches to anyone who would stop to listen to me that I was lost in a sea of noise—most of it my own. I felt I had all the answers to what was wrong with the world, if only the world would listen to me. Fortunately, I eventually realized what was happening. And when I finally did begin to listen to that 'small, still voice' within me, I began to glimpse what my path was meant to be. And that is what led eventually to this place, and this life."

"But how could you leave the city you loved, and all the people who needed you?" Will asked.

Huntington took a minute to respond. "There are many ways to be of service," he said. "I'm sitting here with you right now, helping you to think through your future. Admittedly you're not a poor working man from the slums, but does that make you any less worth my time? And if a handful of the young men who've been here this weekend do a better job of teaching or preaching or being fathers or husbands than they would have otherwise, isn't that useful to society?"

He went on, "My point isn't that you should become a monk, or follow my example. My point is that you must do what God calls you to do, and that may be very different than what you suppose your future to be."

Will was silent. "I understand what you're saying," he said finally. "But to be honest, I don't know if I've ever heard God speak to me. Maybe I, too, have been too busy 'doing.' Or maybe I don't want to hear, because I'm afraid of where that might lead me."

He stopped, clearly troubled by these thoughts. Then, feeling at a loss as to what more to add, he stood up. "Thank you, Father," he said. "I'll try to listen harder. I didn't know what to expect coming here, but you've given me some guidance about how at least to think about these things."

"Kneel down, my son," Father Huntington said. Will did as he was told. Huntington put his hand on Will's head and recited a simple blessing. Will's eyes involuntarily filled with tears, which he tried to fight back as he nodded his thanks and left the room.

Will was grateful that his meeting with Father Huntington meant he was too late to travel back to the city with the other seminarians from General Theological. Alone on the train, he spent the time staring out the window, by turns thinking about Father Huntington's words of advice and, of course, about Ana.

He was back at the seminary in time for Sunday supper. He and Hugh took a walk afterward, during which Will told Hugh a bit about the weekend, leaving out the private discussion at the end. "You probably wouldn't have liked it," Will said. "Too Catholic by far. But I think Father Huntington is a great and wise man."

CHAPTER FOURTEEN

*W*ill awoke Monday morning having made a firm decision about what he was going to do. He knew where Ana worked, in a factory just off Washington Square, and what time she finished, and he was there several minutes before the girls started streaming out.

She was one of the last, by herself and seemingly lost in thought, with her head bent so that he couldn't see her expression.

"Hello, Ana," said Will. "May I walk with you a bit?"

Ana's head shot up. "Hello," she said. Then, seeming at a loss for words, she added unnecessarily, "I didn't expect to see you."

"But I'm here," said Will, "and I'd like to talk to you."

They walked over to a bench in Washington Square Park and sat down.

"Ana," said Will. "I talked this past weekend with someone who helped me to see that maybe I won't even decide to be ordained, in which case any concerns about your being a Jew will be irrelevant. And as for my being religious and you not, I don't really see that that is as important as whether we share a belief that we want to make the world a better place." Taking a breath, he went on, "I'll always be interested in spiritual ideas; it's part of who I am. But that doesn't mean I'll follow one particular way of leading my life."

Seeing Ana looking at him intently, Will plunged ahead. "So

I'd like to make a proposal: Let's put any discussions of a long-term relationship to one side and just go on as we have been these past few weeks, meeting regularly and getting to know each other better. There are so many places I'd like to show you and so many places I'd like you to show me. We don't have to go announcing to the world that we're seeing each other, and maybe no one will care anyway. If they do, well, we'll deal with it."

Ana was silent for a minute, taking in what Will had said.

"I've thought about you all the time since last week," she said finally. "And I think you're right about not getting too far ahead of ourselves. I don't know how easy it would be for us to be together forever, but we haven't really spent enough time together to even know if we want to. I was too quick to see why it couldn't work, and maybe I wasn't allowing for the possibility that our circumstances—not just yours, but mine, too—might change. I think I'm too ready to see everything in black and white"—the last remark caused Will to inwardly smile—"and to assume that how things are is always how they will be."

She paused. "I love you, Will," she said finally. "I couldn't say it when you said it to me because I wasn't sure. But I am sure now."

Will broke into a grin. After pausing to take in this news, and looking into Ana's slightly apprehensive face, he said with a smile, "So now that's settled," and sat back on the bench. Then, unable to hide his happiness, he added with pretended formality, "Miss Ana Markowicz and Mr. William Ingalls, having declared their feelings, are hereby pronounced to be in love."

There didn't seem to be anything more to say, so they sat there in silence for a few minutes, getting accustomed to the new reality. Finally, Will said, "Maybe we could meet next Sunday and you could take me to one of the places you used to go to with your uncle?"

"Yes," Ana said. "That's a good idea. I'll tell my aunt I want to meet a friend, which will be the truth even if not the whole truth. Let's meet in front of the *Forward* building at two o'clock and we'll walk from there."

The week passed uneventfully. Bishop Greer had no evening appointments on his calendar because he was preparing for the Diocesan Convention the following week, and his secretary told Will not to come for his regular Friday appointment. So Will worked on the paper for his Columbia seminar, examining in particular the connections between social and economic conditions in England at the time of the birth of the Shaker movement and the form of community the Shakers developed once they were established in America.

He hadn't realized until he started his research that the start of the Shaker movement coincided with the rise of industrialization in England, and that Mother Ann, the head of the group, worked in a cotton factory when she was a girl. What role did this play, he wondered, in Mother Ann's later decision to establish the Shakers in rural communities? Was it perhaps a rejection of the dehumanizing aspects of industrialization as much as religious impulses that was responsible for the rise of the Shakers and other utopian communities?

On Tuesday, reveling in the sense of having a bit of extra time after a busy few weeks, Will made a point of not rushing off after his University Settlement class, instead staying to talk with several of the students. Among them was Aaron Cohen, the self-confident debater, who was the last to leave.

Cohen asked him whether there was any chance they might organize another debate with College Settlement. "That's a good idea," said Will. "Let me talk to Miss Sperling." Grinning, he added, "But this time we'll insist that it be here and we'll stay away from religion!"

Cohen laughed. "Maybe it's not such a bad thing, religion," he said. "When I see you, studying to be ordained but not like the pompous church officials whose pictures I see in the newspaper, I think maybe the church can actually do some good."

Will smiled. "Well at least I'm making some progress," he said in a joking tone. After a pause, he added, "Maybe in that case you'd be interested in hearing Walter Rauschenbusch, who's speaking at Columbia on Friday night. I'm planning to go with my friend Hugh and if you'd like to join us you'd be very welcome. I'm a big admirer of Rauschenbusch, as you know, but I've only heard him speak once before, and Hugh has never heard him. He lives in Rochester now and doesn't come to the city often."

Cohen said he'd very much like to go, so it was agreed they would meet at the subway station at Columbia.

When they'd all arrived, Will introduced Aaron and Hugh and the three of them walked quickly to the large lecture hall where the talk was to take place. Even though they were half an hour early, the hall was nearly full.

When Rauschenbusch was introduced, the hall erupted into loud applause, making it clear that Rauschenbusch was speaking to a sympathetic audience. He was attractive, in an ascetic looking way, Will thought, and his English, while totally fluent, reflected the fact that German had been his first language.

Rauschenbusch began by talking about his debt to Columbia for having produced Richard Ely, an economist whom he'd come to know while working in a German church in a poor West Side neighborhood. Describing Ely's work as having had a major impact on him and his developing concept of the social gospel, Rauschenbusch said, "He's an Episcopal layman and I'm a Baptist clergyman, but I believe all Christians are engaged at this moment in the same struggle.

"I like to think that it was Ely's academic study in Germany that helped him to reject the claims of English economists that immutable laws govern our economic system," Rauschenbusch went on. "He insisted that it's historical circumstances, not personal qualities, that make some men rich and others poor. It was his book *Social Aspects of Christianity* that helped me to see that Christian churches have taught only a half-gospel—one that has emphasized personal salvation and ignored the Bible's insistence on social righteousness."

Rauschenbusch went on to sketch the outlines of his by now well-known ideas about what the churches needed to do, beginning with recognizing that Western society had become dominated by an economic system in which workers suffered the loss of their health and dignity, while owners, for their part, suffered the loss of those qualities that made them human.

Given this situation, Rauschenbusch argued, the churches needed to take the lead in pressing for socialism, including public ownership of major utilities, and fully support unions. "If society continues to disintegrate and decay, the Church will be carried down with it," Rauschenbusch warned.

Walking out after the lecture was over, Cohen admitted that he'd liked Rauschenbusch's lecture. "What he says seems to be based on common sense," he said, "and on his own experiences."

Hugh agreed, admitting that he, too, had been impressed by Rauschenbusch's down-to-earth style and obvious personal humility. "I'd assumed he would sound like a Communist or anarchist, full of hot air and radical slogans," Hugh said. "But he made it clear that his political views come out of his religious beliefs."

Will nodded in satisfaction. "If either of you gentlemen would care to borrow my copy of Rauschenbusch's *Christianity and the Social Crisis* you have only to ask," he said with a laugh.

On Sunday, Will was a few minutes late for his appointment with Ana, owing to the length of the chapel service. As he rushed up to her, apologizing, she greeted him and said that in fact she'd been a bit late herself because she'd been helping her aunt with the cleaning.

"My aunt is suspicious that something's going on because so often on Sunday now I seem to have something to do in the afternoon," she said. "I'm sure she thinks it's a young man but she doesn't want to appear too nosy so she hasn't asked any questions."

Gesturing toward the *Forward* building, she commented, "I never come here anymore, now that my uncle is dead."

"What do you remember about your uncle's work?" Will asked.

"Well, I actually never saw him at work," said Ana. "If I was going to meet him, it would always be right here, after he'd finished. To me this building was a sort of magical place, not just because of my uncle but because I knew that this was where the newspaper came from."

"Did you read it?" Will asked.

"Oh yes, always," Ana said. "My uncle brought it home with him and I read everything, even though I didn't understand a lot of the political columns, especially when I was young."

"So you always wanted to know about what was going on in the world," Will commented as they started walking in the direction of the cafe Ana had suggested. "I wasn't precocious like you. I was busy drawing and dreaming and reading books about the Roman legions in Britain until I started boarding school when I was twelve. It was only then that I even began to notice that there was a world beyond Greenville, New York, and maybe Boston."

He asked Ana how her week had been. "Like all weeks, long," she said. "Too much work, too many bosses. I hate the way they treat us like children. They even insist on looking through our purses every day in case we are trying to steal anything."

After a pause, she went on, "The best thing was having a cup of tea last night with a girl I met in Miss Sperling's reading group. She lives quite close to me, and also works in a shirtwaist factory, but I never knew her until now. She's interested in the union and in learning more about organizing and I feel sure that we'll be good friends."

Will nodded, and in turn told her about how Aaron Cohen had come with him to the lecture by Rauschenbusch and pronounced himself quite impressed.

"You're a bad influence," said Ana, laughing. "I think I'll have to meet up with Mr. Cohen and set him straight."

"Oh, please don't do that," said Will, with mock seriousness. "I remember how friendly he was toward you after the debate, and I don't want him to have any more chances to impress you."

"Don't worry," said Ana earnestly, missing the point of his humor. "I've made my choice."

The cafe was a large one, filled with people, most of them

men, sitting over glasses of tea or small cups of coffee. Will and Ana found a table off to one side, where they could look around at the other patrons without being too obvious about it. Will let Ana order for both of them while he listened to the conversations, or at least to the sound of them, since they were mostly in Yiddish.

"What did your uncle and his friends discuss?" he asked.

"Politics, mostly," she answered. "Some of his friends had been members of the Bund"—seeing his puzzled look she explained that that was a Polish socialist party—"and they debated endlessly about Polish politics and American politics and whether Jews should form their own groups here or assimilate."

"What was your uncle's position?" Will asked.

"Oh, assimilation, definitely," Ana answered. "He had no time for the Zionists. He thought America was a wonderful country and that the best thing the Jews could do was to learn English and give their children good educations and make new lives for themselves in America."

"And what about you?" asked Will. "Do you feel America is a wonderful country?"

Ana hesitated. "I'm very grateful to be here and not still in Poland," she said. "I don't know what would have become of me there. Many Polish people dislike all Jews and Jews were always worried about whether there would be another pogrom. Here, many Americans might not like us but they aren't going to kill us." She added, "Sometimes, though, I wish I could live somewhere where there are just Jews."

Will was silent for a few moments.

"But that wouldn't mean everything would be perfect," he said. "You told me that the owners of the factory where you work are Jews and yet they make their workers work long hours and pay them poorly."

Ana nodded. "It's true," she said. "We've asked them so many times to cut back on our hours—officially we work fifty-nine hours but sometimes it's more if there's a big contract to fill—but they say if we don't like it there are plenty of others waiting to take our place. And they say the same thing about our wages: I'm making $8 a week, which can't even support my aunt and me, let alone a family, but they say if we don't like it we can leave."

Ana paused for a minute, clearly thinking about what she'd just said. Then she added, "Maybe I just mean that I wish I could live somewhere where people treat each other with respect rather than hating each other, the way bosses and workers do."

Will and Ana sat there for another half-hour, talking idly about books they were reading and what they'd been doing during the week. It turned out that they'd both loved *Looking Backward* by Edward Bellamy, which they'd read when they were young.

"What was your favorite part?" Will asked Ana.

"I liked it when the father of the family explained to Julian that all you have to do if you want to listen to a concert is to call the concert hall and the concert will come to you over the telephone line," Ana replied. "I wonder whether that will really happen by the year 2000."

"I liked the way you could just order whatever you wanted from one huge store and have it delivered to your door," Will said.

Ana laughed. "That's one thing I thought Bellamy got wrong," she said. "Women like to go from shop to shop and see what's there. Part of the enjoyment is the hunt itself. I can't imagine they'll ever want to order things, especially clothes, from just one place."

Eventually they left the cafe, then strolled for another hour as far east as Jackson Street Park, where Will insisted on taking Ana's picture, and then suggested she take one of him, before they headed back along East Houston Street. Along the way they passed several moving picture parlors and dance halls, which Ana explained to Will were very popular among most of the young people she knew.

"There's nowhere to entertain anyone in two or three rooms that you're sharing with your whole family," she explained. "So girls come here to meet the young men they want to spend time with."

"Do you ever go?" Will asked.

"Oh no, I much prefer going to College Settlement and spending time in the library or talking with Miss Sperling or the other girls," said Ana seriously. Will smiled to himself.

"Don't you ever have any fun?" he asked.

"I think going to the Settlement House is fun," said Ana. "But I do remember one time that was so wonderful I'll never forget it. It was just before my uncle died. He took me and my aunt for a week to the Catskill Mountains. We went there on a train and we stayed in a big boarding house and we went for walks every day in the woods. It was the most beautiful place I've ever been."

"Well," said Will, "that's where Greenville, the town I come from, is located—in the Catskills, but right at the very northern end of them, only about thirty miles from Albany. Maybe one day I can take you there."

"I had no idea that's where you lived!" exclaimed Ana. "You're so lucky to have grown up there. I still remember how clean it was, and how the only smell was of leaves or sometimes pine trees. And there were so many birds and squirrels and one time I even saw a fox."

They continued in this vein until they were at Fifth Avenue, at which point, realizing that it was already five o'clock, they agreed it was time to go their separate ways.

"This has been very nice," said Ana. "Just walking and talking and doing nothing special."

"Yes, I agree," said Will. "Until winter sets in, let's try to do this every Sunday. Next time, I want to show you Columbia University and the Cathedral."

Two days later, it was Will's turn to give an interim report on his research paper to the members of his seminar class. He started off by describing the Shakers' origin and growth, then focused on the rural utopian communities they created. "From what I understand so far," Will said, "the Shakers, like many other utopian communities, felt the world was a wicked place and they wanted as little as possible to do with it. And yet, they were not at all opposed to machines; for example, the Shakers in Canterbury,

New Hampshire, patented a washing machine that won a gold medal at the Centennial Exposition in Philadelphia in 1876."

Encouraged by a nod from the instructor, Will continued, "What I conclude from this is that the Shakers had an ambivalent relationship with modernity. And in fact, I plan to argue in the paper that it was their inability to come to terms with urbanization and industrialization, not the celibacy they're so well known for, that doomed them to eventual decline."

"How do you see the Shakers as similar to, or different from, other utopian communities in terms of their attitude toward cities?" one of the other students asked.

"I think for the most part all utopian groups wanted to withdraw from the 'evil' cities," Will answered. "There have been a few efforts to create urban utopias but they never got many supporters. The Shakers may have been the best-placed to try such an experiment but they never did. Instead, they represent yet one more unsuccessful attempt to turn back the clock to what they perceived as a purer, simpler time."

"So do you consider the Shakers a failure?" another student asked.

"They were master craftsmen, clever inventors, and strong believers in equality between races and sexes," Will answered, thinking through his answer as he spoke. "If you put their celibacy to one side, their ideas have a lot to recommend them. But the question of our day is how to create urban societies in which all citizens enjoy clean, safe workplaces and decent housing, and where workers are paid enough that they don't need to put their children to work, too. That's the challenge, or should be, it seems to me, for any social or religious movement. And on that, the Shakers, like the Amish and the Hutterites, have nothing to say."

Will could tell that the other students were interested in his topic from the number of questions they asked. Eventually, in fact, the discussion ended only because the professor called a halt, made a few observations of his own, and dismissed the class. As Will gathered his books, the professor congratulated him on having done a good job of presenting his topic and said he looked forward to the final paper. "I admire the way you've brought a fresh eye to this material," he told Will. "If you should decide to abandon the church and become an academic, I'd be happy to recommend you for a doctoral program."

Surprised, Will expressed his thanks, adding that while he believed he'd made the right choice, he certainly would think over what the professor had said. As he left the building, he realized that his spirits were high not just because of his success with the presentation but because the professor's praise had caused him to realize there might be options involving Ana and the future that he hadn't even thought of: California, certainly, but maybe others as well.

He thought again about what Father Huntington had said about listening for God's voice. He didn't feel he was doing that very well, at least not yet, but he did feel that his mind was opening up to possibilities in the same way that his heart had already done.

CHAPTER FIFTEEN

ednesday morning found Will on Morningside Heights at the opening of the Diocesan Convention, the annual meeting of elected clergy and laity representatives which discussed and voted on church matters. Plans were underway for a new Synod Hall to be built on the Cathedral property but for now, part of the former asylum building housing LaFarge's office and the choir school had been turned into a temporary venue for the event. Mr. Moore, the Bishop's Secretary, had told Will that the Bishop wanted him to be present to help escort those who wanted a tour of the Cathedral and to act as a general guide for the delegates.

The morning began with Holy Communion at ten-thirty in the Cathedral crypt, which had been used as a chapel for some years already while the main construction was underway. Following the service, Bishop Greer formally opened the convention and read his address. Various bits of business were moved including adding two people to Episcopal Fund committee.

Lunch was a hurried affair, with the delegates crowding around two long tables and having to eat standing up. No one seemed to mind, though, since everyone was busy greeting old friends and talking over convention business.

Only half a dozen people had expressed an interest in seeing the state of the construction on the Cathedral, which caused Will to feel relieved at not having to be responsible for too many people but also a bit worried about the level of support for the project. The tour lasted about half an hour, during which only two people asked questions, both having to do with the design and why it wasn't more Gothic.

The afternoon session began with a continuation of the morning's business, and Will could see many eyes drooping until Reverend Ralph Walker, the young rector of a church in the Bronx, unexpectedly stood up and said he wished to propose a resolution. Noting the current strike of transport workers in the city, he proposed that the convention "expresses its sympathy for the striking express men, and recommends that the strike be arbitrated, and that a special committee be appointed by the convention to investigate the conditions existing between the express companies and their employees."

Immediately the hall broke into angry mutterings of disapproval as the delegates craned their necks to see the proposer. A big, bronzed man with a full white beard who identified himself as a lawyer named William Rogers jumped to his feet and cried out, "I move that the resolution be laid on the table. It doesn't come within the province of a church convention to meddle in strikes. We are here to discuss religious and secular affairs. What have we to do with strikes, anyway?"

Walker tried to say something but he was drowned out by calls of "Sit down, sit down." Bishop Greer looked annoyed.

For an hour a verbal battle ensued as to whether the motion would be presented, amended or simply ignored. At one point Will heard a clergyman who was sitting near him comment to another, "I wonder what Mr. Morgan would say if he were here"—Morgan having attended the morning session but not returned in the afternoon.

At length an amended motion was adopted which refrained from any expression of support for the strikers and urged only that the matter be submitted to arbitration.

That evening, after he got back from his University Settlement class, Will stopped in at Hugh's room to fill him in on the events of the day.

"I couldn't believe how much opposition there was to the motion," Will told Hugh. "And it wasn't just the clergy or just the laymen, it was all of them. You'd have thought Walker was proposing that the church begin preaching Communism in place of the Gospel." Pausing a moment, he added, "It made me remember how upset the Bishop was when I suggested ecumenical events at the Cathedral. Now I realize how just how absurd an idea that was."

Hugh nodded. "It's sobering to understand what we'll be up against once we're ordained," he said. "It's fine for us to talk among ourselves about the Knights of Labor or the rights of the working man, but once we're out there we're going to be dealing with congregations that are mainly made up of people who identify with management, not workers, even if they're not managers themselves. We're going to have to satisfy ourselves with very small steps, if we can manage any steps at all."

"Yes," Will agreed. "When you're living among other students and academics, you assume that everyone thinks the way you do, or at least that they're willing to be persuaded by good arguments. But what I saw today was that most people don't want any change and they don't even want to discuss it."

After a pause, Will told Hugh about the conversation he'd had with Henry Dowling after their visit to the tenements, and his realization that it was probably only through tough laws and tough enforcement, not a change of heart on the part of the city's elite, that conditions in the slums would ever improve. "If that's so," Will said, "it makes me wonder whether I should forget about a career in the church and become a political activist."

Hugh's face betrayed his surprise. "Will," he said, "It's clear to me, as I told you before, that you're not by nature comfortable in a public role. You like to weigh things, assemble facts and arguments, not talk to big crowds or be a show-off like Teddy Roosevelt. And besides, if you were a rabble-rouser you'd never be listened to by the kind of people whose hearts need to change. But as someone inside the church, even if you can't completely change their hearts at least you can shame them into not opposing progressive ideas."

Will nodded. "You're right about my inclinations," he said. "But I'm beginning to think that it's cowardly to just stand on the sidelines cheering on the people who are fighting the real battles."

"Such as the Jewish union girl you met?" Hugh asked.

"Yes," Will answered. "But she's only helped me to see what I've been increasingly realizing anyway. Talk really is cheap." After a pause, he added, "If you'd seen those tenements I told you about"—Will shook his head in remembered dismay—"you'd understand how important it is to get rid of them as quickly as possible."

The second day of the convention was much quieter. Of most interest to Will was the report of the church's City Mission Society, which included a discussion of the problems confronting a mission on East Ninety-Fifth Street. Built to minister to the needs of immigrant Germans, it now found itself in a neighborhood consisting mainly of Jews and colored people, the majority of the latter from the West Indies and brought up as Anglicans, the British equivalent of Episcopalians.

These people have a right to be ministered to, the report noted, but it had been found "exceedingly difficult" to combine white and colored in one congregation. The Mission Society would have to decide whether the Chapel would continue to serve only whites, or become a Chapel for the colored people.

Will, remembering Bishop Greer's remarks at the Colony Club, hoped there would be as spirited a debate on the City Mission Society's report as there had been the day before on the motion to support the striking express men. But as with the Colony Club audience, the general feeling among the delegates seemed to be that separation of the races was the right way to ensure social harmony, and the discussion was brief and desultory. In any case, it was clear that no decision was going to be made at the meeting.

The most noteworthy business of the day was the election of Reverend Charles Sumner Burch, the rector of a church in Staten Island, to the new position of Suffragan Bishop for the Diocese.

Mr. Morgan and Dr. William Manning were appointed to formally notify Dr. Burch of his election and escort him to the platform.

Following this, Mr. Morgan presented the report of the committee on finance, of which he was chairman, and, after a few more minor items of business, Bishop Greer rose to make his final remarks.

He was brief, but didn't neglect a plea for additional money for the Cathedral. As they all knew, he said, it had been hoped to have the consecration on St. John's Day in December but owing to the fact that more work needed to be done, the consecration would instead be during Easter Week.

With that, and a benediction, the convention was over.

As Will came out into the close, the sun already descending over the Hudson River, and the sky was beginning to show the dramatic pinks and purples that were a regular sight on winter afternoons. He felt dispirited by the lackluster tone of the past two days.

He wondered to himself whether, if he had been a young rector from the Bronx, he would have had the nerve to offer a resolution like the one Walker had proposed. Walker must have known that it didn't have a chance of passage, and that it would certainly do him no good in career terms to irritate the Bishop. But he'd done it anyway. Why? And would he, Will, have been willing to do likewise? He hoped so, but the thought of standing up publicly as Walker had done filled him with dismay.

When he got back to his room there was a message from Anne Morgan asking whether he could put together a meeting of three or four young shirtwaist workers to meet with her and half a dozen colleagues the following Tuesday at eight o'clock in the evening at the Colony Club. Will noted that she had thoughtfully chosen a time late enough so that the young women would have time to get there after they finished work and even, perhaps, had something to eat.

The first thing Will did when he and Ana met on Sunday was to ask her whether she could organize a group to meet with

Morgan. She said yes, and told Will that in fact she'd been to the Colony Club once already, during the strike the year before. She didn't remember whether Anne Morgan had been there at that meeting, but she did remember that after she and some of her colleagues had spoken, the Colony Club members conducted a fund-raising for the strikers. They'd managed to collect only three hundred dollars, she said. While welcome, that amount hadn't gone far toward paying bail and helping the families of the girls who were on strike.

"Not to defend them," Will said, "but most of the women who belong to the Colony Club don't actually have much money of their own. Their husbands pay the bills for their clothes and everything else they buy, and for the most part the only ones who have any money they can spend as they choose are ones who've been left personal bequests—usually by some maiden aunt."

"So in a way," Ana said thoughtfully, "we factory girls are actually better off than they are. At least we have a skill and can earn money from it."

"Yes," Will said, "I hadn't thought about it that way but you're right. Society is changing but I think it's changing faster at the lower levels than the higher ones—maybe only through necessity, but still at a faster rate."

They agreed that Will would tell Anne Morgan that the meeting was confirmed, and give her Ana's name as the prime organizer, but make it clear that Will himself wouldn't attend. "They don't want to hear from me," Will said. "They want to hear from you."

Will and Ana spent the afternoon touring Morningside Heights. They couldn't actually go into the Cathedral, since it was locked for the weekend, but they walked by it on Amsterdam Avenue and Will pointed out various features.

"Maybe it's nice inside but from the outside it doesn't look very beautiful," Ana observed. "It's too big and cold-looking with all that gray stone."

The weather was raw and windy, but they walked around Columbia and then to Grant's Tomb on Riverside Drive, where they enjoyed the view from the steps and the chance to see the Hudson River. Coming back toward Broadway, they passed the newly-finished buildings of Union Theological Seminary, which like Columbia had moved up from midtown. The first classes in the new location had begun less than three months before.

"Maybe I should have gone to Union," Will commented. "It used to be Presbyterian but the board of directors voted a few years ago to make it non-denominational."

"So why didn't you?" Ana asked.

Will took a minute to respond. "Partly, I suppose, because I was born and bred Episcopalian," he said slowly. "Much as I criticize the seminary and the church, it feels like home." Then, after a pause, he said, "And I suppose, if I'm honest, being Episcopalian is as close as I can get to being Catholic without being Catholic. I thought about converting when I was in England but in the end, I just couldn't do it. But I'm drawn to the sacraments and the mysteries and the Creed."

Ana looked at him soberly. "Oh Will," she said, "When you talk like that I feel as though we're living on different planets."

Will put her arm through his. "I refuse to continue this conversation," he said firmly. "Also, I'm cold and I need a cup of tea."

They stopped at a tearoom on Broadway, where they found a table by a window. Once they were settled, with their tea in front of them, Will asked Ana to tell him more about the strike she'd been involved in and about her work.

"I really don't know what to say about it," said Ana, putting down her cup. "Maybe by describing what it was like when the strike began. That will give you an idea why so many of us were willing to risk what little we had."

Will nodded in encouragement.

"It may be hard to believe but things were much better when I started working than even a few years before," Ana said. "There was one woman who worked at the same factory I did—she was only a few years older than I was—who said that when *she* started they worked seven days a week, from half past seven in the morning until half past six at night when it was not busy, and until nine o'clock when it was. She said she was only ten years old when she started, and there were children even younger than she was. Their job was to trim the threads off the shirtwaists after the operators were through with them. When the inspectors came around, they all had to climb into one of the crates that the material was shipped in, and the bosses covered them over with finished shirtwaists until the inspectors had left, because they were not supposed to be employing children that young."

Ana shook her head in disgust.

"When I started there had already been some strikes and by then it was usual to work only six days a week, and no more than ten hours a day. But conditions were still bad. We had to pay for our own needles and we had to pay for any damaged work. The first company I worked for even charged us for the boxes we sat on and for coat lockers.

"One of the worst things is that there's always so much dust in the air. When the men cut the material, a lot of tiny bits are left over, and sometimes I find it hard to breathe. And I'm not the only one; some girls cough all day long. And the other bad thing is that some of the men like to tease us and say embarrassing things, but the bosses just laugh and join in. I don't mind so much for myself but I feel sorry for the younger girls; they are the ones who are most likely to be targeted."

Will nodded, then said, "Tell me about the business, and about what you actually do."

"I've always worked in shirtwaist factories," Ana said. "It's a huge industry. There are about 500 shirtwaist factories in the city and about 30,000 workers. When I started, shirtwaists had become what you might call the uniform for young working women: a white shirtwaist with a long dark skirt. By now, I've done almost every job except the cutting; that's reserved for men. Most often I do basting or finishing work. Because of knowing how to do so many things, I'm often moved around to wherever help is needed, which is a good thing, because I get to talk to many more girls that way and encourage them to join the union."

"So how did the strike came about?" Will asked.

"Well, first you have to understand that the International Ladies' Garment Workers' Union was still very new at that time," Ana said. "I was active in it almost from the time I started working, but trying to get more workers to join wasn't easy. Many of the girls came from families who were dependent on their wages, and they couldn't afford to risk their jobs. And the union had very little money so everyone knew that if there was a strike, the union couldn't do much to help make up for lost wages.

"At the Triangle Waist Company some of the workers met in secret with officials from Local 25 of the ILGWU to talk about joining. But the company found out and fired the girls and the girls started picketing the shop. In response, the company hired thugs to intimidate and beat the girls, and they also hired prostitutes to stand at the factory door and fight off the pickets so that the scabs could get in to work. Fortunately, at that point some of the women like Anne Morgan from the WTUL got involved, and the newspapers started covering it.

"But things probably would still not have gone anywhere if it hadn't been for Clara Lemlich, a girl I met through the union. She got up at a meeting called to talk about a general strike and, after listening to most of the speakers, even the ones from the ILGWU, urging everyone not to do anything foolish, she started talking about the beating she had received on the picket line two days before. That roused the workers and there was a vote in favor of the general strike.

"I was the first from my company to walk out, but most of the other girls soon followed me. We organized a picket line in front of our shop and we were out there every day for thirteen weeks. The police were always beating us and once I got arrested, along with several others. We were put in a cell with prostitutes and drug addicts who spent the whole night making fun of us and saying we were fools. In the morning one of the women from the WTUL paid our bail."

"I feel so ashamed," said Will ruefully. "I was already here in the seminary, but I hardly paid attention to the strike. I was too new to the city and too wrapped up in my studies. The one thing I do remember, because it made me laugh at the time, is what George Bernard Shaw said about one judge's claim that the girls were on strike against God. Shaw said that he was impressed to see that America was, as he put it, 'always in the intimate confidence of the Almighty.'"

Ana gave him an impatient look. "I don't know who Shaw is and I'm surprised that that's all you remember about the strike," she said tartly. "I thought everyone, even in your world, would be paying attention, if for no other reason than that so many society women were involved."

Will said nothing, and fortunately Ana's irritation was short-lived. "Anyway," she said, picking up her story, "the strike finally ended without a lot to show for it. The employers' committee agreed to a shorter week, four paid holidays a year, and that employers would supply needles. But there was no industry-wide agreement so it was only one by one that the larger shops settled. Triangle, where it all started, refused to agree to the 54-hour week and stuck to 59 hours. And they refused some of the other demands from their workers, like not locking the doors to the fire escapes on some of the floors."

"So why do you keep working there?" Will asked.

"Because I decided that the most useful thing I could do would be to help persuade the Triangle girls to press for the same things that were won in some of the other shops. I got the job because after the strike, the bosses at Triangle were willing to hire just about anyone if they knew how to do the work. But it's no fun every Saturday afternoon hearing girls from other shops passing under our windows calling up that they're going home and we could be, too, if we'd just follow their example."

"And what about the locked doors—you've never mentioned that."

"Oh, that," said Ana. "It worries me quite a lot, especially since so many of the cutters smoke. They're not supposed to, and even the bosses say it's dangerous, but they do it anyway. Legally, the doors are required to be unlocked. But the bosses say that if they leave them open, girls will slip outside and maybe take something. And to make it worse, the doors open in, not out. Not only that but there's only one real fire escape, and even that one doesn't go all the way to the street."

Will, sobered by Ana's comments, stared at the table for a moment, remembering the tenement he'd visited a few days before. That didn't have any fire escape at all, as far as he could remember. How many people in the city, he wondered, were living and working in fire traps.

Ana was silent, too, while Will settled the bill and she gathered her belongings. As they went out the door, Ana took Will's arm, but the conversation and indeed the whole afternoon had left them both in a somber mood.

Neither of them had noticed it, but an older man on his own— probably a retired professor, from his appearance—had been observing them carefully from a few tables away. From the look on his face, you could tell that he was trying to puzzle out their relationship. The young woman didn't look like the Barnard students he was used to seeing in the neighborhood—she seemed a bit shabby, as opposed to bohemian, and her hair, well, rather unusual. But the two appeared earnest in the way young people do when they are discussing Important Things, so perhaps they were merely slightly unconventional in the way young people tended to be nowadays.

But as they left, he looked after them thoughtfully, almost as though he knew that they were heading into a troubled time.

CHAPTER SIXTEEN

The trouble didn't take long in coming. As Ana explained several days later to Will, when she arrived home after their trip to Morningside Heights her aunt was waiting to talk to her, visibly agitated and seeming to waver between anger and tears. A neighbor had told her of seeing Ana and Will together, looking like they were "more than friends," as the neighbor had described it. She'd also told Mrs. Markowicz that Will looked "like a goy." What was going on?

Ana said that she'd first tried to brush off the neighbor's remarks, but in the end, she'd admitted the truth. She'd insisted that she and Will were "just friends," but acknowledged that they were spending time together and had feelings for each other.

To her aunt's credit, Ana said, Mrs. Markowicz hadn't ranted and raved the way many of her friends would have done. But she'd said that Ana was embarrassing her and shaming her by her actions, and that her uncle would have been disappointed in her. How could she be keeping company with a Christian when she knew that these same Christians had been responsible for so much cruelty and even death among Jewish people in Poland and other places? Is this how she paid her uncle back for bringing her to America?

"I really don't know what to do," Ana said miserably. "I have no right to hurt my aunt when she's been so good to me all these years. But at the same time, I don't want to give up seeing you."

Will was struck by the fact that for once, Ana seemed at a loss.

"Do you think it would help if I talked to her, and told her my intentions are honorable?" Will asked anxiously.

Ana shook her head. "It isn't that," she said. "You could be the most wonderful man in the world but you're not Jewish and that's all there is to it. My aunt and uncle grew up fearing for their lives and they believed that the only way for Jews to survive was to keep together. If you go outside the Jewish community you're betraying your family. My aunt reminded me of what happened to the son of one of our neighbors when he took up with an Italian girl: his father threw him out of the house and said he never wanted to see him again."

Now it was Will's turn to be at a loss. Reflecting on how concerned he'd been about Ana's fitting into *his* world, he realized with shame that he'd hardly given a thought to whether he could fit into hers. He'd just assumed that if there were adjustments to be made, they'd come from her side, and that the people in her world would be pleased with his attention. But instead of welcoming him, they wanted him to go away.

Even now, he couldn't think of a solution other than for Ana to move further in his direction.

"Could you stop living with your aunt and board someplace else?" Will asked. "Maybe Lizzy could help you find a place."

"I could never do that," Ana said. "It would hurt my aunt too much. And anyway, how could she pay the rent if I were to leave?" They talked in this vein for a while, Ana explaining more about her uncle and aunt's experiences in Poland and Will coming up with one impractical idea after another about what to do.

Finally, Ana said, more hopefully, "My aunt hasn't said I must never see you again, and I think that if we avoid going any place where we might be seen by her friends—I'm sure that whoever told her about us must have seen us that day we met at the *Forward*—she won't keep asking me about it. She's not an unfeeling person: she and my uncle married for love, not through a match-maker, and she always likes hearing romantic stories. But that doesn't mean there's no problem."

Ana paused. "There's something else I need to tell you, though, which the conversation with my aunt helped me to realize: I know you haven't asked me to marry you, but I need to tell you now that I'm not sure I could ever marry a non-Jew." Seeing the dismayed look on Will's face, she continued, "I told you that I'm not religious, and that's true. But I also said that being Jewish is part of who I am. To marry a non-Jew would be to deny my own identity. I don't see how I could do that. I told my aunt what I've just told you and I think that that made her feel, even though she didn't say so, that she could accept my continuing to see you."

They sat in silence for a minute or two.

Then, deciding that there was nothing more to be said for the moment, and that the best thing to do was to change the subject, Will asked how the meeting had gone with Anne Morgan.

"It was as I expected," Ana said, causing Will to marvel, not for the first time, at how unimpressed Ana was by wealth or social standing. "Miss Morgan is, as you said, serious about wanting to help, but when you're a woman in her position probably the best thing you can do is just give money. You can't run for office, you can't become a judge—you can't even join a picket line without fifty photographers wanting to take your picture."

"But at least you can help her give away her money wisely," Will ventured.

"Oh, we did that," Ana said. "We talked about how, perhaps, she could pay for a program to train women as union organizers, or maybe start a school where women could learn about labor laws and what rights women have. Maybe she could even pay for some working women to go to college and become lawyers who could fight for workers' rights."

"Those all seem like good ideas," said Will. "I hope something will come of them."

"I do, too, but I know that for the most part we have to rely on ourselves," Ana said. "No one else is going to fight our fights for us."

Recalling the huge outcry at the diocesan convention over the modest proposal to offer support for the striking express men, Will nodded his head.

"Do you think you might want to go to college and become a lawyer if you got the chance?" he asked.

Ana looked surprised. "I've never thought about that," she said. Then, after a pause, she added, "I'm sure I'm too old. But even if I'm not, and even if someone paid the cost, there's no way my aunt could manage on her own without my salary."

Will was silent. He was thinking again about California, and about what job he might be able to get there that would pay for Ana's schooling and her aunt's rent. Apart from a knowledge of Latin and Greek, and a considerable familiarity with art, he didn't have a lot to offer. There weren't many jobs apart from the ministry, he thought glumly, in which a theological degree would be considered a useful credential.

Still, there *were* possibilities. With the help of his Columbia professor, perhaps he could find a university in California, or somewhere else, that would take him on in a doctoral program. And perhaps he could get his wealthy aunt or someone else in his family to loan him the money he'd need to get married—he refused to believe there wasn't some way around Ana's objections and those of her aunt—and live on until he and Ana were established.

He began to tell Ana about his ideas, and when she started to protest he said, "I know it's hard to imagine these things, but don't just dismiss them as impossible. Someone told me recently that we need to listen in order to know what God wants us to do. I know you don't believe in God, but maybe it's still possible to hear Him." Then, worrying that he sounded too much as though he was preaching, he added quickly, "And besides that, don't forget the saying, 'Where there's a will there's a way.'"

Ana looked thoughtful. "I'd like you to know that one thing I'm very grateful to you for is that you've made me think about a lot of things that otherwise I wouldn't have," she said. "Until I met you I was completely involved in the labor movement and I didn't see any life for myself beyond the one I had. But you've made me see that there's no reason I can't at least go to Central Park if I want to. Maybe it wasn't so much that my situation was limiting my choices as that I was limiting them myself. When my uncle died I think I felt that the life I had planned for myself was over and that this new life as a factory worker was the only one I'd ever have."

She paused. "It's probably too much for me to think about becoming a lawyer," she said, "but I've started wondering how I can get my high school degree by studying at night. And then, who knows? I didn't tell you but I went back to Columbia University on my own and got some information about what they call extension classes, which are open to outsiders, and to women as well as men. Some of them look very interesting."

Will reacted with surprise. He was, he realized with embarrassment, slightly miffed: he'd thought he was the one introducing Ana to new places and new ideas and here she was, doing it for herself. But at the same time, he was happy, because it meant that Ana was in a small but real sense also starting to become open to change.

He briefly touched her hand. "You're wonderful," he said.

Will told Ana that he'd be leaving town for a few days to spend Thanksgiving with his mother, but suggested that they meet for an hour late in the afternoon on Sunday after he got back. Ana could tell her aunt that she was going a little early to College Settlement for her Sunday evening book group, which wouldn't really be a lie. Ana agreed, and they decided to meet at the same cafe where they'd just been sitting.

As they said good-night Will kissed her lightly, after looking around to make sure no one was nearby. "I love you, Ana," he said. "And for me, the same," she answered, then slipped out of his arms and ran off.

But it was a different Ana who greeted him on the following Sunday. After waiting impatiently for her as the minutes ticked by, Will was taken aback when Ana, her face tear-streaked and full of anger, rushed into the café.

"Ana, what's wrong?" Will asked.

"I'm surprised you haven't heard," she said frostily. "On Friday, there was a fire in a factory in Newark that makes undergarments and twenty-five girls were killed. Six of them burned and nineteen of them jumped from the windows on the fourth floor. The building was over fifty years old. The floors and windows were made of wood that caught fire in seconds, and there was only one door and it was locked."

Ana sat down. "We all heard the news as we were leaving work and I've been busy ever since trying to raise money for the families and organize a protest," she said. "I just came from listening to two of the girls who managed to escape, which is why I've been crying. That could have been us, it could have been any one of a hundred buildings in New York."

"Oh, Ana, I'm so sorry," said Will.

"Thank you," Ana said formally as she stood up. "I can't stay because I have to get back to the organizing meeting. I only came because we'd agreed to meet."

"Is your building really as bad as that one?" Will asked.

"It isn't old but it's just as much of a firetrap," Ana said. "The worst thing is that if there was a fire, the Fire Department ladders wouldn't even be able to reach us because we're on such high floors—above where the ladders could reach us."

Will's face showed his alarm. "I had no idea how dangerous it is," he said. "Please, can't you find another job in a different building that doesn't have so many problems?"

Ana gave a harsh laugh. "I've talked to the men in the firehouse nearest to us and they say our building is better than most. And the owners insist they're in full compliance with the law, which they probably are. It's just that the laws are so weak and no one cares to make better ones or even enforce the ones that exist. To the people in *your* world—here she laughed mirthlessly again—we're less valuable than the company's sewing machines."

With that, and a statement that she'd be too busy to see him for the next week or two, she was gone, leaving Will to stare into his coffee. As so often, she'd been angry with him when she was actually angry with the situation. But at the same time, he recognized that that there was some truth in what she'd said: he might not have any personal responsibility for conditions in the factories, but how much had he ever done to change them?

Deeply troubled, he left the cafe and made his way back to the seminary, where he knocked on Hugh's door. Hugh had heard about the Newark tragedy and told him that there were going to be special prayers at evensong for the victims.

"Prayers?" Will said angrily. "Those girls don't need prayers; they're dead. But there must be something we can do to help make sure what happened to them doesn't happen again."

In the next morning's paper, he read the New York City fire chief's statement that the city could experience a fire as deadly as the one in Newark "at any time." The chief was quoted as saying, "There are buildings in New York where the danger is every bit as great as in the building destroyed in Newark. A fire in the daytime would be accompanied by a terrible loss of life."

By noon, Will had posted a notice in several prominent places around the seminary asking anyone interested in staging a protest march on City Hall to meet that evening at eight o'clock in one of the seminary classrooms. By half past eight only six people, including Hugh and Professor Taylor, had shown up.

Will rose from his seat and looked at the small group. "There certainly aren't many of us," he said, stating the obvious. "I've been asking around at Columbia and elsewhere to find out whether anyone else is planning a march or rally, and the answer is no, so there's not even some other group we could join. It appears that my idea for direct action wasn't very well thought out and isn't going to work. Does anyone have any other ideas?"

Surprisingly, it was Professor Taylor who was the most determined that they shouldn't leave things there. "We may be few in number," he said, "but given that we represent an important institution in this city—I don't mean just the seminary but also, in a broader sense, the churches and the religious community—I think we could get some attention by carrying a petition to City Hall. If Anne Morgan could get so much press coverage for helping the union girls during the strike, why couldn't we get attention for speaking out in support of working girls in New York who are just like the ones who died in Newark?"

Hugh was the first to respond. "For one thing, with all due respect, Professor Taylor, we're not famous," he said. "If we had the Dean with us, or even better the Dean and most of the faculty and students, we might have a chance. But honestly, I don't think anyone is going to care much about our proposed event."

"I agree," said a second-year student named George Hawkins. "And I also think the fact that the fire was in Newark, not New York City, is a big problem. We all know how parochial people in this city are; no one cares what happened in Newark."

The others nodded glumly.

"I'm sorry I've brought you all out for nothing," Will said. "I guess I got carried away with the need to do something more than just talk about what happened."

"Don't blame yourself," Professor Taylor said. "I think it's a very admirable impulse, and one that's shared by at least six of us. Without wanting to be trite, remember that Jesus started with only twelve apostles. I can't speak for the rest of you, but this has made me think hard about what more we—what more *I*—can do. I'm going to pray over this for a few days and hope all of you will do the same, and perhaps we can then meet again and see what else we can come up with."

With that, the group broke up. Will thanked everyone, and in particular Professor Taylor, for coming, and promised that if he heard about any planned actions he'd let everyone know.

Within a few days, however, the public clamor, such as it was, began to die down. Will made no attempt to contact Ana, knowing that she was bound to be busy with her organizing. He was also tired of feeling guilty and he didn't want to risk another tongue-lashing.

He did attend an open meeting of seminary students at Union Theological at which a motion was passed to demand an inquiry into the Newark fire. He also signed his name to a letter to city officials deploring the lack of tougher safety laws. And, at Lizzy's insistence, he went with her to a meeting at which the Consumer League's New York State executive secretary, Frances Perkins, called for legislation that would require fireproof stairways and sprinkler systems in the city's factories. Miss Perkins, Lizzy had explained to Will, was a Mt. Holyoke graduate only a few years older than they were who'd started her career as a volunteer at a settlement house in Chicago. Will was impressed by Perkins' knowledge of her subject as well as her dynamic speaking style.

But his life was also crowded with other concerns, including finishing his paper for his Columbia seminar and making sure LaFarge was pressing on as quickly as possible with the remaining work on the Cathedral. He hadn't seen the architect since LaFarge's father had died earlier in the month, and he sensed that without the constant fear that LaFarge might turn up at any minute, the workmen had slowed their pace. There was still electricity work to be done and some tiles were still missing. More worrying, given the oncoming winter, were several leaks in the roof and problems with some of the steam pipes in the crypt.

The issue of greatest immediate concern was the installation of the organ and pipes. One day, Will arrived at the Cathedral just in time to see the organ console slipping from its rigging amid shouts and curses from the workers. Fortunately, the men were able to halt the slide before much damage had been done, but it seemed clear to Will that the rigging had not been done properly. When he tried to talk to the foreman about it, he received only a brusque reply to the effect that the foreman would appreciate it if Will would just let him get on with the job.

Will was so alarmed by that incident and the general sense of malaise that instead of going directly back to the seminary he stopped by LaFarge's downtown office on Madison Square in the hope of finding LaFarge there. A secretary said LaFarge had gone to lunch but was expected back shortly, so Will waited.

When LaFarge came into the office, he looked nonplussed at seeing Will. The reason, it was quickly evident, was the attractive woman who had come in just behind him, and whom he introduced as Elsie Parsons. Will immediately recognized her as the wife of a local Congressman who had just been defeated for re-election and a well-known reformer in her own right. It was obvious to Will that LaFarge felt awkward about the encounter but Mrs. Parsons was completely at ease, asking Will about his work at the Cathedral and, upon hearing that he also taught a class at University Settlement, mentioning that she'd been one of the founders of a chapter of the College Settlements Association at Barnard.

After a few minutes, she excused herself and LaFarge, still looking slightly flustered, ushered Will into his office. Will told him what he'd witnessed at the Cathedral and LaFarge, his face darkening, promised to go up to investigate first thing in the morning. "Of course," he said, "I don't know why I should be concerned since I've been told on good authority that Ralph Cram is about to replace me. Someone sent me an anonymous letter telling me Cram is scheming behind my back."

Will, surprised by this new development, told LaFarge that he'd been asked by one of the trustees at a dinner party about his opinion of Cram's work, and told that there had been some informal meetings to discuss Cram's ideas for the Cathedral. "That suggests nothing has been decided yet," Will said, "but I have to admit that it raises the possibility that you have grounds for concern." Seeing LaFarge's pained expression he added quickly, "One thing I do know is that Bishop Greer is determined to make no changes, at least for the time being."

LaFarge gave a harsh laugh as Will bade him good-bye.

While he was waiting for the office elevator, Will suddenly realized that LaFarge had come out behind him. "If you don't mind, I'd appreciate your not mentioning to anyone at the Cathedral the fact that you met me in Mrs. Parsons' company," he said. "She and I are just friends, but at the moment I have no doubt that my enemies would be only too happy to claim something more."

Will nodded. "I have no intention of mentioning it to anyone," he said, then added to himself as the elevator door closed behind him, "if for no other reason than that while you may be a fool, the

Cathedral can't do without you right now."

Then, catching himself, he realized that LaFarge was no more of a fool than he was. If there *was* something between LaFarge and Elsie Parsons, who was he, Will Ingalls, to judge its appropriateness when he was behaving with an equal lack of concern about others' opinions and about the possible impact of what he was doing on his career? And in any case, he reflected as he made his way back to the seminary, how could any man criticize another for being in love with the 'wrong' person?

Meanwhile, there was no letup in the Bishop's schedule, and in fact it seemed to pick up in the weeks leading to Christmas. Will thought to himself that if he never attended another dinner at the Waldorf-Astoria after the Cathedral's consecration that would suit him just fine. He'd had no idea how many officials, both public and private, had to be honored upon their promotion or retirement, and how many organizations devoted to worthy causes felt they had to gather their benefactors from time to time to ensure their continued support. All such events were certified as important by Bishop Greer's attendance, and all of them, as Bishop Greer knew well, were likely to draw at least a few wealthy men who had so far managed to avoid making a donation to the Cathedral.

The one positive thing about attending such events, Will told Hugh several times, was the opportunity it gave him to observe, even from the distance of a table near the back of the room, so many famous people. One night it was John D. Rockefeller, who'd come in from his Westchester estate. On another it was William Astor, back from England on one of his infrequent visits. And on yet another it was the industrialist Henry Frick, who, Will had heard, had one of the country's finest collections of Old Masters paintings, which he planned to install in a mansion under construction on Fifth Avenue.

But probably the most exciting, as he reported later that night to Hugh, was seeing Teddy Roosevelt. Will had been standing next to the Bishop at the Lotus Club when Roosevelt came by on his way to the dais, surrounded by friends and local politicians.

Roosevelt had looked very subdued, Will said, not at all the bundle of energy he'd been during the just-concluded campaign. As Roosevelt passed, Will said, he'd heard him tell the man next to him that he thought the American people were feeling "a little tired of me."

It was sobering, Will commented, to realize how Roosevelt, after finishing his presidential term the year before, had gone from being welcomed back from Africa by cheering crowds to being the butt of jokes about political has-beens. The event at which Will had seen him was a dinner honoring Charles Evans Hughes, a decently progressive former New York State governor who had just been appointed by President Taft to the Supreme Court. It was a reasonably grand occasion, Will observed, but not exactly on a par with state dinners at the White House.

When at last Will and Ana did meet, two weeks later, it was only because Will had asked Lizzy if Ana was back attending the weekly reading circle and if so, whether Lizzy thought she'd recovered from the shock of the Newark fire. Upon hearing a yes to both questions, Will ventured down to College Settlement and stood outside, in the same spot where he'd waited on that night he and Ana had first met, until he saw Ana coming out.

"You have a rather quick temper," Will said, his tone accusatory but his face showing a hint of a smile. "I'm very sorry about what happened in Newark. But I can't answer for all the evils of capitalism and the plutocrats, so please don't blame me personally whenever something happens that you don't like." Then, after pausing just long enough for her to have time to worry what was coming next, he added, "And please come with me for a cup of tea or coffee."

Ana looked at him with a rather wan smile and started walking in the direction of the cafe where they had practically become regulars. "I know it isn't fair," she said. "But I was very upset by what happened."

"That's not a good enough excuse," Will said as they sat down. "I think you need to realize that I have feelings just as you do. It takes a lot to upset me, but I wasn't just hurt but angry at the way you treated me. You know perfectly well that I'm in sympathy with you and the union. Yes, I'm not out there on the front lines the way you are, but I do what I can, and I'm trying to figure out how I can do more. I think that I've been much more understanding of your position than you've been of mine."

Ana hung her head. "You're right," she said. "I do have a terrible temper."

"Good, that's agreed then," Will said, making it clear he was ready to move on. "And now I want to tell you something that I hope you'll find more pleasant. I've written to my mother several times about you, and she's invited you to Greenville at Christmas for as long as you can be away from work, which I assume is only a couple of days. Christmas is on Sunday this year."

Will added, "In case you're wondering, I've said that you've become a good friend, but I haven't spelled out our relationship. That's not because I worry about what she'll say but because I really don't know how to describe it myself. You and I have agreed to put off any serious thoughts about the future, and we haven't even agreed that we *have* a future, so I don't know what to tell her. But I want you to meet her and she wants to meet you."

Ana looked at him questioningly. "Your mother wants to meet me?" she asked. "Have you told her I'm Jewish? And that I work in a factory and never even finished high school?"

Will laughed. "Of course I've told her, and I've also told her about the reasons why I'm sure she'll like you."

Ana sat taking in Will's remarks for a minute. Then, looking a little nervous, she said, "I'd very much like to come. The bosses have already told us that owing to their great generosity"—here she gave a small laugh—"even those of us who aren't Christians are going to be given Saturday off."

She paused, obviously thinking. "I could tell my aunt that Miss Sperling has invited me to spend Christmas with her family, who live just outside the city," she said. "My aunt knows how much I admire Miss Sperling and I think it would be better that way."

Then, in a small voice, she added, "I'm very sorry for how I behaved."

Will laughed good-naturedly. "You're helping me to become a better Christian and learn to turn the other cheek," he said. "Maybe that's the main reason why I love you—that and your hair, which is as unruly as your temper."

The next few days passed quickly. He and Ana had agreed that given how busy they both were, they wouldn't meet again until she came to Greenville, but he thought about her often while finishing up several class essays as well as his Columbia seminar paper. There was a Christmas party at University Settlement, and yet another dinner at the Waldorf-Astoria with the Bishop, and then, finally, a choral service and Christmas party at the seminary to mark the end of the term.

By far the nicest of the Christmas celebrations was a party for the Cathedral choristers to which Will had been invited by Canon Voorhis. He'd gotten to know and enjoy talking with Voorhis on his regular visits to inspect the work at the Cathedral, and Voorhis had encouraged him to come to hear the boys sing for their families.

For the choristers, the highlight of the party was a magician whose tricks, which included pulling a live rabbit from the pocket of one of the boys, were met with delighted applause. Surrounded by the boys as well as their siblings and parents, Will thought again about how important the choristers were in bringing life and laughter into the Cathedral close.

After everyone had enjoyed some punch and refreshments, the choristers gathered to sing one of the pieces they'd been preparing for the Christmas service, as well as several carols. Canon Voorhis then made a short speech which ended with his introducing Charles McGirr, a small chorister with cherubic features. He explained for the benefit of those who didn't already know that McGirr had been selected as the model for a small bas-relief on one of the stones meant for an inside Cathedral wall. The choristers themselves had collected the money for the carving. "The stone will remind all those who visit the Cathedral of this wonderful class of 1911," he said.

Will was still smiling as he left the Cathedral grounds.

But if good cheer prevailed on Morningside Heights, the mood was rather the opposite at Gramercy Park when Will met with the Bishop for his last meeting before he traveled upstate for the holidays. "I'll be happy to see this year end," Greer commented, after listening to Will's report. "If there is any Christmas spirit around, I haven't felt it. Nor any Christian spirit, for that matter. The trustees met with LaFarge this week, and to say the discussion was acrimonious would be an understatement."

Will was curious to know more, but thought it best not to ask any direct questions, so he just nodded.

"I think things are coming to a head," Greer said grimly, his earlier reluctance to share information about the situation at the Cathedral seemingly overcome by his need to talk about it. "The trustees—apart from August Belmont, who hired LaFarge and his partner to work on his subway system after being impressed with their design for the Cathedral, and who still remains an enthusiastic supporter—are more or less unanimous in feeling that LaFarge has to go. At first there was more of a difference of opinion, but the ones who were supporting LaFarge have either been worn down by his critics or put off by LaFarge's own high-handedness. He may be a brilliant architect but he doesn't seem to care whether his clients like him or not."

Will was silent for a moment, then asked, "Do you think anything will happen before the dedication?"

"I certainly hope not," Greer answered. "It's something I intend to pray over every day from now on, if for no other reason than the fact that if there is any public discussion of what's going on, it's sure to have an impact on my fund-raising."

CHAPTER SEVENTEEN

*W*ill met Ana at the train station in Catskill, the biggest town in Greene County. Catskill, which was right on the Hudson River, was served by the New York Central's West Shore Service and, during the good weather, by a ferry service from New York as well. Will had insisted on buying Ana's ticket, and had carefully instructed her on how to get the train, but he knew Ana was nervous about what could go wrong. So it was with considerable relief that he saw her alight with her small valise, looking around for him as she did so.

She smiled in response to his wave and accepted his offer of an arm as he took her valise and maneuvered both of them through the small crowd on the platform.

"So was the trip uneventful?" Will asked.

"Oh yes, but in a good way," Ana responded. "There was so much to see that it hardly seemed to take any time at all."

Will had arranged for Matt Rundle, a local farmer, to take them back to Greenville in his cart after making a delivery in town. Ana said she was surprised to see so few automobiles, and confessed to Will and Mr. Rundle that she'd never ridden in a horse-drawn vehicle before. The town of Catskill had paved the main street only the past summer, and from there to Greenville they followed dirt roads that carried a light covering of snow.

"There's only been one real storm so far this winter," Rundle said by way of making conversation. "It was a beaut, though, two weeks ago. I could barely get to the barn to feed the stock, it was snowing so hard. But then it warmed up and since then we've just had dustings, like the one last night."

Ana nodded, clearly fascinated by the landscape, the farmer, and the sheer novelty of it all. "What do you do when there's a lot of snow?" she asked.

The farmer laughed. "We don't *do* much of anything," he said. "From mid-December until mid-March we mostly just stay at home. But we have everything we need in Greenville: three churches and two general stores, plus a drug store and a hardware store."

He looked at her in a not unkindly way. "I expect that being from New York you're used to electric lights and streetcars and nickelodeons. We don't have any of those things here, but we manage to have a good time—especially in the summer, when the boarding houses are full and they're always putting on some kind of entertainment."

Ana smiled at him. "I came to the Catskills once about ten years ago but it wasn't as far north as this," she said. "I liked it very much but not as much as here."

The Ingalls' house was on Greenville's main street, just north of the crossroads and the Episcopal church. As they passed the crossroads, Ana could see a small pond on the left, now covered in ice, and behind it and to the right the buildings of the Greenville Academy. Trees lined both sides of the road, and on one side there was a sidewalk, several feet in from the trees.

Like almost all the other houses, the Ingalls' house was a white frame building with green trim and a metal roof. A porch ran across the front, on the left side of which was a porch swing painted yellow. The house was two stories tall, not as grand as some of its neighbors but comfortable looking. Will had told Ana that it had been built about 60 years before, but that his parents had added an indoor bathroom and a modern woodstove that provided hot water to the bathroom via a pipe along the ceiling from the kitchen.

"So you won't lack for city comforts," Will had told Ana,

thinking that in fact his mother's house offered many more 'comforts' than the apartment in which Ana and her aunt lived.

Mrs. Ingalls came out to greet them as the wagon pulled up. A still attractive woman of medium height in her late fifties, she had an unusually long nose and the same grey-blue eyes as Will. Smiling at Ana, she introduced herself and thanked Mr. Rundle for delivering them safely.

"You must be hungry and tired after your long trip," she said to Ana, holding open the door. "I've made some soup for lunch and there's fresh bread and butter. The butter comes from friends over in Cornwallville who keep a dairy herd for that purpose."

She showed Ana to her room and told her the meal was ready, so she should just wash up and came back to the kitchen. Thanks to the woodstove, the kitchen was warm and cozy and the table, covered with red and white oilcloth, was set for the three of them. In addition to the bread and the hearty soup, which Mrs. Ingalls spooned into their bowls, there were red Cortland apples, which Mrs. Ingalls explained came from a neighbor's farm, and ginger snaps.

Will watched Ana taking it all in as he conveyed the latest town gossip, recounted by Mr. Rundle, to his mother. Ana looked happy, he thought, but a little overwhelmed.

After a few minutes, Mrs. Ingalls turned to Ana and asked her about her family and her work. Ana told Mrs. Ingalls a bit about her uncle and aunt, and about the factory, but left out the details of her organizing activities. "Will has told me that you're involved in union work," Mrs. Ingalls said, obviously noticing the omission and wanting to put Ana at ease. "I want you to know that you have my full support."

Ana smiled at her gratefully and asked in turn about her teaching and how she'd come to live in Greenville. "I know from Will that you were brought up in Boston," she said. "This seems rather far from there."

Mrs. Ingalls nodded. "It's a long story, but I'll give you the brief version," she said. "When I finished college—I went to Mt. Holyoke, too, like Will's cousin and his friend Lizzy—I volunteered to teach in one of the Freedmen's schools in South Carolina. The schools were set up by Northern abolitionists in order to teach the freed slaves and it was the 'done thing' for both men and women from good colleges to teach there for a year or two. It was hard to reach the grownups, most of whom had had no education at all, but the children were eager and quick to learn. Living conditions were fairly difficult, but the work was satisfying and I stayed there for two years."

She paused, then commented, "It's very interesting to me that Will and Lizzy are both involved in the settlement movement, because it strikes me as not so different from what we were doing a generation ago. In a way, you could say that the settlement movement is trying to do for immigrants what the Freedmen's schools did for colored people. It bothers me, though, that apart from a few people like Oswald Villard, most white people seem to think that now that slavery is over, they've done their part. They don't really know or care about conditions in the South."

Ana seemed impressed by Mrs. Ingalls' story. "You must have been very brave to go so far away from home," she said. "How did you get from South Carolina to Greenville?"

"My family assumed I'd return to Boston and marry some eligible young man and settle down," Mrs. Ingalls said with a laugh. "But I'd experienced independence and I didn't want that kind of life. I asked around and found that the Greenville Academy was looking for someone to teach English literature so I applied. Will's father was the principal, and he was open-minded enough to consider an application from a female. He hired me sight unseen."

"And then?" Ana asked.

"And then, he and I fell in love," Mrs. Ingalls said, smiling at the memory and perhaps, Will thought, at Ana's undisguised curiosity. "I admired him very much. When the war began he was over thirty, and already an assistant principal, but he was a passionate abolitionist and was one of the first men in his Ohio town to volunteer. Two years after he joined he was shot in the leg and wounded so badly that he could never walk again without using a cane. After the war he came to Greenville looking for a quiet place. He said that the sights he'd seen during the war were such that it was only in a place like this that he could find enough peace to go on."

All three of them fell silent. "I just wish I could have known him for longer," Will said finally. "I don't think any of us today appreciate what he and the others went through."

Deliberately changing the subject, Will asked his mother whether she had any boots that Ana could borrow so that he could take her out for a walk around the town. His mother laughed, saying that Ana was so small that she could probably fit two of her feet into one boot of hers, but that she was welcome to try. "Let me go find some heavy socks," she said, turning to Ana. "If you put on two pairs maybe you'll be able to manage."

A few minutes later, having concluded that with the two pairs of socks the boots would do, Ana and Will bundled up and started off. Mrs. Ingalls warned them not to go too far as the threatening sky suggested there was another storm coming.

They headed back down toward the center of town, stopping to inspect the school buildings and the pond. Will told Ana that in the summer there was always at least one family of ducks living there and that, as a boy, he'd fed them with old bread that his mother would save for him.

From there they walked by the shops, already closed or getting ready to close for Christmas. There was hardly anyone out, most people having already finished their shopping and preferring a warm house to the increasingly damp and chilly weather outside.

For Will and Ana, though, just being in the fresh air and together was pleasure enough. There had been more snow here than in Catskill, even though Mr. Rundle called it just a dusting, and because there'd been no sun that day it clung to the tree branches and the tops of porch railings in addition to covering the ground.

"It really does look like one of those prints of old country scenes," Ana said wonderingly. "I've seen two of them, by Currier & Ives, hanging in a room at College Settlement. I thought they were just drawn from the artists' imaginations. But looking around I feel as though the pictures are coming to life."

Will slipped her arm through his. "I'm so happy you like it here," he said. "Now you understand why I love this place. And maybe you understand me better, too. It's hard to grow up in a place like this and not be affected positively by it. I don't mean there aren't bad things that happen here, but for the most part my life was reading books and feeding the ducks while you were going to school with children who didn't have enough to eat."

Ana nodded. "I wonder what I would have been like if I'd grown up here," she said thoughtfully. "Maybe I wouldn't have been a labor activist at all. Maybe—oh I don't know—maybe I would have been an apple farmer's wife!"

Will laughed. "I think it's true that where you grow up has a lot to do with who you become," he said. "But I also think we're all born with certain personalities. You were born to be a fighter and I was born to be a supporter, much as I hate to acknowledge that."

"You're probably right," Ana said. "But maybe a little of each of us will rub off on the other, like paint."

They were outside the town now, walking down a small lane where there were no houses anywhere in sight. Ana laid her head on Will's shoulder briefly as she finished speaking. Will immediately stopped and pulled her around in front of him, gently kissing her as he enfolded her in his arms. As they continued to kiss, he felt himself hardening and wondered whether she felt it, too, despite the layers of clothing they both wore.

He realized as he heard her quick intake of breath that she did, and they stood there, wrapped tightly together.

"I just wish it was summer, and we could lie down right here and hold each other," Will said shakily as they finally drew apart.

"Yes," Ana whispered.

They started back then, just as the first few flakes of snow began drifting down. By the time they reached the house, it was snowing hard and their clothes and boots were wet. Mrs. Ingalls met them at the door, helping them out of the sodden layers and draping their clothes over some chairs near the woodstove.

She had just put the kettle on and in a few minutes they were sitting back down at the table, drinking tea and eating more of the ginger snaps. "Don't say I didn't warn you about the snow!" she said with a laugh.

They sat there for half an hour talking and warming up and then, seeing how tired Ana looked, Mrs. Ingalls suggested that she take a rest. Gratefully, Ana agreed. Within minutes, she told Will later, she'd fallen asleep, and by the time she awoke an hour later it was dark.

When Ana came downstairs, the kerosene lamps had been lit in the living room, and Mrs. Ingalls and Will were sitting across from a Christmas tree. On the branches were perched small candles that, Will explained, they usually lit for a few minutes late on Christmas afternoon.

Then it was time for dinner, which they had in the dining room, a pleasant enough spot in the summer but rather chilly and drafty on a cold winter night. With dinner they drank some wine that Mrs. Ingalls said she'd been saving for a special occasion. It wasn't sweet like the wine he knew Ana was used to, and Will could tell that she didn't really like it, but he was glad to see that she and his mother already seemed relaxed enough with each other that even if his mother noticed, it didn't seem to bother her.

In fact, Will thought, Ana and his mother seemed to get along so well that it was hard to believe they'd only known each other a few hours. Perhaps, he thought to himself, his mother could see in Ana the daughter she'd never had.

Through dinner and afterward, the three of them ranged over a large number of subjects, from the vote for women—they were all in favor—to Ana's childhood memories of Poland and his mother's memories of growing up in Boston. Like Ana, Mrs. Ingalls had been orphaned quite young, though in her case her father had died in a boating accident when she was six and her mother had lived ten years more, dying of tuberculosis not long before Mrs. Ingalls had started college. By then her sister had already met and married a British clergyman—they were the ones with whom Will had stayed in London—so she'd moved in with an aunt, the sister of the aunt Will had visited in New York.

The three of them were still at the table when the grandfather clock in the hall chimed ten o'clock, causing Mrs. Ingalls to start in surprise. "My goodness," she said. "The choir will start singing carols at ten-thirty."

After quickly piling the dishes in the sink to be done later, they got themselves ready for church. Will had already asked Ana, while they were still in New York, how she felt about going to the service with him and his mother, and she'd said she'd like to. So all three of them put on their coats, which fortunately in Will and Ana's case had been nicely dried by the woodstove. There was a brief debate about what to do about the fact that there was only one pair of women's boots, but then Will remembered a pair of rubber boots he'd had as a boy. He went down to the cellar and came up a couple minutes later triumphantly displaying the boots, which turned out to fit Ana perfectly.

As they set off, Mrs. Ingalls turned to Ana and said, "I know this might be a bit strange for you, and please don't feel you have to kneel or stand or do anything you don't feel comfortable doing. I know that when I went to the South I had no idea what to do in the churches there, even though we were all Christians, because their services were so different."

Will felt grateful to his mother, and pleased to be escorting them both to church. The snow had already stopped without much accumulation, so walking there took only a few minutes. He could see various neighbors and acquaintances looking at them curiously as they took their places, Ana in the middle and he and his mother on either side. He showed Ana the hymn book and the Book of Common Prayer and she leafed through them as they waited for the service to begin.

Will had always loved Midnight Mass growing up—as much as anything because he got to stay up late. But even now he felt that same sense of excitement as the choir sang the familiar Christmas carols and then, after making its way to the back of the church, processed down the main aisle singing "Once in Royal David's

City" with the vicar and the deacons behind them.

Even the vicar's predictably dull sermon failed to dampen Will's good spirits. Instead of listening, he thought back to the Christmas gospel he'd just heard and, remembering Father Huntington's suggestions about meditation practice, let himself imagine he was one of the shepherds in Bethlehem. He tried to picture himself out on a cold hillside, dozing with his cloak around him, and then abruptly brought awake by the voice of the angel. By the time Will had walked to the manger with his friends, the sermon was drawing to a close.

Half an hour later, after a lengthy communion, the service was over, and they were exchanging greetings and introducing Ana to the other congregants. Some, he realized, were thinking that she didn't look like most people in Greenville but were unable to put their finger on just what it was about her that was different, apart from her odd name. But everyone was polite and expressed the hope that she was enjoying her visit.

By the time they got back home it was well after midnight, but they all agreed they didn't feel ready for bed. Mrs. Ingalls made some hot chocolate and they went back into the sitting room, where Will made a fire and then suggested they light the candles on the Christmas tree since Ana wouldn't be around at the usual candle-lighting time. Mrs. Ingalls agreed and Will carefully lit the fifteen or so candles while Mrs. Ingalls turned the two kerosene lamps down as low as possible. Then they all sat there in the near-darkness, not saying anything.

Finally, Mrs. Ingalls said she thought Will had better blow out the candles while she turned up the kerosene lamps again. Will did as his mother asked, then proposed that they exchange their Christmas presents now. Several small, wrapped packages were sitting under the tree, two of which Will was sure had come with Ana since he recognized neither the shapes nor the wrapping. The other two agreed.

"First," said Will, "for the best mother in the world," handing his mother something that felt distinctly like a book. And in fact, it was a book—Oswald Villard's biography of John Brown, which had just come out in September. At 700 pages, he joked, the book would keep his mother occupied until spring.

Mrs. Ingalls smiled and kissed him, and then gave Ana the present she had knitted for her. It was a blue wool scarf, thick and warm and soft to the touch.

"How did you know I needed one?" Ana asked, clearly delighted.

"I have my spies," Mrs. Ingalls said, smiling.

Then it was Ana's turn to give Will his present. It was a set of handkerchiefs which she had carefully hemmed and embroidered with his initials. "Thank you," Will said, putting one in his pocket. "Now I'll always have a reminder of you nearby." Ana blushed.

Mrs. Ingalls' present to Will was a sweater, and Ana's to Mrs. Ingalls was a set of lavender sachets, which she'd made out of blue and white gingham and filled with dried lavender flowers.

That left only Will's present to Ana. He pulled something from his pocket, hidden inside a small blue velvet bag. When Ana opened the bag, she gasped as she pulled out a gold locket. She opened the tiny catch and smiled as she saw the two pictures inside. They were the photos that Will had insisted they take several weeks before with his Brownie camera, one of her taken by him, and the other of him taken by her. On the back was an inscription: "To Ana from Will, Christmas 1910."

"Oh Will," Ana said, "It's so beautiful." Mrs. Ingalls agreed, then helped Ana to fasten it around her neck. As they sat there for a few more minutes, Will noticed that Ana constantly reached up to touch the locket and each time she did, she smiled.

The next morning passed quickly, and by early afternoon it was time to go. Will had arranged to borrow a horse and cart from a neighbor, and when he arrived back at the door in the driver's seat, Ana thanked Mrs. Ingalls for her hospitality and started to walk toward the wagon. Mrs. Ingalls accompanied her and as Ana reached the cart, she gave her a brisk hug and told her she hoped she would come back again soon.

Thanking her again, Ana clambered up and she and Will started the trip back to Catskill, this time saying little as they came to terms with the fact that the brief holiday was over.

At the station, Will stood with her on the platform until the train pulled in. "I'll be back in the city in a week and I'll come down to College Settlement that same night," he promised. Then, not wanting to draw too much attention, given that it was a public place, he kissed her briefly on the cheek and said, "Just remember every time you touch the locket that it is the proof of how much I love you."

Ana nodded. "I know," she said. "I truly know."

That evening, after dinner, as Will and his mother sat drinking cups of tea before the fire, Mrs. Ingalls asked Will how he saw his future with Ana. "You told me before she came that you were just good friends, but it's clear that that isn't the case," she said. "For one thing, the only other young woman you've ever asked me to invite here is Lizzy, and I knew the minute I met her that there was nothing romantic about that relationship. With Ana, I only had to look at you and her to know this was different. And if I still had any doubts, your present of the locket ended them."

Will took his time replying. He and his mother had always had a relationship that was more one of equals than of parent and child, largely perhaps because of his father's death but also because Mrs. Ingalls treated everyone in the same way. It was part of what had made her able to move easily among people of different backgrounds during her time in the Freedmen's school and to find common ground with everyone from Boston Brahmins to farmers' wives.

"I really don't know where this is heading," Will said finally. "Whenever I try to imagine the future with her I just feel confused or draw a blank."

Will had already told his mother briefly in a letter about the weekend at West Park, but now he described at some length his meeting with Father Huntington. "I've been trying to follow his advice about not becoming too anxious about my career choices," he said. "But so far, while I think I've gotten a bit better at that, the other part of what he talked about—listening in order to understand what plan God has for me—seems not to have produced any results. If and when I can figure that out, I expect that I'll also understand how Ana fits into that."

"Or perhaps," Mrs. Ingalls responded, with a slight hint of criticism in her voice, "once you've decided whether you want to live your lifetime with Ana, the answers to your career questions will follow. It seems to me that that is a far more important decision. I don't know whether or not I believe that God can speak to us individually—I haven't ever myself felt that kind of relationship—but I do believe in listening to one's heart."

Will felt the sting of his mother's mild rebuke.

"I like Ana very much," his mother went on. "She's of course very different than most of the people you've known all your life but I don't see that as an insurmountable problem. When I was teaching in the Freedmen's school I met many colored people to whom I felt closer than the friends I'd had growing up." After a pause, she added, "You're very like your father, Will. Outwardly, you're steady and careful, but you feel things strongly. I can still remember how you cried over the rabbit that the cat killed when you were five or six years old, and I remember the look in your eyes after you made your confirmation that made me think that you might be destined for the Church. I can see why you're drawn to Ana, and she to you. She wears her passions on her sleeve, unlike you, but underneath you two are not so different."

Will was silent for a few minutes as he stared into the flames and thought over what his mother had said. She was right to criticize his self-absorption, and to remind him that it was more important to focus on what was the same about him and Ana, not what was different. It was also helpful to hear her say that she'd never had any strong sense that God had a plan for her. Maybe he wasn't going to hear any voice in the way Father Huntington had. But if so, he'd have to make some hard decisions himself.

Standing up, he walked behind his mother and kissed the top of her head. "Good-night, Mother," he said. "You're right about Ana and, as usual, you're right about me. I have a lot to think about, and I promise you I will."

CHAPTER EIGHTEEN

y the time Will returned to New York, winter had settled in. On the side streets where residents or shop owners hadn't shoveled quickly enough, the snow that had fallen had turned to ice, making the walk to the subway treacherous. Will opted to use the el more often as a result, but waiting for a train often meant standing in the cold, feeling the wind from off the river whip through his winter coat.

One day he read a small article in the newspaper about a report done by the WTUL in the wake of the Newark fire. It had found that almost half of the shirtwaist makers in New York City worked above the seventh floor—meaning they were beyond the reach of the city's fire ladders. For a week or so, there was a small flurry of public concern, and a few editorials calling for better equipment, but then the subject slipped quietly back out of sight, just as the Newark fire had done.

Despite the weather, the city's social life continued unabated, and many evenings found Will riding with Bishop Greer to one or another midtown club or hotel. Toward the end of the month, the Bishop told him that he wanted Will to accompany him to a somewhat different event with no fund-raising agenda: a small dinner at the home of one of the Cathedral trustees for several visiting church officials from England. "Your experience with Toynbee Hall in London and the settlement house movement here in New York will be useful," the Bishop said, "and so will your familiarity with England in general."

When the Bishop's secretary gave Will the address of the trustee's home, Will was intrigued to see that it was the Apthorp, a much talked-about apartment building that had been completed only three years before. Occupying a full city block on the West Side between Seventy-Eighth and Seventy-Ninth Streets, it was an immense limestone creation designed in the Italian Renaissance Revival style. But what made it truly unusual—and which added considerably to the apartments' desirability—was a carefully planned interior courtyard.

Entering the courtyard from Broadway on the night of the dinner through an immense arch, Will noted an ornate iron gate with the name "Apthorp" spelled out in filigree in the center. The courtyard itself, of formal French design, was planted with small shrubbery and adorned with a fountain and stone benches. In addition to providing attractive views from all the windows looking out onto it, the presence of the courtyard meant that the apartments got much greater light than those in more traditional buildings.

Inside, the trustee's apartment was no less grand than the building's exterior: glass-paneled French doors, friezes in the dining room, and a carved marble fireplace in the main salon. Looking around, Will couldn't help thinking that if nothing else, this job with the Bishop was giving him a chance to see and admire some of the city's most impressive architecture.

To Will's surprise, within minutes of their arrival he found himself in conversation with J.P. Morgan, who seemed oddly ill at ease in the gathering and was standing on his own off to one side of the room. Will, seeing him alone, walked up and re-introduced himself, recalling that they'd met at a dinner several months before.

"Oh yes, the young seminarian who is the 'informed appreciator,'" said Morgan, staring at him with that same intense gaze Will remembered. "As I recall, I suggested that you visit me so I could show you a few of the things in my library. How would next Tuesday night do, say around eight?"

Will said that he'd be delighted. For the next few minutes the two of them talked about the Seventeenth Century Barberini tapestries that had been donated to the Cathedral, and what the chances were that they had actually once hung, as some experts claimed, in the Sistine Chapel. Eventually, a visiting bishop from England approached them and insisted that Morgan come to meet a colleague who had known Morgan's father in London.

Will and Morgan didn't speak any more that night. Will was excited by the prospect of the visit to Morgan's house but a bit concerned about what Ana would think of it. Predictably, when he saw her briefly after his Settlement House class, she was unimpressed. "How can you be friends with someone who is the most hard-hearted capitalist in America?" she asked him shortly.

"I'm not friends with him," Will answered. "All he's done is invite me to see some of his art collection. And as for his being hard-hearted, I don't think that's quite fair. Morgan's a banker, and a very shrewd one, probably the cleverest one this country has ever produced. There's no room for feelings of any sort in his kind of business. And in any case, while he assists corporations with their banking needs he's not the one setting workers' salaries.

In the early days of Will and Ana's relationship, an argument would have followed, but now, recognizing where the discussion was headed, both Ana and Will began to laugh. "I'm going to make an anarchist out of you yet," Ana said to Will. "Not before I've seen Mr. Morgan's library," Will responded.

Tuesday was wet and miserable, with snow showers in the afternoon that by evening had turned into a steady mix of snow and rain. Will opted to walk to Morgan's house from the seminary, equipping himself with an umbrella and boots in the belief that he was likely to get there more quickly by walking than if he used public transportation.

"Don't forget to ask him if you could borrow one of his Gutenberg Bibles," Hugh joked as Will set off. "Tell him we want to check it for errors."

Morgan's butler took Will's wet things without comment and showed him to the library, where he found Morgan examining one of his books. The library turned out to be even more beautiful than Will had imagined it. Built only a few years before, and on the outside as austerely elegant as the Metropolitan Club, inside it was like stepping into an Italian palace. Everywhere were lovely things to look at, from the zodiac signs in the ceiling, to the bronze and walnut bookcases, to the Sixteenth Century tapestry over the mantelpiece.

But what seemed to please Morgan most was not showing off the room but rather some of his immense collection of rare books. There were illuminated medieval books of hours, jewel-encrusted books that had belonged to princes and noblemen, and more recent treasures including the manuscript of Charles Dickens' *Christmas Carol*. As he brought out one after another to show Will, Morgan spoke with the excitement of a boy rather than the 73-year-old man he was.

"You're rich when you can buy what you want," Morgan observed at one point. "But for me the thrill is not the buying but the knowing that I have the very best."

After an hour in the library, Morgan took Will to see his study, a large room with an antique wood ceiling and walls covered in red damask. Will, remembering accounts of how Morgan had practically single-handedly saved the American economy in 1907 with a series of meetings held in this room, tried to imagine how the powerful men Morgan had summoned must have felt walking in and finding Morgan sitting behind his desk, glowering.

"I've heard that people call this my uptown office," Morgan said. "But there aren't many offices in which one is surrounded by five-hundred-year-old treasures."

They moved back into the main house then, and Morgan's butler brought them each a glass of port, which they drank sitting in front of a blazing fire. Morgan asked Will a few questions about the progress of work on the Cathedral and then, uncharacteristically, about his family. Will explained that his mother was a widow and he the only child, but that they were very close.

"Your mother is lucky," said Morgan. "I have four children and I can't say I'm close to any of them. My daughter Anne was always my favorite when she was a child—she was bright, fearless and always ready for any challenge—and she should have been the one living here with me now. But she's proved the greatest disappointment of all."

"I've actually met her, sir," Will said, "and I hope you know that she's held in high regard by many of those involved in trying to improve conditions for workers. I know that your politics and hers are quite different, but in my opinion she's a true Christian."

Morgan snorted. "No Christian would engage in the kind of life she's leading," he said brusquely, emptying his glass as a sign that it was time for Will to go. Will thanked him for the tour, and said what a pleasure it was to see objects in the setting of a home, even such a grand one as this, rather than in a museum.

Morgan nodded. "Perhaps one day after I'm gone this whole place will *be* a museum," he said. "I've been thinking recently along those lines."

When Will got back to the seminary, Hugh was waiting for a full report. Will described the place as fully as he could, ending with the observation that if Hugh waited long enough, and if Morgan followed through on his idea of turning the library into a museum, perhaps Hugh would be able to see it for himself.

"J.P. Morgan is so tough that he'll probably outlive both of us," Hugh laughed.

Over the next few weeks, life went on much as before. There were delays at the Cathedral owing to a steamfitters' strike, and some of the tile work still wasn't completed, but most of the marble work was finished. Bishop Greer told Will that the treasurer of the trustees had reported that they still didn't have sufficient money to finish the areas slated to be dedicated in April and that the trustees had discussed a plan to cover continuing costs by getting at least five people in every parish to pledge $100 a year for five years.

One small additional problem for Greer was a speech given by the Reverend John Holmes, a prominent Unitarian pastor, that was highly critical of the Episcopal Church's expenditures on the Cathedral. When Will read a report of the speech the next day in the *New York Times*, his heart sank—not least because part of him agreed with it.

"What will the people of this city think of the Church of God which will spend millions for that tomb of marble on Morningside Heights when people are dying because the Society for the Prevention of Tuberculosis is in need of funds; when the iniquity of child labor exists, and so much remains to be done?" the newspaper account quoted Holmes as having said.

Despite Will's secret agreement with Holmes' sentiments, he was forced to admire the speed with which Bishop Greer and the rest of the church hierarchy mounted a response. The next day, the paper carried detailed remarks by the Reverend Ernest Stires, rector of St. Thomas Episcopal Church, in which Stires pointedly asked what the Unitarians had done for the poor, particularly as compared with the Episcopalians' extensive outreach. He also recalled Judas Iscariot's questioning of why Jesus had allowed Mary Magdalene to anoint his feet with expensive ointment when the money could have been given to the poor.

"Just so it is with the new Cathedral," the report quoted Stires as saying. "It is but right that in this city the great finger should rise on Morningside Heights, as the steeple of old Trinity does at the head of Wall Street, to remind men that all things of worth are not those of the material world."

When Will saw the Bishop at an event a few days later, he asked him how it was that Stires had been the one to respond to Holmes. "Mainly because he's a friend of one of the top editors of the *Times* and was able to call him directly and request the opportunity to be heard," Greer answered.

The Bishop added with satisfaction, "He was quite slashing, wasn't he? I don't think we'll have any more problems with the Reverend Holmes."

For the most part, Will and Ana continued to see each other only briefly during the week after Will's University Settlement class, but they almost always met on Sunday afternoon. Usually it was too cold to spend very long outside so Will began showing Ana some of the city's museums, where he introduced her to his favorite artists. Ana admitted that she found the idea of standing and looking silently at pictures rather dull, but she said she wanted to understand why paintings mattered so much to Will.

"I'm beginning to worry that I might be becoming too much like you, with your tastes and your interests," she said after one visit to the Metropolitan Museum of Art. "And I worry even more that there's no going back."

"Oh Ana," Will said, "I'm sorry if I sometimes seem to want that."

Ana nodded thoughtfully. "No one who is middle class ever chooses to become working class," she said. "When it happens, it's always the other way around."

The one time Ana clearly enjoyed herself was when Will took her to see an exhibit by some of his friends including Bellows and Sloane. One picture in particular, by Sloane, captivated her: it showed three scrubwomen in a library stopping to chat for a moment, while in the background men sat reading at long tables. "I like the fact that it shows workers as real people," she told Will. "They look like they're having fun gossiping. And they look like they're having much more interesting lives than those dull men!"

Will laughed. "You're probably right," he said. "And you've recognized something about Sloane's work, which is that he's political, just like you. The only difference is that he uses art rather than organizing to advance the cause of workers."

The following week, Ana made a surprise announcement: Her aunt wanted Will to come to dinner. Despite Ana's efforts to hide her continuing meetings with Will, Mrs. Markowicz, not being a fool, was aware of what was going on and had decided, she'd told Ana, that she wanted to meet this 'friend' of hers. "She told me that I seemed happy for the first time since my uncle died," Ana said softly.

Friday evening found Will walking toward Ana's apartment building with a mixture of curiosity and nervousness. Ana had warned him that her aunt's English was limited and that the two sisters who were boarders didn't speak any English at all. But beyond that, he was worried about whether he'd know what to do or say. Ana had explained a bit about Shabbat but he was acutely aware of his lack of understanding of almost everything to do with Judaism.

The first thing that struck him when he entered the apartment building were the smells: dust, cabbage cooking, and a faint smell of urine that reminded him of the tenement he'd visited with Dowling. The hallways and stairwell were dark, too, just like the tenement, but clean and obviously looked after.

Two floors up, he knocked at the door to his left, as Ana had instructed him. The door was almost immediately opened by Ana. Mrs. Markowicz, who was standing in the background, came forward to shake his hand, as did the two boarders. "Pleased to meet you," Mrs. Markowicz said. Or at least Will thought that's what she said, but her English was so heavily accented he couldn't be sure.

She was a thin woman, her face careworn and her dress carefully brushed but more than a little out-of-date. When she saw the small box of chocolates Will had brought as a present, she gave him a pleased smile.

There was nowhere to sit in the small room except at the table, since the only two comfortable chairs had been pushed out of the way to make space in the center of the small room for the table and five upright chairs, only three of which matched. So they all took their places and the three older women looked at Will expectantly.

"Thank you for inviting me," Will said, somewhat awkwardly. "I'm glad to be here and I'm sorry that I can't speak Yiddish. But maybe one day Ana will teach me."

Ana, throwing him a look of surprise, turned to the two boarders and translated, prompting them to smile. As this was going on, Will had time to notice the two candles, the covered loaves of challah and the wine that had been set out on the table, which itself was covered with a white tablecloth. The room doubled as the kitchen and living room, Will realized; the dishes of food, neatly covered with clothes, sat next to the sink off to one side. Except for formal occasions, he guessed, the table was pushed up against the wall and they ate their meals there.

Mrs. Markowicz stood up and reached for a box of matches next to her place. Reciting the Shabbat blessing, she lit the candles and then uncovered one of the loaves and broke it into several pieces before handing it around. After this was done, she brought over the dishes and carefully uncovered them: there was a stewed chicken, cabbage and dumplings.

Mrs. Markowicz indicated that Will should help himself first, which he did, making sure to take only a little chicken as he could see there wasn't a lot to go around. Everyone helped themselves and began to eat, while Will racked his brain for something to say.

"Ana has probably told you that I teach a class at University Settlement," he said. "That is how I met her, because we had a debate with College Settlement. Ana was the best debater and her side won."

Again, Ana translated and there were smiles all around. A minute later one of the boarders said something and her sister and Mrs. Markowicz laughed. "What did she say?" Will asked Ana.

"She said that you are nice-looking," Ana said, embarrassed.

After they'd finished the meal, the eating interspersed with a few halting attempts at conversation, Mrs. Markowicz said, in English, "You two go for a walk," gesturing toward Ana and Will.

They did so, after Will had expressed his thanks for the meal and Ana had retrieved her oversized coat from a hook by the door. As they came out of the building, Will commented that the pot of zinnias was still on the first-floor windowsill, even though most of the flowers had died.

"Oh yes," said Ana. "Mrs. Simkovic will look after them until they all freeze. She brings them inside at night and somehow, there is enough heat during the day that a few of them are still alive."

"Did I pass the test?" Will asked.

"I think so," said Ana with a nervous smile. "It's never easy knowing quite what my aunt is thinking, but she seemed to like you. The most important thing is that she could see you were not a golem—a monster—who was going to snatch me away. But I know that in the end, that doesn't count; she won't change her mind. We are Jewish and you're not, and so while she's willing to allow us to spend time together, as far as she's concerned there can't be anything more."

Pausing briefly, she added, "Also, as you know, I've realized that I feel more strongly about being Jewish than I ever thought I did before I met you."

Will looked sobered by her comments. All through the following week, he kept thinking about what his mother had said about the need to first resolve his relationship with Ana and then everything else would follow. Perhaps if Ana and he were both to decide that being together was more important than anything else—more important than careers, or the workers' union, or being Christian or Jewish, or what their relatives or friends might think—then together they would be able to find a way to do it. But it would almost certainly mean wrenching changes for both of them. Was he ready to make those changes? Was she?

Finally, in early March, Will made up his mind. "Ana," he said one night as they were saying good-bye, "please meet me next Sunday at this address"—he slid into her hand a piece of paper with the name of the restaurant at the 'Flatiron' building—"and we'll have a fine lunch to celebrate the fact that winter is nearly over. After lunch, I have an idea that I'll tell you about then."

Ana nodded, a little doubtfully.

When the time came, Will found Ana standing by the elevators in the lobby, dressed in her best dress but still looking a bit out of place among the fashionable women around her. The view from the dining room was just as wonderful as Will had imagined, and Ana reacted excitedly as Will pointed out one landmark after another. At Ana's suggestion, Will ordered for them both from the extensive menu: consommé, followed by roast duck with roast potatoes and applesauce, and for dessert, cheesecake.

The setting somehow made conversation a bit awkward until

they happened upon the topic of a new book they'd both just read called *Howards End*. It was the story of a well-meaning young upper-class Englishwoman who befriends a young clerk trying to make his way up in the world, but who carelessly causes him a financial setback that ends in disaster.

"I couldn't help but think of us as I read it," Ana said. "Not that you'd be as thoughtless as she was but because she and he were so different."

"Yes," Will said, "I remember that comment by one of the characters about standing on an island made of money and never thinking about it while all around are poor people sinking under the waves. The ones standing on the islands aren't even aware of what is going on."

Both of them were silent for a minute. "Enough of these gloomy topics," Will finally declared. "Let's talk about happier things." Ana nodded her agreement and started by recalling her visit to Greenville. "The best thing apart from meeting your mother was the Christmas tree," she said. "And the second-best was the ginger snaps." They talked about their discussions with Will's mother, and laughed about the too-large boots, and chatted happily through the rest of the meal.

As they were drinking their coffee Will reached into his pocket and pulled out a small box.

"Another present!" Ana exclaimed.

Will opened it and took out a small ring that consisted of a little circle of inexpensive turquoise stones. Slipping it on Ana's finger, he said, "This isn't an engagement ring because I can't formally ask you to marry me until I've figured out how and where we can get married and what we can live on. But I would like you to marry me, Miss Ana Markowicz, and I hope, when the time comes, you will say yes."

Plunging ahead, Will told her about what he'd been thinking: that if she was willing, as he was, to put their relationship before everything else, he was sure that they could find a way. Certainly he'd have to give up his career in the church. Possibly they could move to California. Maybe he could become an academic, maybe she could become a lawyer—he just didn't know, but he found these ideas exciting rather than alarming.

Perhaps, he continued, they could both join the Society for Ethical Culture, which was home to many former Jews and former Christians, all of whom believed that morality should be separate from theology and that meetings shouldn't be for worship but for educating themselves and their children on right living. He'd attended one of their services a few days ago, he said, just to see what it was like, and had come away impressed with the emphasis the Society put on social reform and on 'deeds, not words.' He'd felt comfortable there, he said, and he thought she would, too.

"It doesn't mean that I wouldn't go to Episcopal services any more than that you would never go to High Holy Day services," he said. "But it could be a place where we were comfortable together and—and a place we could bring our children."

At this Ana's eyes widened but she continued to say nothing, sitting absolutely still. Her whole demeanor, however, showed her intent focus on everything he was saying. Thus encouraged, he repeated that the one thing he felt sure of was that they could do it if they wanted it enough. And in the end, he said, if they truly loved each other, he felt certain that their families and friends would come around to accepting their decision, even if it took them a long time to get there.

"I love you, Ana," Will said, simply, "and I want to be with you always."

In response, Ana nodded thoughtfully, put her hand up to the locket and said, "You already are."

CHAPTER NINETEEN

"*W*ill!"

The urgency in Hugh's voice as he rushed up to Will in the library the following Saturday afternoon told Will immediately that something was wrong. Will quickly closed his book and followed Hugh outside.

"Will, I just heard that there's been a terrible fire at a factory near Washington Square Park and I remember you said Ana works around there," Hugh said.

"What's the name of the factory?" Will demanded.

"Triangle, I think it's called," Hugh said.

Will put his hand out to steady himself against the wall. "That's where she works," he said, the blood draining from his face. "I've got to go there."

"I'll come with you," Hugh said.

As they ran down the stairs, grabbed their jackets, and hurried through streets already touched by the first signs of spring, Hugh told Will the little he knew. The fire had broken out in one of the three floors occupied by the factory just as the Triangle workers were finishing for the day, and within a few minutes the whole place was in flames. Some workers had managed to escape either down the stairs to the street or up to the roof, but some were trapped and many had jumped to their deaths.

As Will and Hugh approached the park, at first they could see nothing amiss. On the north side, the century-old red brick townhouses stood glowing in the late afternoon sun. But to the east, crowds were rushing toward Greene Street, just a block off the park. There, at the corner of Greene and Washington Place, stood the ten-story Asch building that housed Triangle in its upper floors.

By the time Will and Hugh arrived, the fire was under control—astonishingly the worst of it had lasted no more than about twenty minutes—but firemen were still pouring water into the building. The water cascaded out of the windows and down the sides of the building, turning bloody as it rushed toward the gutters. One of the policeman told them that the fire had probably started in a scrap bin under a cutter's table, most likely from a match or cigarette butt. Thanks to being fed by hundreds of pounds of scraps and the thin tissue used for the patterns, it had spread rapidly and burned with ferocious intensity.

On the sidewalks on Greene Street and Washington Place Will and Hugh saw dozens of bodies, most already covered by coats or tarpaulins, while police carried other bodies out of the building. The ones being carried out were, for the most part, unrecognizable as human beings.

There was little Will and Hugh could do except helplessly look on from behind the line of police that was keeping the huge crowd of relatives, friends and gawkers at bay. Will noticed that the firemen's ladders had been too short to reach the factory floors, just as Ana had said, and he heard one bystander say that many of the workers had crowded around the windows, watching as the ladders stopped at the sixth floor. A few had tried jumping into a firemen's net, but because they were jumping from such a height they had ripped through the net.

Pressed for more details, the bystander said that while the firemen were extending their tallest ladder, a girl on the ninth-floor ledge slowly waved a handkerchief as the ladder inched toward her. But then the ladder halted its rise—three floors below her. The girl stopped waving her handkerchief as a flame caught the edge of her skirt. She leaped for the top of the ladder almost thirty feet below, missed, and hit the sidewalk, the man said, "like a flaming comet."

Other bystanders talked of seeing girls hanging onto the ledges below the windows or jumping from the windows as the flames licked out toward them. One described seeing a young man and woman jump together as the flames touched the woman's long hair. Another talked of seeing two and three young women at a time, arms linked, coming down together, while a third described seeing a young man help several young women out a window, then hold each carefully in turn away from the building before letting them drop. Finally, the man recalled, came a girl who kissed the young man before he dropped her, after which he perched on the window sill himself and stepped off. "His coat fluttered upward and the air filled his trouser legs as he came down," the onlooker reported. "I could see he wore tan shoes."

The Greene Street side had been the worst, according to Frances Perkins, whom they unexpectedly met on the sidewalk and whom Will recognized from the meeting after the Newark fire that he'd attended with Lizzy. Miss Perkins explained that she'd been having tea with a friend who lived on Washington Square when they heard the sirens and decided to investigate. "People had just begun to jump as we got here," she said. "They had been holding until that time, standing in the windowsills, being crowded by others behind them." All around her, Perkins said, people were calling, "Don't jump! Help is coming!" But she knew, even if they didn't, Perkins said, that there was little the fire department could do.

Those who hadn't jumped had been subjected to an even more horrible fate than those who did. When the window jams broke, their bodies had come down in showers, burning and smoking as they fell. So many bodies on the sidewalk were still burning that at one point the firemen had turned their hoses on them before going back to aiming at the flames above.

After hearing their fill of ghastly stories, Will and Hugh decided to see if they could find Ana among the workers who had managed to escape. For the next forty-five minutes they walked up and down the periphery of the crowd while Will asked those who looked like possible survivors whether they had seen Ana, describing her in terms that barely distinguished her from dozens of her co-workers. For the most part, all he got in response were dull stares, some of them hostile, and shakes of the head.

"What do you care about some factory girl?" asked one man in a surly voice, taking in Will and Hugh's obvious middle-class appearance. "Go back uptown where you belong."

Just at that moment, a wild-eyed young woman came staggering around the corner, her long hair loose and her clothing torn and smoke-stained. Seemingly deranged by what she'd experienced, she kept shouting, "Don't let them hurt me! Don't let them hurt me!" as the crowd parted before her. Falling into the arms of a policeman who had hurried over to help her, she sobbed out her name and her address, at which point two women came forward and led her away, still sobbing and barely able to stand.

By now it was dark, but the several thousand people who had been drawn to the disaster showed no sign of dispersing, and in fact the crowd continued to grow. From time to time the crowd threatened to break through the police lines and twice they did, shrieking and shouting, as police used their billy clubs to beat them back.

Meanwhile, efforts were underway to locate any workers who were still alive. When a policeman thought he saw signs of life, he and his colleagues would burrow through a pile of corpses and sometimes bring out a ragged but still-breathing body. At one point a woman who was being carried toward an ambulance began shrieking so piteously that many in the crowd covered their ears to shut out her cries.

On the east side of Greene Street, across from the Asch building, police had spread a huge canvas on which they had placed about forty bodies. As the bodies lay, waiting for coffins, the police added the handbags, combs, hair ribbons and cheap jewelry that they kept picking up from the sidewalk where the girls had landed after they jumped. In one corner lay a shoe, its heel half ripped off, in another, a pair of rosary beads.

Finally, Will asked a policeman where the injured were being taken, and he was told most were at St. Vincent's Hospital. He and Hugh hurried there, only to be told that no one by the name of Ana Markowicz was among those who'd been brought in. "But some are so badly injured, and without any identification, that she might still be here," a sympathetic desk clerk explained.

On the sidewalk outside the hospital, Will and Hugh stood trying to decide what to do next. "It's possible she's at home," said Will. "Her aunt has probably heard about the fire by now so we wouldn't be the first to tell her. And if Ana did manage to escape she might be there."

Turning to Hugh, he said, "There's not a lot more you can do right now. I very much appreciate your coming with me. But there's no need to come to her aunt's house with me, too. I'll find you back at the seminary later."

Hugh looked uncertain. "Will, I'm happy to go with you anywhere you want," he said. "But if you think it's best if you go by yourself, that's fine."

Will looked dazed. "Hugh, I have no idea what's best," he said.

Hugh briefly put his arm around Will. "I'll go to the chapel and pray that she's safe," he said. "Come to my room as soon as you get back." Then he turned and headed off.

As Will approached Ana's street he could see small knots of people in front of some of the buildings, each, he surmised, the home of one of the workers. From the buildings, he heard wailing and sobbing, and he assumed that meant that those inside already knew the worst. It seemed as though the whole of the Lower East Side was in an agony of uncertainty, or in mourning.

In front of one building, he saw a large crowd standing in a circle around a young woman who, it was obvious from her disheveled appearance, was one of the survivors. She was recounting, in a strangled voice, what had happened to her and her friends.

She'd been in the dressing room on the eighth floor when the fire started, she said. She'd just put on her hat when her friend Rose ran into the room screaming, took her by the hand, and began to drag her through the shop and toward a window. "I saw men pouring water on the fire on the cutting tables but the fire was quickly getting hotter and more and more tables were on fire," she said. "Suddenly I felt I was going in the wrong direction. I couldn't go with her. Always, even as a child, I had a great fear of heights. And that's what saved me. I turned back into the shop but my friend jumped from the window."

At the memory, the young woman started to cry. But then, seeming driven by the need to tell what she had seen, she went on, "Just then one of the men managed to get the Washington Place stairway door open and we all started to rush through. I don't remember how I got down but I know I was screaming all the time. When we came to the bottom the firemen wouldn't let us out because they were afraid we'd be killed by the falling bodies. Finally, two men carried me across the street and into a store. I lay there on the floor and all the time I could see through the store window the burning bodies falling."

Will shuddered as he listened to the story, then pushed his way through the crowd to Ana's building and climbed the stairs to her apartment. When he got there, the door was open and he saw many neighbors crowded inside. In the midst of them, he found Ana's aunt sitting, staring blankly.

When she saw Will, she beckoned him over. "No news," she said. "Nobody see Ana. You see her?"

Will shook his head, then explained with the help of a neighbor who translated that he'd gone to the hospital and that Ana might be there but right now they didn't know. "I'm going to go back there, and also back to the factory, to see if I can find out anything more," he said. "I'll return if I do."

Then he wrote the phone number of the seminary on a piece of paper and gave it to one of the boarders, who was standing next to Mrs. Markowicz, for safekeeping. "Please call this number if you have any news," he told Mrs. Markowicz. "Someone will get a message to me." Gesturing toward the boarder, he said, "She has the number."

When he reached the street, Will stopped to take a few deep

breaths. Ana's aunt was lucky, he thought; at least she had neighbors she could talk to and who would be a constant source of fresh scraps of news. He had no one. He wasn't part of this world.

But then he realized that he knew at least one person. He headed over to College Settlement, where he found Lizzy talking quietly about the fire with some of the other volunteers and a few people from the neighborhood. Lizzy saw him as he came in and immediately went over to him.

"No news," she said, shaking her head. "I've already heard about half a dozen girls from the neighborhood who are dead, but nothing about Ana."

Then, seeing Will's stricken face, she said, "Oh Will, I'm so sorry." She urged him to rest for a few minutes and have a cup of coffee but he shook his head and, after asking her to please let him know if she heard anything, started back uptown.

By now it was well into the evening but the crowd around the Triangle building was still enormous. Some relatives wailed, others sobbed softly, and some walked up and down wringing their hands and calling out the names of relatives. Will again asked if anyone had seen Ana, but with the same results as earlier.

A fire engine with a searchlight had been brought in and Will could see it follow the path of each body as it was lowered down from the upper floors. A fireman was on duty at each window it passed in its descent and he reached out and swung it clear of the sills. After the bodies were lowered and tagged, they were deposited in coffins and placed on wagons that then moved off into the night. Will asked one of the police guarding the site where the coffins were being taken and was told that a temporary morgue had been set up on a pier at the foot of East Twenty-Sixth Street.

After checking at the hospital again, and this time being told that all the victims who'd been brought there had been identified and Ana was not among them, Will decided to go to the temporary morgue. But unsure whether they would let him in since he had no proof that he was connected to any of the victims, he returned to Ana's apartment. The place was still full of neighbors and friends, some of whom had brought food and chairs in the expectation of a long wait ahead.

Will explained what little he had learned to Mrs. Markowicz, and asked if she would come with him to the morgue. She nodded and got up. The neighbors stood back as she and Will left the apartment, with Will giving her his arm once they were on the street. Two blocks away, he found a taxicab and directed the driver to take them to Twenty-Sixth Street.

The pier was covered by an iron-frame enclosure, black and gloomy against the sullen sky. Every few minutes a patrol wagon or ambulance filled with coffins drove up to the huge doors and was allowed through.

Already a long line of people had gathered, snaking back from the pier entrance down Twenty-Sixth Street. Will and Mrs. Markowicz took their places at the end of the line and began their wait in silence. The night was cold, and many in the crowd were shivering.

After an hour or so, a policeman came out and began to walk the length of the waiting line. "Who seeks a girl with a ring bearing the initials G.S.?" A shriek and an old woman staggered forward. "Who seeks a girl whose pay envelope bears the name of Kaplan?" Another shout, this one from a middle-aged man. Finally, after calling out about twenty-five such identifications, and gesturing to those who responded that they should proceed inside, the policeman disappeared.

At midnight, the great iron gates swung open and, after a pause, the crowd began to move forward. They were admitted in groups of twenty, each accompanied by several policemen.

Inside, the corpses had been propped up in coffins in two long lines, the scene lit by lights hung high in the rafters and by lanterns held by the policemen. People shuffled up and down the rows, and occasionally one of them shouted in surprise or anguish as he or she recognized a sister or daughter or wife. Some of the bodies—the ones of people who had jumped—were relatively easy to identify. But those of people who had burned to death were in most cases so charred that it was only through shreds of clothing or jewelry that their relatives could identify them. Every bit of clothing on dozens of bodies had been burned off and the body of one girl was headless.

Will and Mrs. Markowicz walked up and down the rows twice, Mrs. Markowicz clutching Will's arm but otherwise stoically calm as she and Will peered at the disfigured faces. Will felt torn between wanting to find Ana and wanting not to, because if they didn't, that meant she might still be alive. All around them, families were wailing in Yiddish or Italian, punctuated by the screams of those who had just found loved ones.

As soon as an identification was made, an officer put the lid on the coffin and tacked onto it a small card on which he wrote the name of the victim. He then sent the relatives, with a corresponding slip, to the temporary office of the coroner, where permits were being issued to remove identified bodies.

As Will and Mrs. Markowicz were about to give up, the officer in charge announced that one more set of coffins was on its way. Most of the crowd, including Will and Mrs. Markowicz, stayed on, milling around outside until the wagon had pulled up and the coffins taken inside. Then, the doors were opened again and they filed back in.

Will and Mrs. Markowicz peered at the new coffins as they had the old ones, but agreed that Ana wasn't among them. Will suggested that they walk one more time up and down the two rows they'd already examined, and Mrs. Markowicz nodded. It was at the far end of the first row that Will spotted what both of them had completely missed before: a locket, blackened but still recognizable, around the neck of a body whose hair and skin were mostly gone.

"Ana," Will gasped, involuntarily recoiling. Mrs. Markowicz, seeing what he was seeing, buckled at the knees and Will had to hold her up.

One of the policemen helpfully held his lantern closer to the coffin so they could see better, but Will closed his eyes. When he opened them, the man had moved off, realizing that what they needed was not more light but more time.

Mrs. Markowicz was crying now, softly, her shoulders heaving as she stood there. Will tried to comfort her by putting his arm around her, but he had no words to offer. Another policeman came up and asked whether they could make a positive identification. Will nodded, and gave Ana's name, address and age, along with that of her aunt.

The policeman, after filling out the identification card, told them that Local 25 was making arrangements for a funeral procession and would assist with burial costs, and that they should be in touch with officials there on Monday morning. Perhaps moved by Mrs. Markowicz's dignified distress, he said he would pass on the identification slip to the coroner's office. Will nodded and thanked him, then led Mrs. Markowicz out of the building.

"I will make the arrangements with the union," he told her slowly. "For now, you should decide where you would like her buried." Mrs. Markowicz nodded numbly.

Will had only a few coins left in his pocket after paying for a cab back to Mrs. Markowicz' apartment, and so, after having first made sure that there were people to look after her, he began the long walk to the seminary. By the time he arrived, the sky was just beginning to lighten, but it was evident that it would be an overcast day.

His plan was to slip into his room and not wake Hugh, but Hugh had clearly been listening for him and came out of his room as Will passed his door. They went into Will's room, where Will sat down heavily on the bed, his head bowed.

"Did you find her?" Hugh asked.

Will nodded.

"Is she alive?"

Will shook his head.

"Oh Will," said Hugh. "What happened?"

Will talked then, talking and talking as though he would never run out of words: about the morgue, and the charred bodies, and the crowds of people on the streets. He told Hugh how he and Mrs. Markowicz had hunted and hunted for Ana and how he was unable to recognize her apart from the locket he'd given her.

"I can't believe that what I saw in that coffin was Ana," he said, despair in his voice. "Ana has long hair and that body had almost no hair."

"Stop it," Hugh said firmly. "You're on the verge of hysteria. I wish I had some sleeping aid to give you but I don't. Instead, I'm going to sit here until you go and wash up and then I'm going to stay with you until you fall asleep."

Will did as he was told. When he came back to the room, Hugh had turned down the blankets and put a chair beside the bed.

"Get in," Hugh said. Once he had, Hugh began to read to him, not from the Bible but from a travel book about New England. At first Will couldn't even grasp the words, but gradually the descriptions of small towns in the mountains of New Hampshire and little-known fishing villages in Maine began to soothe his spirit.

Every now and then, the grief rose up in a great wave and he found himself gasping for breath. At first he gave himself over to the sensation, almost welcoming the idea that he was suffocating. But gradually, the waves subsided and grew less frequent, as exhaustion overcame anguish.

It took well over an hour, but in the end, he fell asleep.

CHAPTER TWENTY

y Sunday morning, the total of the dead in the Triangle fire stood at one hundred and forty-six and the efforts to avoid blame were already well underway. Joseph Asch, owner of the building, first went into hiding but later emerged to declare publicly that he'd done everything legally required by way of safety precautions. Triangle partners Max Blanck and Isaac Harris vehemently denied having done anything wrong.

Throughout the city the mood ranged from anguished to angry. At Grace Church, the rector, Reverend Charles Slattery, preached a sermon in which he said that he hoped that the tragedy "would make New York stop to think whether it was not allowing men to go too madly and disastrously and selfishly in pursuit of money." At the headquarters of the Women's Trade Union League, Rabbi Stephen Wise called for an investigation.

One of the first to disclaim responsibility was Governor Dix, who declared that he was "appalled by the terrible disaster in New York" but that it was the job of city officials to conduct an inquiry. The State Labor Commissioner "deplored" the tragedy but said his office bore no responsibility. The City Building Department explained that it normally inspected buildings like the Asch building only when violations were called to its attention.

One of the few public officials to admit there were problems with existing policies was Fire Department Chief Edward Croker.

He maintained that the laws on fire escapes were too weak, and said that he had been warning about the possibilities of a serious fire such as the one at Triangle for a long time. "There wasn't a fire escape anywhere fronting on the street by which these unfortunate girls could escape," he said.

Will took no notice of any of this, keeping mainly to his room and to the chapel for the next two days. Devastated but feeling unable to talk about Ana or the fire with anyone but Hugh, he spent hours sitting in one of the choir stalls in the chapel doing little other than staring at the cover of the hymn book in front of him. No matter how hard he tried to push it away, the ghastly memory of Ana in the coffin kept returning, at once wrenching and terrifying.

By Wednesday, he'd recovered enough to attend a memorial meeting called by Local 25 at the Grand Central Palace on Lexington Avenue. Thousands of people were crammed into the hall and the mood was tense. When Abraham Cahan, the editor of the *Forward*, spoke critically of a worker who'd come into his office and told him that only planting a few bombs in the right places would bring redress for what had happened, it was immediately clear that Cahan had badly misjudged the crowd. Shouts of "Throw a bomb under City Hall!" and "Blow the place up!" rang throughout the auditorium. Will left feeling shaken by the depth of the crowd's anger.

The following Sunday, Bishop Greer was to address another large gathering, this one at the Metropolitan Opera House, which had been rented by Anne Morgan on behalf of the Women's Trade Union League. The meeting started at three o'clock, and drew people from all classes of New York City; the galleries were filled mostly with workers and the main floor with men in high hats and women in furs. Although he knew that several people from the seminary were planning on attending, Will deliberately went on his own, slipping into a seat in the very last row of the main section, where he was unlikely to be seen by anyone he knew.

Greer spoke well, Will thought, talking about the need for fire protection laws that "must be enforced not for a few weeks or a few months but for all time, faithfully, continuously, and effectively." If this were not done, the Bishop warned, "the responsibility—the sin—is on the public, on us."

Greer's words were met with loud applause, and followed by adoption of a resolution calling for the creation of a Bureau of Fire Prevention, along with creation of a system of workmen's compensation. But not everyone was satisfied. To many, including Will, it sounded like a replay of what had happened after the Newark fire: plenty of speeches, plenty of resolutions, but in the end, nothing.

When a slight young woman, Rose Schneiderman, who reminded Will of Ana, and who, he knew, had been a colleague of hers in the 1909 strike, rose to speak on behalf of the Women's Trade Union League, he leaned forward to pay attention.

"I would be a traitor to those poor burned bodies," she began, her fiery red hair matching the intensity of her words, "if I were to come here to talk good fellowship. We have tried you good people of the public—and we have found you wanting."

At this, the hall became very quiet, not just those in the main floor seats but in the galleries, too.

"This is not the first time girls have been burned alive in this city," Schneiderman said angrily. "But there are so many of us for one job, it matters little if one hundred and forty-odd are burned to death. I can't talk fellowship to you who are gathered here. Too much blood has been spilled. I know from experience it is up to the working people to save themselves. And the only way is through a strong working-class movement."

For a moment, Will was transported back to the debate at College Settlement a few months before and it was Ana he heard speaking those words. Then, for the first time, he cried—silently but so profoundly that his whole body shook with the pain.

Rose Schneiderman was followed by a city councilman, and during the latter's remarks Will slowly regained his composure. As the councilman droned on, an idea came to him and, rising unobtrusively from his seat, he made his way up the aisle toward the stage. Most people, assuming he was part of the organizing committee, paid him little attention until, after climbing the stairs to the stage, he waited until the city councilman had finished his remarks and then swiftly moved to the podium. Apologizing for inserting himself into the proceedings, he introduced himself simply as a seminary student and said he'd appreciate the chance to make a brief statement.

Surprised but clearly intent on avoiding a scene, the master of ceremonies gestured to him to continue.

"One of the people who died in the fire was named Ana Markowicz," he said in a clear voice. "When I met her, I was convinced that the petitions we signed, the letters we wrote, the resolutions that we passed, represented a major contribution to changing the conditions of workers. Ana taught me better. As Miss Schneiderman has said, workers know enough not to depend on the good-will of people like me, and like many of you in the audience.

"Why? Because what we do is so puny compared with what is needed: laws—real laws that send people to jail for the murder of girls like Ana. Getting such laws passed may require measures that many of you find objectionable—registering millions of new voters, even if they're recent immigrants and their command of English is minimal; fighting hard to unseat public officials who are less than one hundred percent behind the movement; joining strikers on the picket lines, in the jails and in the courts. But there can be no turning back."

There was a stir in the audience as people craned their necks to get a look at the young man whose militant words seemed so at odds with his refined demeanor.

"This isn't to say that the efforts of well-meaning people haven't been important," Will went on. "The people like Anne Morgan, who paid for this hall today, and Reverend Ralph Walker, who demanded a show of solidarity with striking expressmen at a recent Episcopal convention, have all played supporting roles. But until now, we've left the real battles to the workers to fight on their own. The time has come for all of us to join that fight, not just to support it."

Then, looking out over the crowd, Will said quietly, "I loved Ana Markowicz and I was hoping and planning to make my life with her. She was Jewish and I'm Christian but that didn't matter; what mattered was that we loved each other and we wanted to help build a world in which every person has a right to a decent life. Instead"—and here Will's voice dropped nearly to a whisper—"the last view I had of her was of a charred corpse."

Then, after a slight pause to collect himself, Will concluded, "I pledge to devote my life to ensuring that what happened to Ana and the others will never happen again."

With that, Will bowed his head briefly in thanks to the master of ceremonies and left the stage. The crowd was silent as he walked down the aisle and pushed aside the curtain to the lobby. As he did so, he could hear the speeches resuming and he wondered whether his remarks would have any effect at all. But he didn't really care; what mattered to him was that he had found his path. It was certainly not a path he had contemplated at the time of his talk with Father Huntington, and he wouldn't have been able to say whether he felt God speaking to him or not. And he wasn't even clear what his pledge would involve. But his mind was made up.

Word of what he'd done quickly spread through the seminary, thanks to the other students who'd been at the meeting, but perhaps out of respect for his loss, no one brought up the subject of Ana or of his remarks. Several newspapers briefly mentioned his appearance on the stage but none had learned his name. Most of the space devoted to the meeting was taken up by accounts of the speeches by the Bishop and other notable public figures. A dogged reporter from a weekly union newspaper sought him out at the seminary a few days later and he reluctantly gave a brief interview, but the story that resulted ran on an inside page and wasn't read beyond the union membership. All the focus among the big newspapers was on who was to blame and the horror of what had happened.

Will didn't attend the mass march and funeral a few days later organized by the unions; Ana had already been buried, in the same cemetery in Brooklyn as her uncle, in a small ceremony attended only by him, Ana's aunt, and a few of the aunt's friends. Ana's aunt had insisted that Will take back the locket he had given Ana and he gratefully accepted. He kept it in his pocket, except at night when he held it in his hand as he went to sleep, the way small children hold a blanket.

Hugh behaved like an anxious parent, making sure Will showed up for meals and insisting that they take walks around the neighborhood after dinner. Will obligingly agreed, but for the most part he was silent, letting Hugh talk about classes and seminary gossip and his recent decision, after much thought, to seek a church position back home in New Jersey. "I've decided the city is just too harsh for me," Hugh said.

Will's mother wrote him a long letter, telling him how much she'd liked Ana and how hard she knew it must be for him to lose her. "I know something about losing someone you love, because I loved your father very much," she said. "We shared not only intellectual interests but moral concerns as well, just as you and Ana did. When he died I was devastated. But eventually, I was able to move on with my life in the knowledge that, just like your father, I had a role to play in trying to change the world for the better. I'm certain that in time you'll do the same, gaining inspiration from Ana's example."

Will went through the motions of teaching his class at University Settlement, and once accepted Lizzy's invitation to join her for a meal. There were no evening events for the next few days, many having been cancelled out of respect to the dead workers, and Will didn't see Bishop Greer for a Friday meeting until two weeks after the fire.

When he did, Bishop Greer listened to his report on the Cathedral with a slight frown, then said, "Mr. Ingalls, I was touched by your remarks at the meeting about the young woman who died. Obviously, I had no idea of what was going on between you and her, and if I had, I would have counseled against it in the strongest possible terms. Now, of course, that's irrelevant. I don't know what you're thinking about in terms of your future—you made a reference to devoting yourself to the workers' struggle—but I believe you could be more effective within the church than outside it and I'd be happy to recommend you for any post to which you decide to apply."

After a pause, he added, "I'll say a special prayer for Miss Markowicz during the Cathedral consecration next week. I've very much appreciated your assistance over these past few months and I'm sorry to see you so affected by the tragedy."

Will thanked him, then walked out into the spring-like evening thinking how much his life had changed since his first visit here six months before. Then, he had been a young man 'on the way up.' And now? Instead of contemplating the prospect of building a life with Ana—a life very different from the one he'd imagined when he joined the seminary—he now had to decide how to honor the pledge he'd made.

At the moment, however, it was all he could do to go through the motions of living. Head down, shoulders hunched despite the warmth in the air, he headed home.

Over the next few days, Will visited the Cathedral several times to watch the finishing touches being administered before the consecration. The high altar was covered with linens that had been specially made in England, and a palm in a large pot had been placed near the pulpit. Two of the Barberini tapestries had been hung behind the main altar and another over the window on the right.

Late in the afternoon two days before the ceremony, Will was sitting in one the pews watching two workmen standing on a scaffolding as they cleaned the clear glass windows on the north side of the crossing when an idea came to him. He touched the locket in his pocket, then got up quickly and went out of the building and walked down Amsterdam Avenue until he came to a hardware store. There, he bought a small jar of putty and a putty knife, then returned to the Cathedral and entered St. Saviour's Chapel, where he found a spot to sit where he was unlikely to be observed by anyone walking by.

He waited until all sounds of activity in the Cathedral had

ceased, indicating that the workers had left for the day, and then cautiously emerged into the crossing. Seeing no one around, he walked quickly to the scaffolding and climbed up. Just under one of the windows, he found what he was looking for: a small crack in the cement which, with the help of the putty knife, he was able to enlarge.

Taking the locket out of his pocket, he pushed it into the opening, then quickly opened the putty jar and filled up the hole. When he'd finished, the work was hardly visible, and in any case, he thought, the window cleaners wouldn't be looking below the window as they hurried to finish the job.

As long as the Cathedral stands, he thought to himself as he left, the memory of Ana will be safe within its walls.

By ten o'clock on the morning of the consecration, almost every one of the nearly two thousand seats in the Cathedral crossing had been filled. Governor Dix was there, along with many state and local politicians and large numbers of the clergy. Will spotted two of the trustees, August Belmont and Levi Morton, as well as a former governor of New York State and several men he'd met on his evenings out with the Bishop. The high altar looked beautiful, adorned with white roses and lilies that conveyed a message of spring and new beginnings.

Admission was by invitation only, but at least five thousand people were gathered outside, hoping for a glimpse of the dignitaries as they entered. The Bishop had personally given Will an invitation card, thanking him again for his assistance and saying he looked forward to presiding at Will's ordination.

Promptly at ten-thirty the organ began the entrance hymn and the doors of the Cathedral opened, allowing in the choir and a procession of twenty-two Bishops who slowly made their way to the front of the church. All the clergy were dressed in black cassocks and white surplices, but among the women in the congregation, large hats in various colors were the order of the day.

Bishop Greer's sermon was on the text of "Love the

brotherhood, fear God, Honor the King," and he spoke of the Cathedral as a manifestation of a determination "to give our best" to God and country.

The ceremony, while impressive, went on much too long— four-and-a-half hours, by Will's watch. Will noted with interest the late entry of Andrew Carnegie, and wondered whether Carnegie had got wind of the expected length of the service and adjusted his arrival accordingly. In addition to the dedication of the main space, there was also a dedication ceremony for the two completed chapels. The offertory, it was explained, was for the creation of a third.

By half past twelve some people began to slip out, while others looked increasingly bored or studied their programs with an air of resignation. Will felt sorry for the choir boys, remembering how hungry he'd always been by noon when he was their age. Will couldn't help thinking that the gusto with which the congregation sang the final hymn, "Onward Christian Soldiers," was more a reflection of everyone's desire to get out of the building as quickly as possible than an excess of religious zeal.

And then it was over. Will joined the crowd streaming out onto Amsterdam Avenue and made his way to Broadway. The rest of the city, he observed, was going about its business without so much as a thought about the morning's events.

Once back at the seminary, he spent what was left of the afternoon doing some reading for one of his classes, then made his way to the chapel for evensong. As he entered, he heard Mr. Goodhue practicing a new piece that Will assumed was intended for the Sunday service. Soothed by the familiar sounds and surroundings, he sat there in the gathering darkness, watching the disappearance of the last beams of light.

CHAPTER TWENTY-ONE

*W*ill graduated in June with the rest of his class, but he had already decided against being ordained. In mid-May, a few days after Frank Hastings announced he was resigning as head resident at University Settlement to take up an unexpected job offer, Will was asked to fill in on a one-year temporary basis. With no other plan in mind, he readily agreed.

By the end of that year, he felt that his heart had healed enough to allow him to move on with his life. He was firm in his resolve to carry on the work that Ana had done, but accepting at last that he wasn't meant for front-line activism, he got a job with the special state Factory Investigating Commission that had been set up a few months after the fire. It was a real commission, with powerful backers, and its four-year term resulted in dozens of new state laws touching not only on fire prevention but also on child labor and other matters. One of the most significant new laws established workmen's compensation for workers injured on the job.

Will started out by helping to recruit witnesses to testify at the Commission's hearings and later moved on to a role in drafting bills and lobbying for their passage in Albany. He found that the combination of tasks, which involved him in meetings with workers' groups as well as in reviewing all the hearing testimony, and then strategizing on how to get the bills passed, suited him very well.

In particular he appreciated the chance to work with Frances Perkins, the Commission's chief investigator. She organized numerous factory tours for commission members that drove home the dangerous conditions that were rife throughout the state. Will was inspired by Perkins' combination of careful, on-the-ground research and passionate commitment to the cause. In one late-night conversation in Buffalo, the two talked about their shared experience at the site of the Triangle fire, and it was clear to Will that Perkins, too, had been deeply affected. Years later, Will was interested to read that Perkins had referred to Triangle as "a torch that lighted up the industrial scene."

The pay on the Commission staff was poor, but Will saved on housing costs by sharing an apartment in a run-down neighborhood in Brooklyn with two other men, one a union organizer and the other an assistant to a reform leader in the city council. In time, he became close to the chairman and vice chairman of the Commission, two young Tammany Hall politicians, Robert F. Wagner, Sr. and Alfred E. Smith, who ended up being life-long friends.

When the state subsequently created an industrial commission under the Department of Labor to set safety and health rules administratively, Perkins was named as one of the commissioners and recruited Will to assist her. In time he became one of the leading experts on workplace health and safety in the Northeast, taking a particular interest in the dangers posed by the chemical industry. For the most part he shied away from public speaking— too much like giving a sermon, he would smilingly explain when asked—but he wrote often and well about issues of public concern and was frequently called on by members of the New York State Assembly and Senate to brief them.

Will developed a reputation for always treating people with respect and, while not naturally given to small talk, never being too busy to share a cup of coffee with anyone from a factory worker to a legislator. It occurred to him more than once that he had learned from Bishop Greer the importance of taking time to listen to people, even when one had little to offer except a bit of advice or a sympathetic ear. Out of the material from his factory visits and interviews with families who had lost their breadwinners to industrial diseases, Will wrote powerfully-argued articles and provided guidance to reformers at the city and state levels.

People came to admire Will not just for his knowledge but also for his frugal lifestyle and his single-minded commitment to the reform cause. Whatever money he made from his writing or speaking he donated to various workers' funds, taking only a small salary from a citizens' group devoted to labor and housing matters. When Frances Perkins become Secretary of Labor under President Franklin Roosevelt, she asked Will to join her staff in Washington, but he declined on the grounds that he wanted to remain closer to his mother.

It wasn't until Will was in his late thirties that he finally got married, to a woman his age who'd been widowed some years before and who had two school-age children. She was a Wellesley graduate from a family not unlike his own, but she'd worked both before and after her marriage as a lawyer for the Children's Aid Society and was so independent that she'd always kept her own name. She and Will made a good team, respectful of each other's opinions and work. Will told her about Ana very early on in their relationship, and he was grateful for her response: she made it clear that she didn't feel threatened and that she had no interest in pressing him for details.

Will was active in his parish church but never in any public way. In times of difficulty, he tended to be the one who found a way toward consensus and acted as a steadying hand. Once or twice a year, he spent a weekend at West Park, participating in the life of the monastery much as he had as a young seminarian. A few times on these visits, he wondered what his life would have been like if he'd become a monk in the way Father Huntington had done, but then he would remind himself that he needed to live out Ana's dreams, not just his own. And besides that, he knew that he liked having a family and work whose results he could see in the cleaner homes and brighter faces of poor children.

Hugh Prescott got married right after graduation, in the seminary chapel, and served all his life at one or another church in western New Jersey. He and Will always stayed in touch, and their families often visited each other at Christmas. A few times through the years, when the two of them were sitting together late in the evening after the others had gone to bed, they would speak about the fire. Will talked occasionally about Ana, but always carefully, hesitant to disturb a wound which, like his father's war wound, would never completely heal.

Once, in a conversation at Hugh's house in New Jersey, Will confessed that he sometimes worried that he wasn't doing enough to fulfill his pledge to work toward Ana's goals.

Hugh responded in his typically common-sense way. "Who's to say that marching on a picket line outside a factory that employs children is 'action' but lobbying for a bill to outlaw child labor in Albany is 'support'?" he asked. "They're both important, but there are times when you might actually be moving things along more quickly by being in Albany."

Pausing briefly, Hugh continued, "And without wanting to sound self-serving, any movement also needs people like me who sign petitions and vote for reform candidates but spend most of their lives pursuing their careers. The world couldn't survive if everyone was doing nothing but protesting—or lobbying, for that matter. I don't apologize for my life any more than you should for yours. Of course it's not morally acceptable to do nothing. But we all choose the level of involvement that seems right for us. And you've not only chosen a life of full-time involvement, but you've also given up the chance to achieve a level of worldly success that isn't even on offer to most of us. To me, that makes what you've done particularly admirable."

Will stared into the fire, thinking over what Hugh had said. Finally, he replied, "You're right, of course, about all of us having to choose the path that's appropriate for us, and thank you for helping me not to become too self-dramatizing or falsely modest. I know Ana changed me, but that doesn't mean I could become like her—or should even try to." After another minute of staring into the fire, he added quietly, "Still, I think I'll always feel that what I'm doing can never be enough."

And with that they ended the conversation and went to bed.

Will's mother continued living in Greenville until she was well into her eighties. She often visited Will and his family in the city, and Will's step-children grew to love roaming the countryside around Greenville just as Will himself had done.

Will visited Ana's aunt several times during the year he was at University Settlement, and helped her to apply for assistance from a fund set up by union supporters including Anne Morgan that allowed her to stay in her apartment. He and Mrs. Markowicz continued to see each other once every year or so until, about ten years after Ana's death, Mrs. Markowicz died, too.

Will was touched at how many people came up to him at Mrs. Markowicz's funeral and told him they remembered hearing about him from Mrs. Markowicz, or seeing him at her apartment after the fire. "She used to say that you were a good man," one of the older women told him. "She often talked about how you had helped her get through that terrible night, and how much she appreciated your help afterward. Once, only a couple of years ago, she told me that if Ana had lived, even though you were not Jewish, she would have been happy for you and Ana to marry."

Surprised and moved deeply by the comment, and by the memories it evoked, Will had to turn aside for a moment to regain his composure.

Lizzy became a teacher at a private girls' school in Manhattan. She had some modest success as a writer; two of her books for children remained in print for years. She never married but acted as an unofficial aunt to many of her friends' children and maintained a life-long friendship with Will and his wife.

EPILOGUE: JULY 2002

*K*en Breaknell, the young Cathedral priest who acquired Ana's locket after the 2001 Cathedral fire, never did find out where the locket had come from. For several months, he kept it in a drawer in his desk while he read obsessively through old newspapers and the Cathedral archives searching for clues. The closest he came, based on the damage to the locket and general appearance of the two people whose pictures were inside it, was to guess that it had been in a fire that occurred sometime not long after the Christmas of 1910, when, according to the inscription, Will had given it to Ana.

That led him to reading about various fires including the one in Newark and the one at the Triangle Waist Company, but he couldn't find anything to tie the locket to anyone who had died in either. Still, as he read about the young women from the Lower East Side who had perished in the Triangle blaze, something made him feel that there might be a connection. This was reinforced by two accounts he found of the big Sunday meeting addressed by Bishop Greer, neither of which included Will's name but both of which described a young seminarian who openly expressed his love for one of the young women who had died. The image prompted him to recall the similar reactions he and the crew boss he'd met after the fire had had to the pictures in the locket: "They look like they don't belong together and yet they do."

To the few people who knew about Ken's search and asked why he was so dogged about it, Ken explained that it was just because it seemed to him an interesting bit of Cathedral history. But he admitted to himself that he found the parallels between 2001 and 1911 compelling. In a roundabout way, his search was helping him to probe the questions that had been plaguing him before the Cathedral fire and the events of September 11: What does it mean to lead a committed life? What was he being called to do?

Finally, in July, after many discussions with his friends and some of his Cathedral colleagues, Ken decided to leave the priesthood and take a job with a small non-profit group that was trying to raise awareness about inequality and the links between inequality and race. "I've come to realize," he told the Dean, "that what attracted me to the priesthood was primarily the chance to work on social issues. I love the church and will always be a part of it, but I recognize that my real passion is public policy. Right now, terrorism and anti-Muslim sentiment are on everyone's mind, but in the long term my greatest concern is that we seem to be returning to a time like the Gilded Age, when the rich just get richer and the poor, particularly poor minority people, are left behind."

The Dean, after a half-hearted effort to dissuade him, told Ken that his door would always be open if Ken changed his mind, and wished him well in his new life.

Ken's final act before he left was to give the locket to the Cathedral archivist, who had taken an active interest in Ken's unsuccessful efforts to discover its story. "I'll always feel disappointed that I wasn't a better detective," Ken told him. "But it's time for me to move on to other things." Then, fingering the small gold item one last time before reluctantly handing it over, he said, "Maybe one day someone will unlock the secret."

THE REAL CHARACTERS

Bishop David Greer lived to be 75, remaining Bishop of New York until his death in 1919. Among his admirers was Helen Keller, whom he knew from the time she was a student. She recalled that she "never had a truer friend" than Greer.

Canon Ernest Voorhis was headmaster of the Cathedral Choir School for eleven years. His gently amusing description of life on the Cathedral grounds, written some years later and used here, suggests why he was well-suited to his role.

Grant LaFarge was fired as Cathedral architect only thirty-five days after the consecration ceremony while he was travelling in Europe. The trustees appointed Ralph Cram as the new architect before even notifying LaFarge of his removal, a move that was much criticized. LaFarge never commented publicly about what had happened but in a private letter to Cram ten years later he referred to the entire episode as a "greasy performance."

Ralph Cram, a strong proponent of the Gothic Revival style, became the architect of the Cathedral after LaFarge's departure. He was responsible for the soaring nave, which was completed in 1941, and for introducing Gothic elements into already-completed areas. He was a partner in a Boston-based architectural firm and, for several years, head of the MIT Department of Architecture.

August Belmont was the son of a Jewish immigrant by the same name who established a banking house in New York City and, at the time of his marriage to the daughter of Commodore Matthew Perry, adopted the Episcopal faith. The younger Belmont, in addition to being a Cathedral trustee, was the founder of the city's first subway line and a horse-racing enthusiast who built Belmont Park.

Gutzon Borglum, who created the lovely angel statuary in the Cathedral's St. Saviour's Chapel, later took on a much grander project: creating the Presidential likenesses on Mt. Rushmore.

Father James Huntington, the founder of the Order of the Holy Cross, an Anglican Benedictine monastic order for men, died in 1935 and is buried on the monastery grounds in West Park, New York.

Wilford Lash Robbins continued as Dean of the General Theological Seminary until 1916.

Elsie Clews Parsons was an eminent anthropologist and pioneering feminist as well as a fearless challenger of social and sexual mores. Her relationships, including with Grant LaFarge, were part of an effort to live freely at a time when women were for the most part still bound by traditional rules.

Phillips Brooks, a descendent of a distinguished Massachusetts family, was a renowned preacher and the long-time rector of Trinity Church in Boston. He is probably best remembered as the author of the words to the hymn "O Little Town of Bethlehem."

J.P. Morgan was the dominant American financier of the late 19th and early 20th Centuries, playing a key role in the creation of the US Steel Corporation and AT&T and virtually single-handedly stopping the panic of 1907. He died in 1913, having narrowly escaped being on the Titanic the year before as a result of changing his travel plans.

Anne Morgan became internationally known as a philanthropist, particularly for her efforts to assist France and French troops during World War I. In 1932 she became the first American woman appointed a commander of the French Legion of Honor. In her later years, she was active in trying to organize US peace groups and was a member of the National Urban League.

Walter Rauschenbusch was regarded in his time as the country's foremost thinker on Christians' responsibility to respond to social conditions. While *The Social Gospel* was attacked in some circles for its severe critique of capitalism, the fact that it sold more than 50,000 copies attested to its popularity. Rauschenbusch criticized both the Germans and the Allies in World War I, thereby losing many supporters, before dying in 1918.

John Sloan and **George Bellows** were members of what came to be known as the "Ashcan School" of painters, who broke with the prevailing genteel tradition and attempted to show that there was beauty to be found in the most humble of occupations and settings. They and many of their colleagues were active socialists and worked for magazines such as *The Masses*.

Upton Sinclair, **Ray Stannard Baker** and **Lincoln Steffens** were among the "muckrakers," as they were pejoratively referred to, who brought to the country's attention horrific workplace conditions and widespread corruption. Many of them had strong religious upbringings or impulses which were reflected in the moral indignation they brought to their work.

Theodore Roosevelt, who became President of the United States upon the assassination of President William McKinley in

1901 and was elected in 1904 to a full term, tried unsuccessfully to block William Howard Taft's re-election in 1912. He then formed what came to be known as the Bull Moose Party, opening the way for the election of Democrat Woodrow Wilson. He died in 1919.

Emma Goldman, who was born in Lithuania and emigrated to the United States in 1885, was an ardent anarchist and tireless campaigner and lecturer on behalf of many causes including prison reform and atheism as well as workers' rights. In 1917, after being convicted in connection with her opposition to the draft, she was deported to Russia, where she at first embraced the Bolshevik revolution but later became disillusioned with it. She died in Canada in 1940.

Clara Lemlich and **Rose Schneiderman**, who both played important roles in organizing women workers in the garment industry, were also strong supporters of women's suffrage. Late in life, Lemlich persuaded the management of her retirement home to join in the United Farm Workers' boycotts of grapes and lettuce. Schneiderman is credited with the phrase "The worker must have bread, but she must have roses, too" which, as "Bread and Roses," became the rallying cry of workers during a 1912 textile strike.

Oswald Garrison Villard, a grandson of abolitionist William Lloyd Garrison, was a pioneer civil rights leader and a co-founder of the NAACP. His family owned a New York City newspaper as well as *The Nation* magazine, where he served as editor beginning in 1918.

Max Blanck and **Isaac Harris**, the owners of the Triangle Waist Company, were indicted on manslaughter charges shortly after the fire but acquitted by a jury some months later. Their lawyers were so skillful in raising doubts about details including whether the two men were aware of a locked door on the

Washington Place staircase, and even if so whether the locked door was responsible for the deaths, that one juror later said that the fire "seems to me to have been an act of the Almighty." Several civil lawsuits were filed against the pair by relatives of the fire victims, but the litigants at most received small insurance settlements. Still, the fire did produce significant change, most notably in the form of the Factory Investigating Commission's work.

Despite all the new laws, however, factory fires still occurred. In 1958, only a few blocks from the Triangle building, twenty-four workers perished when a fire broke out in an old building with no sprinklers and a weak floor that collapsed. Among the onlookers was a survivor of the Triangle fire.

Frances Perkins become Secretary of Labor under President Franklin Roosevelt, the first woman to hold a cabinet position. Some years after the Triangle fire, she said that the New Deal's foundations lay in the stricken consciences of those whose lives had been touched by the 1911 fire.

The Cathedral of St. John the Divine, under Cram's direction, became far more Gothic in style. The enormous nave he designed includes fourteen bays, one of which pays tribute to labor in the form of a stained-glass window that portrays vocations ranging from fisherman to printer to construction engineer. The crossing tower designed by Cram was never built and the transepts never completed. But while the building of the Cathedral languished, its role in the life of the city grew; beginning in the last quarter of the 20th century it became a center of interfaith and international activities with a strong emphasis on human rights.

HISTORICAL NOTE

I've read widely about the historical events portrayed in this book, and tried my best to accurately reflect both the events themselves and the individuals who figured in them. I've scoured maps of transportation lines, taken a course in Episcopal Church history, and donned white gloves in order to be allowed to touch photographs of old city neighborhoods at the New York Historical Society. On the Lower East Side, I walked the route from University Settlement House to College Settlement House, as well as the nearby streets that Ana knew so well. My interest in the history of the Cathedral and in the role of the Episcopal Church in the progressive moment began while I was living on Morningside Heights and was a member of the Cathedral's Congregation of St. Saviour.

But this is a work of fiction and I've taken liberties where they seemed acceptable. For example, Lincoln Steffens did indeed speak about contending with God but not, obviously, in a conversation with Will Ingalls; similarly, Frances Perkins did describe her first-person experience of the Triangle fire, but not in a conversation with Will. Strictly speaking, the Settlement House movement had accomplished a considerable amount in terms of legislative change before the time period in which the novel is set, but I wanted to highlight the debates over tactics. In some cases, I've based descriptions on published accounts of events, e.g. Rev. Ralph Walker's speech in support of striking workers at the

Diocesan Convention and Rev. John Holmes' criticisms of the Cathedral. In other cases I've imagined, based on my research, what an actual person might well have said, e.g. the conversation between Will and Cathedral trustee Henry Lewis Morris about LaFarge, and Bishop Greer's remarks about how best to serve the non-white community. If sometimes historical characters speak in fictional terms, the opposite is also true; for example, Ana, in her speech at the College Settlement House debate, employs Emma Goldman's language about anarchism and also public remarks made by organizer Clara Lemlich.

The language people used not just in speeches but in letters and everyday exchanges a hundred years ago was much more formal and ornate than the language we use today. I've tried to capture some of that, even though it may at times sound strange to modern ears. The terms used in Will's time to refer to African-Americans also sound dated. Due to the efforts of W.E.B. DuBois and others, "Negro" replaced "colored" as the preferred usage in the early part of the 20th Century, only to be replaced later by other terms.

Still on the subject of changing terminology, and changing values as well, "progressives" of Will's era were not always so progressive, judged by today's standards: many supported segregation—of Native Americans and immigrants as well as African-Americans—on the grounds that it preserved social tranquility and protected these groups from harsh competition. The "progressives" also promoted their own middle-class values as the ones to which all groups should aspire.

In trying to remain true to the spirit of 1910-11 if not always to the precise letter, I've been guided by the example of Jack Finney, whose captivating historical murder mystery *Time and Again* (published in 1970) was set in New York City in the 1880s. In his own historical note, Finney wrote that while he had tried to be scrupulously accurate about most things, "If I needed a fine old Dakota apartment building in 1882, and found it wasn't finished till 1885, I just moved it back a little; sue me." I hope no one did, and in my own case, I hope no one will.

The Locket

ACKNOWLEDGEMENTS

My research included interviews with a number of people connected to the Cathedral of St. John the Divine in the early 2000s to whom I owe many thanks. These include Steve Facey, former executive vice-president, and the Rev. Storm Swain, former Canon Pastor.

Father Huntington's discussion of Christian meditation is based on remarks by Rev. Susan Cannon, a former member of the Cathedral staff, during a retreat she led at West Park.

Michael Cantwell, a New York City fireman at the time of the 2001 Cathedral fire, provided an invaluable account of how he and his colleagues fought the blaze.

Wayne Kempton, Cathedral archivist, searched out and generously shared many pictures and documents from the early years of the Cathedral.

I drew heavily on two outstanding books for the description of the Triangle fire: *Triangle: The fire that changed America* by David Von Drehle, and *The Triangle Fire* by Leon Stein; I owe a great debt to both of them. Other books that I found of particular value were *Morningside Heights: A history of its architecture & development* by Andrew S. Dolkart, and *A Fierce Discontent: The rise and fall of the progressive moment in America 1870-1920* by Michael McGeer.

Early versions of this book were read by a number of people; I'd particularly like to thank Wendy Karmali, Constance Rosenbloom, and Bernard Rivers.

ABOUT THE AUTHOR

Karen R. Rivers was a career journalist (under her professional name, Karen Rothmyer) at news organizations ranging from *The Wall St. Journal* to *The Nation* magazine. She served in the Peace Corps in Kenya in the 1960s and returned to work there for ten years in the early 2000s. She and her husband lived for many years in New York City and now live in the Catskills.

www.ingramcontent.com/pod-product-compliance
Lightning Source LLC
Chambersburg PA
CBHW070620130626
46556CB00001B/421